NOT THE WAY A
MARRIED LADY BEHAVES

"Why did you come to the dance tonight?" Anora asked Jesse.

"What do you mean?"

"I looked for you earlier on. You weren't here. Naturally I assumed . . ."

"Assumed what?"

"That you had someone . . . something else to keep you entertained this evening."

He laughed, a rich, amused rumble in the dusky air. "Maybe I did. Looking for me, were you?"

Anora bit her lower lip. "I only meant—"

"I know what you meant. Come on. Let's go try out that dance floor, shall we?"

She was torn between a longing to feel Jesse's arms around her and her sense of what was proper. "Do you think we should? I mean if you and I go up there and share a dance, folks are bound to talk."

Books by Kathleen Webb

Callie's Honor
Anora's Pride

Published by HarperPaperbacks

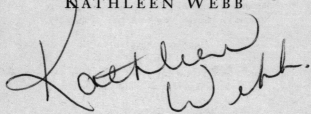

Harper Monogram

Enjoy!

Anora's Pride

❦

KATHLEEN WEBB

Kathleen Webb

HarperPaperbacks
A Division of HarperCollinsPublishers

![HarperPaperbacks logo] **HarperPaperbacks**
A Division of HarperCollins*Publishers*
10 East 53rd Street, New York, N.Y. 10022-5299

This is a work of fiction. The characters, incidents, and
dialogues are products of the author's imagination and are not to
be construed as real. Any resemblance to actual events or
persons, living or dead, is entirely coincidental.

ISBN 0-06-108521-9

HarperCollins®, ![logo]®, HarperPaperbacks™, and HarperMonogram®
are trademarks of HarperCollins*Publishers* Inc.

Cover illustration: by Vittoria Dangelico

First printing: July 1997

Printed in the United States of America

Visit HarperPaperbacks on the World Wide Web at
http://www.harpercollins.com

❖ 10 9 8 7 6 5 4 3 2 1

To my daughter, Reyna, with sincere thanks for her endless support and enthusiasm.

And to my father, Robert Shandley, whose example taught me about inner strength, hard work, and sense of self.

1

The train was late.

Anora tapped her foot, aware that a larger crowd than usual had turned out to meet the 12:10 out of St. Louis. She noticed the Reverend Fish on hand, standing alongside the mayor of Boulder Springs. Neither of them had greeted the noon train before.

Penny skidded to a stop alongside Anora. Breathless from her run from the schoolhouse, between gasps she asked, "Am I too late?"

Anora smiled at her friend's unexpected arrival. "You're supposed to be at the school, aren't you?"

"I know," Penny said in a loud whisper, tugging at her bonnet brim as if she were trying to hide. "I just couldn't resist running down to get a peek at the new marshal."

"What new marshal?"

"Lord, girl, where you been? The whole town's been talking about nothing else for weeks."

Just then the scream of the steam whistle was followed by the sight of the gleaming black locomotive gliding into the station. Anora automatically straightened her bonnet and pasted a smile on her face as she stood alongside her rickety wooden wheelbarrow full of cheesecloth-wrapped sandwiches and boxed lunches.

"I declare!" Penny grabbed her friend's arm and squeezed hard. "That must be him. I heard he was tall, dark, and very, very handsome. Not that you'd care. Being married and all. But as a single gal I—"

Anora shook off Penny's arm as the first flurry of customers approached. As she passed out sandwiches and collected coins she tried unsuccessfully to tune out Penny's magpie chatter.

"The mayor's shaking his hand. So's the reverend."

" 'Lo, Anora. I'll take six, today."

"Hi, Butch." Anora scooped six sandwiches from the wheelbarrow and exchanged them for precious money.

"Who's that?" Penny asked with an interested gleam in her eye as the young man hopped nimbly back on board.

"Butch." Anora checked the station tower clock. Five minutes, tops, to sell the rest of her lunches.

"What's he do?"

"Rides the train. Sells peanuts and drinks and my sandwiches to the passengers."

"Look!" Penny exclaimed.

Anora followed her friend's gaze to where a dark-haired man, dressed top-to-toe in black city clothes, stood head and shoulders above most of the people mingling around the station. His gaze was riveted on her in a way that made her skin flush.

At that second a woman dressed in an eye-catching red and black gown launched herself at the stranger, who scooped her up in his arms, swung her around, then set her back on her feet before he bent down to plant a lingering kiss on her painted lips.

Anora shifted her gaze. How dare the stranger watch her at the same time he kissed another woman?

"Gotta go!" Penny said. The train whistle sounded two short blasts, setting off a final brief flurry of activity, and Anora stared down at half a dozen unsold sandwiches. Maybe she could sell the rest in town. As she grasped the handles of her wheelbarrow and turned it around she passed the dark-haired man, who didn't take any notice. He was busy talking to the stunning woman hanging on his arm. Richelle, the bordello queen whom Anora knew by reputation alone, was obviously no stranger to the new marshal.

Jesse found his interest piqued by the young woman who trudged past him and Ricki as if they were invisible. "Who's that, Ricki?"

"Where?"

"Little gal with the lunch wagon."

Ricki pinched Jesse playfully on the arm. "Nice try, Casanova, except for you're barking up the wrong tree this time. Anora King lives over yonder with her husband."

"Married, is she?"

"Wife to one sorry excuse for a man. And I've seen some real gems in my day."

Jesse frowned. "She doesn't look married." He'd caught the way the young woman had lowered her eyes as he kissed Ricki. A maidenly gesture if ever he'd seen one.

"Can't be much of a marriage," Ricki said blithely. "Given that Ben King's lame and spends most of his nights in the Maverick."

Jesse turned to meet her gaze. "That a fact?"

"As the town's new marshal, you'll no doubt be meeting Ben King in person real soon."

"How long have the Kings lived in Boulder Springs?"

"Not long. Three, four months, maybe. Showed up after old Dan King drank hisself to death, claiming to be his kin. Moved into his shack on the edge of town." Ricki shuddered. "I gotta hand it to the gal. Word is she's one hard worker. Got to be, I guess, saddled with a shiftless husband."

Jesse laid an affectionate arm across Ricki's shoulders. "Have I told you yet how stunning you look?"

Ricki managed a fretful pout. "Not yet. And I had this frock made special."

"You're more beautiful now than the day I first laid eyes on you."

Ricki tapped his chest with her folded fan. "Twenty years ago. And even if you're too polite to remind me of time passing by, I do own a looking glass."

Jesse laughed. "Twenty years. Has it really been that long?"

"You were the randiest fifteen-year-old boy I ever met. Even if your ma was my best friend." Her voice dropped. "She never found out about us, did she?"

Jesse shook his head. "She died without suspecting a thing."

Ricki blew out a breath. "That's good. Now, I've made arrangements for you to stay in the boarding-house closest to your office, like you asked. Fetch your bag like a good boy and I'll walk down there with you."

"Yes'm," Jesse said with a mock salute. "While we walk you can fill me in about this gang of outlaws that's stirring folks up in these parts."

"Don't you expect the mayor'd be the one doing that?"

"I'm willing to bet your sources are a sight more reliable than anyone else's in town."

"I declare, Jesse Quantrill, you've gotten more cunning as you've grown."

"Got to, if a body wants to stay alive."

When Anora glanced over her shoulder she saw the new marshal and that woman locked in conversation, their heads near about touching. Observing the way he bent attentively over Richelle, Anora felt a momentary twinge of envy. To have a man look at you as if you actually had something to say worth listening to, hanging on your every word that way. Even Ben, who at one time had minded what she said, went his own way now that they were established in Boulder Springs. She knew he was drinking more than was good for him, even if the liquor did help dull the pain of his childhood injury. She just had to get enough money to send him to those special doctors.

The door to the general store stood open and she stepped inside, out of the noonday sun. The blinds were half-drawn to help keep the interior cool. The store was crowded the way it tended to be after the train came through, on account of Lettie was also the town's postmistress. And just about the sweetest woman Anora had ever met.

Anora made her way through the cluttered shop, careful not to knock anything with her basket. The smell of freshly ground coffee and cinnamon wafted through the crowd as she approached the counter to purchase some rice and tea.

"Did you see him?" Lettie asked with a bawdy wink.

"See who?" Anora peered inside her money pouch, pretending she had no idea who Lettie meant.

"The new marshal. Jesse Quantrill. Came all the way from Philadelphia. Retired, he was, with a spotless reputation. This here town won't know what hit it."

"I wonder what prompted him out of retirement," she said innocently.

"Sweetcheeks, that ain't no secret. Him and Richelle are old, old friends."

"I guess she won't be worried about him closing her down then," Anora said.

Lettie shot her a sharp look and Anora squirmed beneath that knowing gaze. "That don't sound like the gutsy young woman who marched in here, cocky as you please. The one who convinced me and Sam to let her have supplies on credit so's she could make up lunch packets for the train passengers. Didn't I hear you say a woman has a right and a responsibility to provide for herself the best way she knows how?"

Anora flushed. Lettie was right. Could it be she was jealous of the attention the new marshal paid to Richelle?

"Richelle's just doing the same. Woman has a heart of gold under all that rouge and kohl she wears." Deftly Lettie weighed out a scoop of rice and a handful of tea leaves, which she wrapped in brown paper and tied with string.

"You're right," Anora said quickly. "How much do I owe you?"

"You got any sandwiches left?" Lettie asked.

"Six," Anora admitted.

Lettie held out her hand. "Let me have them."

"Lettie, you don't have to." Anora reached into her basket and passed over the foodstuffs reluctantly.

"Anyone says I do? More than likely some old boy will wander in later and buy them. If not, I'll just feed them to Sam for dinner tonight. It's too hot to cook, anyway."

Anora dug into her money pouch. "I want to pay some on my account." She passed Lettie a handful of coins, most of the money she'd taken in today.

Lettie looked Anora square in the eye. "Ben was in earlier. Bought some tobacco and some beef jerky and some other stuff. Put it on your account."

Anora's heart grew heavy. Some days Ben acted as if money grew on trees here in Boulder Springs, running up her tab with Lettie faster than she could pay it off.

She returned Lettie's level look. "That's fine. I told you before. Whatever he needs, just put it on my account."

"I heard you," Lettie grumbled, picking up a rag and rubbing at an imaginary speck of grit on her spotless counter. After a surreptitious glance over her shoulder to where Sam was busy with several customers, she leaned toward Anora. "We both know who brings in the money. And who spends it. Just you say the word and—"

"I won't hear of it," Anora said briskly. "A man has needs."

Lettie compressed her lips into a thin line, her look implying she thought she knew exactly what Ben needed, and it wasn't stocked in her store. "Mollycoddling ain't never turned no boy into a man." Her look softened on Anora and she changed the subject. "Penny down to the station checking out his nibs?"

Anora smiled as she gathered up her purchases. "Yes, she was there."

Lettie shook her head. "I declare. That girl is just itching to get herself hitched. You might consider having a friendly word with her."

Anora fumbled the rice. "Me? Have a talk with her? What about?"

"Marriage. You know. Woman to woman."

Anora blanched, wondering what her new friends would say if they were to learn the truth. "Why, I wouldn't know what to say."

"Honey," drawled a whiskey-smooth female

voice from behind her. "You're the first woman I ever heard make such a claim. Ask any woman about being married and usually you can't shut her up."

Anora spun around, purchases clutched to her chest, belatedly aware the store had grown unusually silent with the arrival of the infamous Richelle, new marshal in tow.

Seemingly unaware of the stir she was causing, Richelle addressed Lettie.

"Lettie, this here is Jesse Quantrill. The man who'll be putting a little law and order back into these parts."

" 'Bout time someone did," Lettie said. Raising her voice she called, "Sam, get your sorry hide over here and say how d'you do to the new marshal."

As Lettie's husband Sam approached, Anora tried unsuccessfully to sidle unnoticed past the gathering crowd. "Mrs. King," Richelle said. "Don't go yet. Jesse was just saying he was a tad peckish. I expect one of your famous sandwiches'd hit the spot."

Anora's tongue stuck to the roof of her mouth. She tried to point to Lettie, but the packet of tea slid from her grasp. When she bent down to pick it up, the marshal beat her to it and her head bumped into his as he straightened.

"Sorry," Anora stammered, aware her face was redder than Richelle's gown.

"No harm done," Jesse said, passing her the tea. His lean brown fingers brushed her open palm in a way that set a couple of dozen butterflies batting about her insides. Lord, what a smile the man had. And his eyes. He had a way of looking clear through a body, leaving Anora with the uncomfortable feeling that in a few intense seconds he'd unearthed every one of her carefully guarded secrets and ferreted out a few new ones besides.

As Jesse's eyes remained on Anora she felt a wave of heat creep up her neck. Beneath her bonnet her ears were burning.

"Marshal Quantrill, meet *Mrs*. King," Richelle said pointedly.

"A pleasure," he said, clasping her hand, tea and all in both his hands. "Ricki tells me you live on the outskirts of town. Any problems out your way with Rosco and his boys?"

"No, sir."

"You let me know if that changes, you understand? 'Cause I hear tell they've rustled cattle from several of your neighbors."

"Don't have much in the way of livestock at Three Boulders," Anora said. "So I guess they won't be coming around bothering us none."

"Never can tell what a group like that will do," he said, releasing her hand and turning his attention to Lettie and Sam. Packages clutched tight, Anora pushed her way through the crowded store, feeling a deep abiding sense of having narrowly escaped. Escaped from what, she hadn't the faintest idea.

The following day Anora was once more in position at the train station, her trusty wheelbarrow filled with lunches. In a moment of inspiration she had made mini–bread loaves, splitting and filling each loaf with Lettie's finest smoked ham, fresh-churned butter, a slab of cheese, and a dill pickle slice. The result was different from her usual lunch fare and she was contemplating raising her prices a nickel when her heart skipped a beat then sped right up at the sight of the marshal.

"Good day, Mrs. King." As he spoke Jesse tipped his hat and Anora realized that, until this moment, a gentleman had never in her entire twenty years tipped his hat to her. Folks had treated her differently since that first day someone called her Mrs. King and she didn't make the correction. She liked the freedom her alleged marital status fetched her, even if she did feel guilt over the deceit.

At the admiring look in Jesse's dark brown eyes she felt a slow warmth of approval chug through her veins. "Good day, Marshal. Are you meeting the train?"

Jesse nodded.

"Me, too. I mean, I'm here every day. Folks been telling me lately that they know to look out for me at this stop."

"And how do they know that?"

"I don't rightly know. The conductors, I guess. And the spotters."

Jesse nodded. "Word of mouth. Usually a businessperson's most effective advertising."

Lord almighty. He was talking to her like she was somebody important. Someone who mattered. "Who's on the train?" she blurted out, then bit her lip, aware it was hardly any of her business.

"A lawman's best friend. In this instance my horse, Sully." He cocked his head. "Don't you have a parasol? To keep the sun off you? You're getting freckles."

Anora rubbed the back of her hand self-consciously across the bridge of her nose, resolving to attack the much-hated freckles with some fresh-squeezed lemon juice. "Parasol'd just get in the way," she said. "I need both hands." She didn't add that the price for such a luxury was far beyond her reach.

Jesse just smiled a slow spreading smile as he continued to observe her. "I like them. The freckles. They suit you."

Anora felt herself blushing what had to be twenty different shades of crimson. Desperately she sought to change the subject. "Why'd you name your horse Sully?"

" 'Cause when I got him he was the sullenest thing on four legs. He's a lot more mellow now. In fact he's a right good old boy."

"Why didn't he come with you yesterday?"

"Old Sully had a bit of unfinished business to attend to. Male-type business, if you get what I mean."

Anora didn't get what he meant in the least, and her face must have registered the fact.

Jesse laughed as if greatly amused. "He's been hard at work. Studded out."

"Oh." If Anora felt embarrassed earlier, it was nothing compared to now. What an idiot he must think her. More than that, she received a sudden, clear picture of Sully, doing his manly duty to some receptive filly. The image strangely excited her.

"He's got offspring from one coast to the other, old Sully does." Jesse winked. "I told him more than once, whenever he gets tired of the job to let me know and I'll retire him. So far it hasn't happened."

Anora cleared her throat. "I'm not sure this is a proper conversation for us to be having."

Jesse just flashed her an incorrigible look. "You think on it. Once you decide, you just let me know, you hear?" That said, he turned and sauntered back the way he'd come, hands clasped behind his back, elegant long coattails swaying with every step he took. Anora wondered if he always dressed in black.

She didn't have time to wonder more than that because the train arrived and she was busier than ever. Her new creation was enthusiastically received and she sold every last one of her miniloaves at the higher price. She glanced down the tracks only once, in time to see Jesse leading a magnificent-looking animal out of a boxcar.

Lord, it was hot. After the train left and the station slowly emptied she whipped off her bonnet, blotting the dampness from her forehead with a slightly grubby cuff. She'd best get home. If she didn't get the laundry washed she wouldn't have anything clean to wear tomorrow.

She was about halfway home, thinking longing thoughts about a tall cool glass of lemonade, each step raising hazy plumes of dust on the parched road, when the front wheel rolled right off her wheelbarrow and flopped onto the roadway.

"Pish, tish, and bother," Anora said as she squatted next to the crippled wheelbarrow. The nut and bolt had come out. She spotted the bolt right away lying in the dust next to the wheelbarrow, but hard as she looked she didn't see the nut anyplace. Could be it had fallen out back at the train station, the bolt slowly working its way loose till now. That being the case, surely she could just reattach the wheel. With luck, it would last till she reached the ranch. She was in the middle of the road wrestling with the uncooperative rusty bolt, when she heard the sound of approaching horses.

Four men, riding abreast, rounded a curve in the road ahead and came toward her. The sun was behind them, throwing their faces in shadow. Anora eyed them warily. It seemed to her that the countryside had suddenly gone deathly still. Not an insect buzzed. Not a bird chirped. Not a leaf rustled. Surrounding Anora from every direction was the overwhelming scent of danger.

2

The feeling of danger cut deep in the pit of her stomach, heightened as three riders lagged back and one lone man approached, bringing with him the scent of unwashed flesh and stale urine. Anora held her ground, aware she had little hope of losing herself in the cover of the underbrush.

"Looks like you got yourself a bit of a problem." The rider leaned over his saddle horn toward her but showed no sign of dismounting or lending a helping hand.

"It's almost fixed to rights," Anora said, telling herself that as long as she didn't panic, didn't display her fear, she'd be just fine. Still, she couldn't control the slight trembling of her hands as she fiddled with the bolt, recalling a similar encounter with the gambler who'd killed her pa. Ben had saved her then. This time she had to save herself. She straightened, praying the bolt would hold. "Good as new."

"You hear that, boys? The little lady done fixed the problem all by herself. No need for us to be stopping to help." He grinned at Anora, revealing a gap where two teeth were missing. "That being the case, I was wondering if maybe you could be helping us out."

"I don't—"

"See, me and the boys, we're a little strapped for cash. If you was to see your way clear to untie that pouch under your apron, we'd just relieve you of it and be on our way. Sweet and simple."

He unholstered his gun. "On the other hand, if you was to do something foolish . . . Well, it's hard to say how things might turn out."

Anora fought back her fear, trading it for anger. Why hadn't she stopped at Lettie's on the way home like she did most days? If she had, her losses would be minimal.

She jerked the cord around her waist and tossed the pouch to the outlaw. He caught it in his free hand, his grin widening at the weight of it.

"Much obliged to you, ma'am." Spinning his horse around, he and the others disappeared through the bushes at the side of the road.

Anora was down at the creek scrubbing clothes when she heard Ben arrive home. After one look at the way she was smashing her petticoat against a flat rock he rushed to kneel at her side. "What's wrong?"

She kept her eyes on her underpinnings. "Today, on the road from town, four men rode up and took my money."

"Did they hurt you?"

"Nope. Never touched me." She looked up at him. "Just took my money pouch and rode off."

Ben sat back awkwardly on his heels. "How much they get?"

"I hadn't counted it." She eyed her brother closely. He didn't seem half so upset as her. Maybe if he knew she was saving every dime she could to send him to that new hospital . . . No, she didn't want to go getting his hopes up. Best to wait and surprise him with the news.

Ben shrugged philosophically and rose. "No sense crying over spilt milk. You'll get more money tomorrow, right?"

Anora rose as well, resisting the urge to take hold of her brother and give him a bone-rattling shake. Lettie was right. She did mollycoddle him. She just felt so bad, ever since the accident, that he'd been the one who was hurt when the wagon flipped over, while she'd been thrown clear. "What's wrong with you? I was robbed! All my hard-earned money is gone."

"You got lots," Ben said.

"Is that what you think?"

"Never give me any."

"You want money, get your own job." Anora turned and stomped back toward the shack.

"Who's going to be hiring a cripple?" Ben said. "Besides, I'm fixing up the place. Remember?"

"And a right splendid job you've done so far,"

Anora snapped. "Look here!" She waved an arm to encompass their sorry surroundings; fallen-over fences, dead trees, a ramshackle shack and run-down barn. The few scabby-looking chickens they'd bought when they arrived ran wild across the rutted, dusty yard. "We got ourselves a real nice cozy home." Hopelessness threatened to overwhelm her. All she'd ever wanted was a real home and to see her brother healthy and strong. Today that dream seemed farther away than ever.

"I'm doing my best," Ben said. "Don't know nothing about being a rancher."

"You know lots about the saloon, though, I'll wager. And the poker tables."

Ben gave her his best little-boy look. One he used when he wanted his own way. "You're just hot and upset. You don't mean what you're saying."

"I mean every blessed word. It's time you took some responsibility around here. Past time."

Ben's head shot up. His eyes narrowed. "You want responsibility? I'll give you responsibility." Turning, he started toward his horse.

"Where are you going?"

Favoring his good leg, Ben mounted his sway-backed nag, jerking the reins so hard the poor animal's eyes rolled back in its head, ears flat. "Going to tell the marshal what happened. Let him do his job. Catch those crooks and get you your money back."

"Ben King, you come back here this instant. I mean it. I . . ." Sending her a final rebellious look, Ben dug his heels into the horse's flanks and rode off in a cloud of dust. She stared at his retreating back and knew the robbery was just an excuse. Like as not he'd wind up in the saloon, having forgotten everything she'd just said.

Anora thought back to their arrival in Boulder Springs. For the umpteenth time she regretted the misunderstanding that originated when she and Ben first moved to Three Boulder, the desolate ranch that was now their home. At the time it had seemed fairly harmless to pass themselves off as husband and wife rather than orphans. Lately, though, not a day passed when she didn't regret the lie she lived.

It was late afternoon by the time Anora had pegged her wash to dry on the line she'd strung out in back of the shack. Ben hadn't returned and a part of her was glad. He was getting awfully difficult to be around these days. She'd thought once they had a home that he'd settle down. Instead, his temper seemed to grow shorter with each passing day. She reminded herself she had no ken what it felt like to live with constant pain the way Ben did.

With towel and clean gown in hand she returned to the creek, acutely aware that the Three Boulder Ranch was hardly the lush and prosperous spread she'd envisioned on the trip west. The parched and barren landscape was too rocky to farm. A meager one-room shack afforded the barest of shelter, and although Anora had spent the first week scrubbing every square inch of the place, it was still dark and dingy. The barn was missing more than a few boards and listing to one side in a way that made her fear it might blow over in a strong wind.

In fact the only thing the ranch really had going

for it was this pretty creek that meandered through the middle of it. The crystal-clear waters were ideal for a hot summer day's swim. And although Anora didn't know how to swim she splashed and paddled with great abandon, after first scrubbing herself clean with a scented bar of soap Penny had given her for her birthday.

Back on shore, Anora dressed quickly and pinned her wet hair atop her head. She had no business feeling sorry for herself. For the first time ever she had not only a home, but good friends like Lettie and Penny. She was earning a living. Once Ben's leg was fixed he'd settle down and help her buy some livestock to raise on the ranch.

Rounding the side of the cabin, head down, Anora barreled straight into the arms of a man. She gasped, stumbled, then felt his steadying hands grip her bare arms. When she looked up she let out a relieved breath. It was the marshal.

"Mrs. King. I didn't mean to startle you. I knocked on the door but no one answered."

"I was . . ." Anora paused, aware of the picture she made, her feet bare, clad in her oldest, nearly threadbare gown, with a ratty pile of wet hair dripping rivulets of water down her neck. "I was out back. I wasn't expecting anyone."

"Your husband stopped by my office. Reported that you'd been robbed. Are you all right?"

She nodded. "Where's Ben?"

"Last I saw him, he was headed in the direction of the Maverick."

Anora felt no surprise at Jesse's naming the town's seediest saloon.

"Did you get a good look at the men who robbed you?"

"One of them."

"Why don't we go inside? You can tell me what you recall."

Anora thought quickly. She couldn't ask him in. The place was a hovel. Besides which the marshal was no doubt an observant man. Wouldn't take much to figure out that Anora, alone, occupied the shack, while Ben slept out in the barn.

"It's a dreadful mess. Washday and all. Why don't we talk out here instead?"

Jesse saw the brief flash of panic in her eyes. Plainly, the thought of inviting him inside threw Mrs. King into a tizzy. Which made him wonder what she had to hide. For no matter how bad her housekeeping, he'd be willing to bet he'd seen worse. Glancing around, his gaze lighted on a makeshift bench, a slightly bowed board nailed between two tree stumps. "Shall we sit over there?"

"Good idea." Anora didn't hide her relief at his suggestion. As she led the way to the bench he noticed her bare feet and the sight stirred up an unwanted memory in him. He couldn't help thinking about his sister Rose, who'd had the same intelligent but unworldly air as Anora King.

This here's a married woman, he reminded himself. Can't be half so unworldly as the airs she puts on.

Her hair was pinned up, displaying the slender column of her neck, and where her gown dipped low in back he could see the vertebrae in her neck and spine. A shaft of sunlight pierced fabric worn nearly transparent and revealed the fact that she didn't have a stitch on underneath. His body responded to the knowledge in a predictable way. Not only was Anora King, with her cinnamon-colored curls and green eyes, a fetching morsel, he'd always been a sucker for that beguiling air that reminded him of Rose.

Except he didn't get hard looking at his sister. And he wasn't the sort to be lusting after another man's wife.

Anora sat and smoothed her skirt, dainty bare feet dangling just inches above the ground. The bench was narrower than he'd first thought and as Jesse settled himself next to her his thigh brushed hers. There was barely enough room for the two of them and he could feel her jutting hipbone through a gown so thin she might as well have been wearing nothing at all.

"You didn't have to come all this way out here, Marshal." She glanced at him through her lashes in a way that struck Jesse as totally unaffected. She had delicate fine features, strongly marked brows and the hint of a dimple in her chin. While he counted two dozen freckles marching across the bridge of her nose, she lowered her gaze to her lap, only to glance up, flushing when she saw that his eyes lingered on her face. "We don't get many visitors."

"Tell me about the robbery." Jesse shifted, but his movements only put him in closer bodily contact, his arm brushing the indentation of her waist.

"I was about halfway home. The wheel came off my barrow, so I stopped to fix it."

"*You* stopped to fix it?"

"There wasn't anyone else."

"I see."

"That's when they came along. Four altogether. The sun was in back of them, so their faces were shadowed. Three hung back. The fourth rode right up to me." She frowned, her brow wrinkling prettily. "Didn't seem real surprised to see me, now that I think about it."

"Do you come the same way every day?"

"It's the only way."

"Same time?"

"Fair close, I guess." She cocked her head at him. "You thinking they knew I'd be by about then?"

"It's one possibility."

" 'Cause they knew about my money pouch. I wear it around my middle under my apron."

"What did the man look like? The one who spoke to you?"

Anora shuddered delicately. "He smelled something awful. Like a privy on a hot day."

Jesse bit back a grin, keenly aware of Anora's scent, fresh and clean, with just the faintest hint of honeysuckle or wild rose. Tendrils of escaped hair framed her face in springy curls and he was tempted to reach out and remove the confining pins, to watch the tresses tumble about her shoulders, see the sparks of deep color stabbed to life by the sun's rays.

"Couldn't tell how tall he was," Anora was saying, "on account of he never got down from his horse. Had a hat on, so's I couldn't see the color of his hair, either. Whiskers were darkish. Mean, slitty little eyes. Oh, and he was missing some teeth. Right here."

Parting her lips, she pressed an index finger against her small, even teeth. Her lips were soft and rosy. Moist. Kissable lips. With difficulty Jesse pulled his attention away from her mouth and back to the matter at hand.

"Any idea how much money they made off with?"

Anora shook her head. "Oftentimes I stop at Lettie's and pay some on my account. But I didn't today on account of it being so hot and all, I just wanted to get home."

"They might have known that," Jesse said finally. "One of them could have been in town, watching you. That would explain how they knew where you kept the money." Suddenly restless, he stood. It didn't seem to be such a good idea, sitting so close to her. "This the wheelbarrow that broke on you?"

"That's it, all right." Anora followed as Jesse hunkered down next to the wheelbarrow. The wood was warped and peeling, the metal rusted so bad it was a wonder she made it into town and back every day. "Nut's gone." He moved the barrow slightly and Anora gave a little squeal of pain. Glancing down he saw he had rolled the wheel on her foot.

"Lord, I'm sorry. I had no idea you were standing so close." Anora bit her lower lip. Her luminescent green eyes shone with unshed tears. Seeing the bright red outline of the wheel and cursing his clumsiness, Jesse swept her into his arms. Felt like she weighed no more than a handful of feathers. "You have any ice in the house?"

Anora shook her head.

Looking around, Jesse determined the way to the creek and made his way there, ducking under the line of laundry and following the slightly overgrown pathway at the back of the shack.

"Where are you taking me?" It seemed to take Anora forever to find her voice. First had come the sudden pain, stealing her breath, followed by the heady sensation of being caught up in this man's arms and cradled against his firmly muscled chest like a heroine in one of those novels Penny was teaching her to read. The books described perfectly the way she was feeling right this minute. Flushed and dizzy. Butterflies batting at her insides. Difficulty with speech. She felt all those things and more.

"We'll get some cold water on your foot so it doesn't swell. I hope nothing's broken. Can you feel your toes?"

Anora couldn't feel a thing aside from the banded strength of his arms beneath her bottom. The steady, even beat of his heart where her arm pressed his chest. Echoed by the erratic fluttering of her own heart.

"I'm not sure."

They reached the creek and Jesse deposited her on a sun-warmed boulder, setting her down as gently as if she were a newborn babe. Without a thought to her modesty he pushed her skirt up past her knees and plunged her foot into the icy water.

Anora sucked in her breath.

Jesse's concerned gaze flew to her face. "Did I hurt you again?"

"Not a bit." She spoke candidly. "In fact, I think maybe you're the most gentle man I've ever met."

"That's a strange thing to say, considering how I

near abouts crushed every bone in your foot. Can you move your toes?"

He raised her foot gently. Anora obligingly wiggled her toes, wincing at the discomfort. Despite the cold water, the flesh was swelling and Jesse guided it back into the cold water. "That's a relief. I guess it's just bruised."

He held her foot in the water, cupping her heel, his thumbnail absently grazing her instep. The warmth that his touch triggered, spiraling up the length of her leg, was in direct contrast to the icy water rushing over her foot. As he squatted alongside her, Anora focused on his hat, below which his glossy dark hair escaped and brushed the collar of his jacket. Having the sudden urge to reach out and twine her fingers through a handful of his hair, she clasped her hands tightly in her lap as if she didn't trust her own limbs.

"How's that feel?" Jesse lifted her foot from the water.

"Frozen solid." Her foot and ankle were bright red from the cold. When she realized it wasn't her foot Jesse was looking at, but the exposed length of her legs, Anora brushed her skirt down below her knees. A lady never revealed her legs to a strange man this way. Well, only women like Richelle, the type whose company Jesse was no doubt accustomed to.

"Put your arms around my neck," Jesse said, as he made to lift her back in his arms.

"That really isn't necessary. I can walk perfectly fine."

Slanting her a dark, enigmatic look, Jesse took

her arms and looped them around his neck. There went her breath again; stolen right out of her lungs. Then he lifted her, one arm behind her back, the other beneath her bottom. His gaze never left hers and Anora couldn't look away either. There was something in his eyes, something she'd never seen before, and it was having an awfully strange effect on her.

Instead of pulling away, she felt herself lean closer against him. Tightening her arms. She could feel the pulse beating in the corded vein on the side of his neck, keeping time with his heartbeat, which felt slow and heavy against her breasts.

Her breasts didn't feel normal either. They felt hot. Swollen. Her hardened nipples brushed against Jesse's shirtfront as if no barrier of clothing separated them. Her breath caught in her throat. Her entire body was suffused with warmth. Her eyes widened at the way Jesse looked at her. Like he was hungry and she was food. Unconsciously she moistened her lips, stared up at his. Fascinated she watched as he slowly lowered his head and captured her mouth beneath his own.

3

His mouth atop hers was hot, invasive, fueling a steadily growing whirlpool of sensation deep within her. A whirlpool of emotions that, instead of warning her to pull away, encouraged her tentative response.

Jesse was the one who pulled away, setting Anora abruptly on her feet as if he were burned by the feel of her. She swayed slightly and caught her balance, still off-kilter from the aftermath of his kiss.

Jesse looked severe. "Mrs. King, I apologize with every fiber of my being. I had no right to do that and I wouldn't blame you one bit if you slapped my face."

Belatedly Anora remembered she was supposed to be married. Married women didn't go around kissing other men. She struggled to regain her composure.

She supposed she ought to act all offended, when what she really felt was curiosity. He'd ended the kiss much too abruptly for her liking.

She raised her chin a notch and met his gaze. "You're right. You ought not to have done that, Marshal. I would suggest neither of us makes mention of it ever again."

"Agreed." Taking a deep breath he scooped her back in his arms. This time Anora was aware of a difference in the way he held her, arms stretched out as far as possible, holding her away from himself as if she smelled bad.

She couldn't think of one single thing to say while he carried her back to the shack, but when he set foot on the sagging front stairs she struggled for release. "Please put me down."

"Right after I carry you inside."

Panic edged its way into Anora's tone. "I said put me down."

When Jesse continued as if he hadn't heard her Anora did the first thing she thought of. She reached into his holster and tugged out his gun. That got his attention. He stopped so abruptly she almost tumbled from his arms, and set her down as if she were a rock. As they stood on the rickety porch, eye-to-eye, inches apart, Anora noted a new look in Jesse's eyes. A dangerous look, as he narrowed his gaze and took her measure. When he moved, it was lightning-bolt swift. A blur of motion and the gun was wrested from her grasp. He continued to eye her steadily as he slid his gun back into his holster.

"A word of advice. Never point a gun at a man unless you have every intention of using it."

Anora crossed her arms over her chest. "What makes you think I wouldn't?"

"Anyone who's ever handled a gun could tell you've never had one in your hand before today."

"Oh." Anora's bluster faded. It was true her pa had refused to teach her to shoot. Told her that with him and Ben to protect her, she had no need. "Maybe I ought to get me a lesson or two. Deal with those robbers on my own terms."

"You leave the robbers to me," Jesse said grimly. "Although if I was you, till I get them behind bars, I'd have that husband of yours escort you back and forth from town."

"That's a sound idea, Marshal. A very sound idea."

Jesse mounted Sully and headed back to town in a thoughtful mood. It had been obvious there was something in that shack Anora didn't want him to see. Which made him wonder if perhaps she was linked in with Rosco's gang somehow. The whole robbery story could have been concocted by Ben King to throw him off the scent.

Jesse frowned. No. He had a good instinct for when someone was lying and he'd swear Anora was telling the truth. Still, her story didn't make much sense. Her description of the robber, sketchy as it was, matched Rosco. The outlaw and his boys had never struck in the daylight before, let alone bothered with the kind of money Anora would have been carrying. Which left Jesse feeling, deep in his gut, that at least one King, if not both, figured into the equation somehow. He just couldn't fit the pieces together.

Yet.

But he would. Given time he'd get to the bottom of things, including Anora King's big secret hidden in the ramshackle cabin she called home.

The one thing he refused to dwell upon was just how good she'd felt trussed up tight against him today, nothing between him and her except that flimsy gown. The way she started to respond when he kissed her. He remembered Ricki saying how Ben King spent most evenings up at the saloon. In all likelihood Anora King was lonely and looking for some man to keep her company. That being the case, she could go do her looking someplace else.

He shook his head. Love. It was a strange bird to figure. But one thing was for sure. Love made ready fools out of anyone dumb enough to get hooked up in its clutches. He thought of his mother. His sister. Other men and women he'd known who'd succumbed to the malaise. Not for him. Never had been, never would be.

The hour approached midnight as Jesse made his rounds through the town. It had been a quiet night so far but he was smart enough not to be lulled into a false sense of complacency. Rosco and his boys had an unpredictable way to them.

He was just passing by the Maverick when the door opened and a drunk staggered out, stumbled, did a few clumsy dance steps, tipped off the boardwalk and landed facedown in the dirt. Seconds later he was snoring loudly. Jesse walked over and nudged him with the toe of his boot, turning his face into the thin stream of light spilling through the saloon doors. Ben King.

For some reason all he could think of was Anora,

alone in that dismal shack, waiting for a husband who never showed up. Straightening, he pushed open the swinging doors into the saloon and walked up to the bar.

"Drink for you, Marshal?" asked the bartender, a man Jesse knew to have an unsavory reputation.

"Just saw Ben King stumble outta here. That his horse tied out front?"

"That sorry-looking gray? Kinda suits him, don't you think?"

Jesse took a breath and a chance. "Understand King was here last night as well."

The bartender's eyes shifted sideways. "Can't say as I recall."

Jesse leaned closer. "Sure you do, Mac. He was playing poker with a couple of Rosco's boys. Never did climb on a winning streak, now did he?"

"Never does," Mac muttered.

"It's last night, interests me. I want to know what was said when King left. Everything that was said."

"They were sitting at the back. Couldn't rightly hear."

Jesse grabbed a handful of sweat-stained shirt-front. "That's not like you, Mac. You hear everything. I know. 'Cause I hear everything, too. Like how there's a warrant out for you in Texas. The right word from me and there'll be a couple of big, ugly bounty hunters in here before dawn. The type's not too particular if they bring a man in dead or alive."

A new line of perspiration broke out along Mac's shiny forehead. "That warrant's years old."

"Some of us got long memories. Now you

gonna tell me what went down in here last night, or do I go over and wake up Jake over at the telegraph office?"

Mac licked his lips, cast his gaze sideways to see if anyone was in earshot. "It's like you said. King and a couple of Rosco's boys. Rosco was up at Ricki's. The boys took King's IOU. Said they'd be collecting the money by noon today, or he'd be minus a couple of fingers."

"What did King say?"

Mac's voice dropped an octave. "He made 'em promise not to hurt her."

Jesse recoiled as if he'd just received a fist in the gut. "Hurt who?"

"The missus. King told the boys where she'd be and when. Told 'em she wears a money pouch 'round her middle 'neath her apron."

Not until Mac's eyes started to bulge, his Adam's apple bobbing erratically in his throat, did Jesse realize he'd unconsciously tightened his grip. Slowly he released the other man and dusted the wrinkled front of Mac's shirt.

He gave a grievous sigh. "I guessed it might be something like that."

Mac licked his lips nervously. "The warrant," he said, low-voiced. "That stays 'tween me and you. I got your word?"

"My word," Jesse said, as he turned and left the saloon.

Outside, King was sprawled exactly where Jesse had left him, snoring loudly enough to wake the neighborhood. Except no one bedded down till dawn in this part of town. Jesse considered tossing him in the drunk tank, aware that Eddy, his deputy, would complain long and loud. Any of the prisoners got sick in the cells, Eddy was the poor sot who cleaned up the mess.

An image of Anora came to mind, her pert little nose with its smattering of freckles, the way her hair dried in fetching corkscrews around her head. He glanced again at King, shook his head, then reached down and plucked the man from the street. He hauled King over to a rain barrel and took a certain perverse satisfaction out of pushing him underwater, head first. On the count of three, King stiffened, tried to bellow, and took in a mouthful of water. Jesse hauled him up by the scruff of his neck, shook him, waited till he finished coughing, then dunked him again. It seemed to do the trick.

"What the . . . ?"

"Go home, King." Jesse tossed the other man onto his nag, put the reins in his hand, and gave the horse a wallop on its flank. He watched till they disappeared from sight. Then he turned and made his way to Ricki's.

"Darling, this is a pleasure," Richelle gushed, as she breezed into what she referred to as her "salon." "Naturally I had hoped we might get together, but I had no idea it would be so soon. Dare I hope you missed me more than you let on?"

"Save it, Ricki," Jesse said shortly. He crossed the nauseatingly pink room and helped himself to a hefty measure of her best whiskey, tossing the liquor down his throat in a single swallow. It smoked its way down to his knees in a slow burn.

Ricki arranged herself on a padded chaise, taking

pains to display a goodly portion of her shapely calf. Her movements weren't lost on Jesse, who couldn't help comparing Ricki's lush curves to Anora's slender limbs. The realization of what he was doing deepened his frown and Ricki sat forward.

"Must be something mighty important to crease up your poor old forehead like that," she said.

"You had Rosco here last night."

"Really? That's funny, I don't recall as to—"

Jesse closed the distance between them and planted himself in front of her, legs apart, arms crossed over his chest. "It's late and I'm not in much of a mood. You sent for me because of Rosco and his thugs terrorizing the good citizens of Boulder Springs. Why would you even let him through the doors, Ricki? Why?"

Ricki swung her legs out of the way and patted the spot next to her. After a brief hesitation Jesse sat down. "Surely you haven't been out of the game that long, Jesse. You have any idea what Rosco would do if I refused him entry? Like as not he'd burn the place down and me along with it. Healthiest thing I can do is roll out the red carpet for the vermin." She patted Jesse's knee. "Now that you're here you'll catch the bastard red-handed. Save me and everyone else in Boulder Springs from worrying our poor little heads about him anymore."

"I just picked Ben King up out of the gutter drunk as a skunk."

"What'd you do then?" Ricki watched him closely. Too closely. Jesse took care to keep his expression unreadable.

"Threw him on his horse and sent him on his way."

Ricki shrugged her narrow shoulders. "I guess that's better than him spending the night in the jail. Can't help feeling sorry for that little gal he's married to, though."

"You don't know the half of it," Jesse said tightly. "You think she married him for love or pity?"

"What's the difference?" Ricki sat forward, eyes bright with sudden interest. "Hear she got robbed, in broad daylight, no less. Has Rosco no shame?"

"It appears not," Jesse said, his lips tightening in a thin line. Same as Ben King.

The doors on the back of the schoolhouse flew open. A herd of children, some young, others nearly grown, scampered down the steps and nearly bowled Anora over. After the youngsters had scattered Anora made her way inside to where Penny stood, her back to Anora, erasing the chalkboard.

"I don't know how you do it," Anora said, lowering herself into a front row desk. "Manage to keep them cooped up in here all day."

"It's more like keeping me cooped up in here with them," Penny said, as she moved to her friend's side. " 'Specially now it's so hot. But it's almost time for summer vacation." She gave Anora a critical glance. "You sure you're all right? 'Cause we can make it another day if you'd rather."

Anora blew out a long breath. "I just want to forget about what happened. Darn near impossible the way folks keep reminding me of it day and night."

Penny picked up a well-worn copy of *Little Women* and took a seat next to Anora. "Folks are just worried about you. That's all. Goodness, you could have been killed, or worse."

Anora gave her a puzzled look. "What's worse?"

Penny bobbed her head. "You know."

At Anora's blank look she shook her head. "I declare, Anora, some days you act so naive, I do believe some of my students got more smarts than you do about certain things. I'm talking about those horrid men forcing themselves on you."

"Oh, that. Rest assured, they didn't."

"But they could have. And I don't see how you can stand making that trip home alone every day after your close call."

"I don't carry money anymore."

Penny rolled her eyes skyward. "Land sakes, girl. Maybe next time it won't be your money that catches their interest."

Anora pinkened. "I hardly think I'm the type to, you know, fuel a man's lust." Even as she spoke she recalled the breathless feeling of being caught tight in Jesse's arms. The hungry look in his eyes, seconds before his lips captured hers . . . Belatedly she realized Penny was prattling on.

". . . don't understand that husband of yours. What good is he if he never does or says anything that lets you know you're a woman?"

Anora shrugged and pulled the novel toward her in an attempt to change the subject. "Now, where were we?"

Penny snatched the book back and slammed its cover. "I mean it, Anora. One of these days some man is going to come along and sweep you clean off your feet. And when that happens, look out, girl. Your life will never be the same."

Anora flushed deeper. "That only happens in books."

Penny straightened and pounced. "You're blushing! Something happened. What? More important, who? You can tell me. I'm your best friend."

"It was nothing."

"I'm not teaching you to read another word until you tell me what happened." She stared at the ceiling. "Some man made eyes at you. That must mean . . ." She gave an excited squeal and leaned forward. "Not the new marshal. Say it isn't so."

Anora couldn't stem the tide of color flooding her face. "It was nothing. After the robbery, he came out to the ranch, is all. Then he accidentally ran over my foot, so he picked me up–"

"He picked you up. In his arms? Oh, you lucky thing, you." Genuine envy colored Penny's words. "Then what?"

"Nothing really," Anora fibbed. "Except it felt really funny. You know. Kind of hot and cold and dizzy all at the same time."

"And Ben never made you feel that way, I wager?"

Anora shook her head. Confidentially, she leaned forward. "I never felt that way before. It kind of scared me."

"Just tell me one thing. Do you think he felt it, too?"

Anora pressed her lips together thoughtfully. "I think he felt something. 'Cause he looked at me, kind of, I don't know. Like he was seeing me for the first time. Then he set me down sudden like, as if he couldn't stand to touch me."

"More like couldn't trust himself to touch you," Penny said with a knowing nod. "That's the way it happens. I remember Johnny, my first beau. . . ." Penny launched into a lengthy yarn of her first love and Anora stared longingly at the novel. She had so hoped to find out what had happened between Jo and Laurie. But once Penny got started it was easiest to just let her go on till she wound herself down like a big, old clock.

4

Another chapter of *Little Women* successfully completed, Anora stood and made ready to leave. As the two women descended the school steps to the street, who should come along right then but Jesse Quantrill, larger than life astride his glossy-coated mount.

To Anora's chagrin she heard Penny flag down man and horse. "Why, Marshal, what a coincidence. Not two minutes have gone by since your name passed between us."

"Penny!" Anora felt the telltale warmth creep over her jawline to her cheeks. A quick look at Jesse revealed the worst. His gaze was nailed to hers, eyes narrowed with suspicion. Like as not he thought she'd told Penny all about *the kiss*. And Penny wasn't helping things a bit, glancing from Jesse to Anora, a big grin stretched across her prominent front teeth.

"Good day, ladies."

She relaxed slightly when Jesse let Penny's comment go unchallenged. Maybe she had him pegged wrong. Nope. A quick, sideways glance told her he was keeping his emotions under tightly leashed control.

It was his own fault, Anora told herself righteously. After all, he'd been the one to sweep her up in his arms. He'd been the one to start the kiss. And end it, she reminded herself, flushing anew as his gaze wandered over her face. Could he read her thoughts?

"Any more problems on the road home, Mrs. King?"

"Not a one, thank you, Marshal."

"I was just telling Anora she's powerful lucky not to have been compromised as well as robbed," Penny piped up. "Matter of fact, she's heading home now, and I was just saying I don't think it's such a good idea, her walking alone." Penny paused for effect. "How lucky you just happened along now when you did. That way you can see to it that Anora gets back safe."

Jesse slanted her a cool glance. "I believe I suggested to Mrs. King that's a responsibility her husband ought to undertake."

Penny continued on, ignoring him. "Everyone hereabouts knows Ben King can't hardly get himself home in one piece. Imagine if Anora had to rely on him."

"Point well taken, ma'am." Jesse dismounted and

stood directly in front of her. His confident stance had Anora quaking in her boots. He stood tall, dashing, and debonair, and every single maid's dream. She also recognized that, while meeting Jesse Quantrill was exciting, it was also far and away the worst thing that had ever happened to her.

"How about it, Mrs. King? Do you accept my offer of safe escort?"

Safe escort!

Funny, but she found very little safety in the thought of being alone with Jesse Quantrill.

Quit being a goose! He thinks I'm a married woman. As long as he continues to believe that, I'm quite safe.

Anora's gaze skipped from the top of Jesse's wide-brimmed black hat to the tips of his dusty black boots, and for one ridiculous second she wished he knew the truth.

But how could she bear the ridicule that was certain to result if the truth became known? Her new friends would never believe another word she said. Especially Jesse Quantrill.

As he waited expectantly for her response, she sought to give him an easy out. "No doubt you're busy with far more pressing matters, Marshal."

Jesse took one long-legged step closer. Close enough for her to see the inordinately thick line of lashes rimming his dark eyes. "Actually, I feel it could be helpful in apprehending the thieves if we were to review, one more time, the particulars of the incident. I'd like you to show me the exact spot where the robbery took place."

"Then it's settled." Penny stepped back, looking

infinitely pleased with herself. "I know I, for one, will sleep better knowing Anora's in such capable hands." Sending Anora a saucy wink, which Jesse couldn't fail to miss, Penny took her leave.

Anora glanced back to Jesse in time to catch his disapproving frown. "It's not what you think."

"You have no idea what I'm thinking."

"On the contrary, I believe I have a fairly accurate idea as to the direction of your thoughts." It was a lofty sentence, sounding rather like something Louisa May Alcott might have written for Jo to say, and Anora relished the idea that she sounded schooled and well read.

With a telling look Jesse bent and linked his fingers low to the ground to give her a leg up. By the time she'd taken in the fact that her perch atop the horse's broad back was actually much higher up than it looked from the ground, Jesse had positioned himself behind her. She felt the warmth of his body as he reached around her for the reins. When they started moving she grabbed a handful of Sully's mane and hung on.

"You mistakenly believe I ran around like some giddy schoolgirl, spreading tales we both agreed were best left unspoken." The horse's swaying movement beneath her seemed to heighten the disquieting sensation of Jesse's nearness. She found it difficult to keep her balance without leaning back against him. He held the reins loosely in his fingers. His arms circled her waist in an intimate way and she swore she could feel his warm breath stir the hair on the top of her head, causing little prickles of awareness to whisper across her scalp.

"And from whence, pray tell, might I have garnered such an impression?"

"Penny has a flair for melodrama," Anora said. "We were talking about you only insofar as the robbery was concerned."

"Ah, yes. The robbery," Jesse mused. "I see you failed to heed my advice to have your husband accompany you on your trips to town."

"Sometimes he does," Anora said quickly. "For the most part, Ben tends to get involved with what he's doing."

"Something he judges more important than his wife's safety?"

"I wouldn't put it that way, exactly."

"Tell me something, Anora."

Anora caught her breath at the sound of her given name on his lips. He made it sound different from most folks. Throaty. Sensual.

"Is your husband acquainted with Rosco and his cohorts? Any of them ever visit him at the ranch?"

"No one visits the ranch. What are you getting at?"

"It's possible the thieves were lying in wait, knowing you'd pass along the road at a certain time. Traveling alone. They also knew exactly where you carry your money."

"Are you implying Ben tipped them off? That my own b . . . That he knew about the robbery in advance?"

Jesse remained silent.

"Ben wouldn't do such a thing," Anora stated flatly. She felt him shift in the saddle.

"Pardon my bluntness, but exactly how long have the two of you been married?"

"Not long," Anora said evasively. "But I've known Ben all my life. I admit he's got his faults same as the next person. But you're wrong about this. No way did Ben have anything to do with the robbery."

"I commend your loyalty," Jesse said stiffly. "Let's both hope I don't discover something that proves it's been misplaced."

Anora wished she could see Jesse's face. His words were so wooden she couldn't help but feel there was something he wasn't telling her.

Just as Anora started to relax and enjoy the ride, Jesse opened another uncomfortable subject. "Just why did your friend the schoolteacher go out of her way to have me escort you home?"

Anora thought quickly. Rather than lie she settled for a partial truth. "Tell you the truth, Marshal, I do believe Penny's a wee bit sweet on you. I think she hopes you might reveal certain things to me."

"Things?" Jesse echoed.

"Things which I can, in turn, pass along to her."

She heard him chuckle. "You mean if I was to tell you I'm partial to auburn hair she might up and color hers with henna?"

"Something like that," Anora said, relieved he'd bought her story so readily.

"And if I was to tell you how much I'm taken with those freckles of yours, your friend might be inclined to go out without her parasol."

"She might."

"And if I was to tell you how I fall asleep every night remembering the way it felt to catch you up in my arms, to hold you against me, the feel of your lips pressed against mine–"

"You agreed we wouldn't mention that," Anora interrupted in a rush.

"So I did," Jesse said. "You can tell her the rest of it, though."

"What rest of it?"

"The part about the auburn hair and the freckles."

"Oh, I wouldn't dream of it," Anora said quickly. "She might get the wrong impression."

"Wrong impression?"

"Since I possess both auburn hair and freckles, why Penny might think . . ."

"Might think what?" Jesse prompted. When Anora didn't respond he answered for her. "Your friend might think I find you attractive, Anora? It just so happens, I do. I find you extremely attractive indeed." He heaved a huge sigh. "Course, you being a married woman and me not being one to poach on another man's wife . . . well, I'm left with no choice but to admire you from afar."

Anora craned her head around to look at him. "I do believe you're teasing me, Marshal."

"The name's Jesse," he said, his arms at her waist seeming to snug her just the slightest big tighter. "I'd be much obliged if you'd call me that. Leastways when we're alone."

Jesse watched the intriguing flush of color creep up Anora's slender neck and knew he had effectively nonplused her once and for all. She was too damn easy to toy with. Easy to tease. He wished she were a trifle less naive, for it would make what he was planning to do easier. Maybe not easier, exactly, but at least he wouldn't feel so guilty about the fact that he intended to use Anora. More precisely, Anora and Ben King's connection to Rosco's gang.

Rosco was wily. No surprise no one had caught him up to this point. Ben King, on the other hand, was a decided weak link. And the deeper King got in with Rosco, the easier it would be for Jesse to apprehend the outlaw gang in a lawless act.

Anora stirred and the scent of her filled his nostrils. Warm and womanly, underscored with that same faint floral fragrance as the other day. If he'd shown up at the ranch earlier, he well might have come across her bathing in the creek. He imagined her naked, rivulets of water cascading down her perfectly formed breasts, over her abdomen, then disappearing into the tangle of auburn curls at the juncture of her legs.

He was enjoying the mental picture so much it took him aback to hear Anora's voice. "Right up ahead there. That's where I stopped. Wasn't more than two minutes before I heard the sound of horses approaching."

"Which means they were waiting just ahead." Jesse reined Sully to a halt and scanned the surrounding countryside.

"What makes you say that?"

"If they'd been riding toward you, you would have heard them sooner." He pointed. "Good chance one of them was sitting watch up over there. That way he could signal to the others when you got close. Make sure you were alone, nobody else on the road."

Anora pivoted to face him, worrying her full bottom lip in a fetching way. "It's no secret Ben and me are dirt poor. Why would anyone set out to rob me?"

Jesse touched his heels to Sully's flanks, urging the animal forward. "I have a few different theories on that score." He felt the instinctive stiffening in her spine and knew he'd have a tough go convincing her that her husband was involved in any way. Women were such fools when it came to their menfolk. He thought again of his baby sister, Rose. And the part he'd played in killing the man who had abused her innocence and trust. Love. It sure as hell made a mishmash of people's lives.

They reached the Three Boulder Ranch shortly, an uncomfortable silence stretched between them. Jesse stopped Sully in front of the cabin and dismounted. Anora clung to the saddle horn, wondering if there was any possible way she could reach the ground without Jesse's help.

In her heart she truly believed he was teasing when he stated that he found her attractive. Trouble was, that same traitorous heart had taken on the annoying habit of skipping a beat or two whenever he was around, then speeding up in a way that left her breathless. If she hadn't experienced it firsthand, she wouldn't have thought just the sight of him could have such an effect.

Exhibiting considerably more poise than she was inwardly feeling, she managed, with Jesse's help, to slide down from Sully's back. "Thank you for seeing me home safe, Marshal."

Jesse touched two fingers to the brim of his hat.

"Believe me, the pleasure was all mine." He seemed to be waiting for her to open up the door and go inside. Anora was determined not to give him the satisfaction. A long, silent look passed between them. A look that told her she hadn't seen the last of Jesse Quantrill. Not by a long shot. It was a look that unsettled Anora clear down to the tips of her toes.

Only after she was certain Jesse was well on his way did she venture inside. The sight of Ben, his back to her as he rifled through her trunk, stopped her cold.

"Just what do you think you're doing?"

Ben straightened and slowly swung about. The half light filtered in through the open door and revealed her brother's face, desperation twisting his boyish features. His hands were clenched into tight-fisted balls at his sides, an extension of the tension running through his body.

"Where is it?"

"Where is what?" Anora crossed the room, displaying more calm than she felt as she removed her shawl and hung it on a peg.

"I need money. And I need it now."

His words spiked a terrible premonition of doom. She felt her insides tremble as she turned to face him. "I don't have any."

"You're lying." Ben advanced, one fist raised. Anora held her ground, her gaze steady on him until he seemed to realize what he was doing and lowered his arm.

"Lettie's keeping my money in her safe at the store. I couldn't chance getting robbed again." Her voice softened. This was Ben, her little brother, life-long companion, and the only kin she had. She bit back the urge to tell him about the money. How she was saving for him to go to Boston and get his leg fixed by those good doctors there. She'd vowed from the first not to say a word till she had the means. "Ben. What's happened?"

Ben crumpled into a chair. "They're going to kill me, Nory."

Anora rushed to kneel at his side. His thin shoulders were shaking with silent sobs and she laid her cheek against his back. She and Ben had to stick together. They were all each other had.

She stayed like that till he seemed to have himself under control, then she rose and lit the fire. The coffeepot was still half-full from the morning so she set it to heat. Nothing like a nice cup of coffee to make things look less bleak.

"Now then," she said briskly, as she set a cup in front of Ben and added two spoonfuls of sugar, the way he liked. "What's all this about someone wanting to kill you? Sounds more like a misunderstanding to me. Who is it making these threats?"

Ben slurped his coffee noisily. "Just some guys. Don't rightly know their names."

"Where did you meet up with them?"

"In town. The saloon," he added, as if Anora didn't already know that for herself. "We were just having a friendly game."

Anora exhaled sharply.

"I know, I know." Ben held up a hand as if to stem her unvoiced objections. "Like father, like son. But I was winning all night, Nory. Doing real well.

Then I got dealt me an awesome full house." His face registered his disappointment. "Beat out by a royal flush."

"I thought you said you were winning."

Ben shrugged. "I was. Last hand of the night, though, the stakes went real high. Fellas agreed to take my IOU." He clutched her hand. "I didn't think I could lose, Nory. All that money. I did it for us. For you. I know you hanker after nice things. I wanted to make you proud. Buy you the fanciest gown this here town has ever seen. And a horse." He waved a hand through the air. "Fix up this dump."

Anora's breath whistled through her teeth as she exhaled. It was a familiar refrain, one she had heard countless times over the years from their pa. Only the fancy gown and nice home never quite appeared as promised. Always having been just within his grasp, whisked away by the turn of a card. Instead, all she got was a life filled with uncertainty. A life Ben was threatening to take her back to.

"You sound just like Pa. You want to end up like him? 'Cause you're well and good on your way."

"I learned my lesson, I swear. Never again. If you could help me out, just this once."

"How much do you owe?"

"Two hundred dollars."

Anora blanched. No way could she manage that much and save for his operation at the same time. She *had* to get him to that hospital. And if he felt more able-bodied he wouldn't get had by smooth-talking card sharks. "I don't have that kind of money. And even if I did I wouldn't countenance you handing it over to some trickster. Sounds to me like you were being cheated all along. Dealt a half-good hand, only the other fellow's is better."

"You think I'm some poor dumb schmuck who lets himself be cheated?"

Anora pushed his hair out of his eyes. "I think you were playing with dishonest men."

Ben straightened. "A gentleman always pays his debt."

Anora smiled weakly. Ben really was doing his best to be the man of the family. It wasn't his fault the gambling was in his blood. "You find these fellas tomorrow. Tell them you'll pay, you just need a little time. Give them some, I'll get it from Lettie, so they know you're sincere. I mean, if they up and kill you, they won't ever get paid, now will they? I'm sure they've already thought of that."

5

Lettie made no secret of her disapproval as she watched Anora count out twenty dollars and pass it to Ben, who clutched the money in his fist and ambled off.

"Throwin' good money after bad, is what you're doing," the older woman muttered.

"This is none of your concern, Lettie. Much as I value your friendship, I won't have you talking that way about Ben."

Lettie pulled a face and changed the subject. "You hear the latest?"

"What latest?"

"Big rustling over at the Bar X. Smithy don't rightly know yet how many head gone missing. Marshal's out there now. Smithy wanted to put together a posse to follow them. 'Pears Quantrill has something else in mind."

It struck Anora that Jesse had himself several "something elses" in mind. Telling herself it didn't matter, she said her good-byes to Lettie and was preparing to go down to the train station, when Jake from the telegraph office burst into the store.

"Just got a message here from Philly," he said, waving a scrap of paper in the air as if it were a flag. "'Pears we got ourselves a full-broiled railway strike."

"A strike?" Anora glanced in disbelief from Lettie to Jake and back to Lettie. "That can't be."

Jake nodded emphatically, the few remaining hairs atop his head, which he attempted to spread as far as possible, lifting with the movement. "The AFL has been trying to negotiate higher wages for the unskilled workers. Earlier today in Texas a couple dozen masked men forced their way on board and tossed the fireman and engineer off. They disabled the engine."

"Texas?" So far away. "Surely that doesn't mean—"

"This here strike has been brewing for some time clear across the country. I predict we'll see plenty more violence before it's ended."

Anora lowered herself stiffly into a rocking chair near the big old unlit woodstove. A strike spelled disaster. It meant unemployment for those of the townspeople who counted on the railway for their livelihood. Including her. She thought of the twenty dollars she'd just given Ben to buy some time for his gambling debts. A rail strike meant no customers for her wares. No money. No operation to fix Ben's leg. She felt nauseous.

The store was unnaturally silent as, all around her, the citizens of Boulder Springs digested this latest bit of news. Anora's insides were awhirl with panic. The same feeling of helplessness had assailed her every time Pa had announced they were pulling up stakes. Not this time, she vowed. This time she was staying put. Strike or no, she'd get that money. She'd find a way.

Ben, his face solemn, was making his way toward her.

"Anora, what is it?"

She tried to moisten her dry lips. To form words of reassurance the way she always did, but none would come.

"There's a rail strike."

She watched his gaze lower to the twenty dollars still clutched in his fist, before he straightened and turned away.

"Where are you going?"

His voice, when it came back to her, was faintly muffled. "Doin' what I got to do."

As she watched him retreat with his off-kilter gait, a feeling of infinite sadness welled up inside her. A short time ago she would have tried to stop him. Would have done her darnedest to pretend things were fine even though everything was a mess.

She felt a reassuring squeeze on her shoulder and looked up to see Lettie, concern registered on her kindly face. The first time she'd met Lettie, with her jutting jaw and thin-pinched features, she'd expected to be skewered by an equally sharp tongue.

Nothing could be farther from the truth. Lettie had a heart of pure melted gold, and an equally soft spot for strays.

"I expect old Jake's mostly blowing his horn. Makes him feel important, hon. Leave your lunches out back in the icebox. I bet your weight in beans the old iron horse will be back on schedule tomorrow."

"You think so, Lettie?"

"I do. Now why don't you run along and have yourself some fun. Treat today like a holiday."

Anora left the store in somewhat of a daze. Outside it felt as if the entire town was shrouded in a subdued air, preparing for changes in the offing. Do something fun, Lettie had said. Trouble was, Anora had never in her life done anything that could be called "fun." Occasionally over the years she'd met young women near her age. She'd overheard them giggling about beaus. Jawing about a town dance. Singing in the choir. Shopping for a new hat or some satin hair ribbons. No room in her life for such doings. Never had been and never would be.

Still, Anora couldn't resist a slight detour past the marshal's office, her pace slowing to a crawl as she tilted her head just enough to peer through the window without appearing obvious. Alas, Jesse wasn't anywhere to be seen, and at the sight of his unoccupied desk she couldn't quite credit the disappointment that seeped through her. Guiltily she speeded up her pace, glancing from left to right to make sure she was unobserved. What would folks think? 'Specially Jesse if he caught her mooning outside his office like some schoolgirl with a giant crush. For shame!

Back at the Three Boulders, Anora was too distracted to settle in to any of the chores that would normally hold her interest. Instead, she took a slim novel out to read on the porch. Under Penny's tutelage her reading skills had improved immensely.

Unfortunately, the book failed to capture her interest for long. It was a fanciful tale of a family whose life was so improbably perfect that Anora wound up feeling worse off than before she knew how to read. The fictional mother's love and support of her young children was as foreign to Anora as the soft, new sheets and abundant food also made mention of. No one lived that way. Did they?

Anora recalled her own mother, who'd died from a snakebite in the middle of nowhere. No matter how unhappy Ma had been, being dragged from town to town with their pa, the thought of finding herself left alone had thrown her into some kind of vapor. Trouble was, except for herself and Ben, their mother had died alone. Pa had stumbled back to camp three days later, hungover and broke.

That was the same year as Ben's accident. Pa had set her brother's broken leg, made such a mess of it, it had healed crooked, getting worse as he got older. In her heart of hearts she just knew that famous surgeon in Boston could help Ben if anyone could.

At an early age Anora had learned she had only herself to rely on. Wasn't anyone else going to come along and make things rosy for her. Least of all a man. More than likely, fixing her sights on a fellow would only weaken her resolve to do right by herself. She liked being alone. Enjoyed her solitude just fine.

No sooner had the thought taken root before her solitude was interrupted by the sound of an approaching rider. At first she thought it must be Ben, come home early for a change. Except Ben's nag had never moved so fast, and her view of the approaching horse and rider confirmed the worst. Jesse Quantrill, come to make her life a misery. How, she didn't rightly know. But her instinct sounded a warning she didn't dare ignore.

"Good day, Mrs. King. Is your husband about?"

" 'Fraid not, Marshal. Shame you rode all this way for nothing."

Jesse took his time as he dismounted and climbed the rickety steps to the porch. Each tread creaked ominously under his weight. He flashed her a smile, the likes of which nearly took her breath clean away. "I wouldn't say for nothing, exactly. Not when it affords me a chance to gaze upon you."

His compliment unfurled something warm and fuzzy deep inside Anora. Before she could enjoy the sensation it shifted abruptly, turned into a voice that screamed "danger." The man before her, with his glib tongue and ready smile, represented a threat on some primitive emotional level, the likes of which she'd never come up against. The security and independence she prized would be no more if ever a man like Jesse Quantrill gained entry into her life. Into her heart.

"Such a hot, dusty day, Marshal. Could I offer you a glass of lemonade before you head back into town?"

"Much obliged. A glass of lemonade'd go down real good right about now."

"I'll be right back."

Anora set her book aside and went into the cabin, careful to pull the door firmly shut behind her. Looking down she was dismayed to see her hands were shaking worse than she thought.

He can't hurt me, she told herself firmly. *Not if I don't give him the chance.*

She couldn't live her life steeped in fear, either. Which was why she fought down her earlier instinct to jump up and run inside. To cower in the cabin till he left. Lord almighty. What might happen if the man had the faintest inkling he had that sort of power over her?

Jesse propped himself against the porch railing, but feeling the flimsy post sway beneath his weight he quickly altered his stance. He picked up the book Anora'd set down and flipped through the pages, curious to see what kind of reading a woman like her would be doing. He wasn't surprised to find it was the fairy-tale variety. Folks like these fictional characters didn't exist in this world. Leastways, none that he'd run across.

When Anora returned he was leaning against the shack's front wall, a scant arm's length from her stool. He took the glass of lemonade she held toward him, hoisted it in a silent toast and downed the tart liquid. She didn't resume her seat and Jesse had the distinct feeling she was waiting for him to drink up and go. Something he had no intention of doing just yet.

"Any news on the strike?" she asked, her hands burrowing in the folds of her apron.

"No good news, I'm afraid. A crowd gathered earlier in Big Spring Creek. Hundreds of them got together and pushed the cars off the tracks. After which they set the property on fire."

"Oh, dear."

"Emotional times, these. On the one hand you've got your rail line owners, who the unions feel are taking unfair advantage of their workers and pocketing huge profits. The employers feel they're being more than fair, reinvesting their profits back into the rail lines and creating more jobs. The poor unfortunate workers get caught in the middle."

Anora nodded silently, her lower lip clamped between her teeth.

"None of which bodes well for the businessperson such as yourself, what with your livelihood dependent on having the line run."

"Will it be a long strike, do you suppose?"

"I hope not. It's bad all ways around for the town. Whereabouts did you say your husband was?"

"I didn't say. Why?"

Jesse inhaled deeply. "The men who rustled Smithy's cattle last night. One of them was spotted standing watch. I'm afraid the description matches your husband. Right down to the horse he rides."

Jesse knew he didn't imagine the coldness that crept into her voice. "Ben was here with me last night. All night."

"You're certain he didn't leave? Even for a short while?"

"Look around you, Marshal." Anora waved her arm. The movement stretched the fabric of her bodice, pulled it tight across her breasts. "Do you see any rustled cattle? Any signs that Ben and I are living a life of luxury on ill-gotten gains?"

"So you don't mind if I have myself a look around?"

She did mind. He could see it by the brief flash of panic in her eyes. Anora King was scared spitless of what he'd find on this ranch. Something that she'd prefer remain unfound.

She raised her chin a notch, her eyes meeting his. "I've got nothing to hide. And neither does Ben." In that instant he felt a stab of sympathy for her. She would be old and used up way before her time, same as his ma. Unhappy, too, the same way as Rose.

Jesse didn't cotton to being lied to, but he gave her credit for the way she did her best to sound like she meant it when she said she had nothing to hide. Still, her eyes gave her away; wide-open and shadowed by fear. A slight tremble rocked her slender frame.

He flashed her a grin that was designed to help put her at her ease. "Good. I believe I'll start with having a look-see in the barn."

To his dismay she placed herself directly in front of him, blocking his way to the barn.

"There's nothing in there."

He took a determined step forward, feeling like a bully. Telling himself he was only doing his job. "Then it won't matter if I take a little look."

"I tell you, you're wasting your time. You should be out catching those thieves, instead of harassing innocent citizens."

Before he had a chance to respond, a second horse and rider appeared at the top of the drive.

"Here's Ben now. You can ask him yourself about last night, seeing as how you don't believe me." They both turned and watched Ben King ride up and execute his awkward dismount. Ben's shuttered glance settled on Anora.

"What's going on?"

"Where were you last night?" Jesse asked. Wherever he'd been, King didn't look as if he'd gotten much sleep. His eyes were red-rimmed and bloodshot. His clothing was dirty and rumpled.

When Anora opened her mouth to speak, Jesse laid a restraining hand on her arm.

"Let him answer for himself."

"I was here on the ranch all night. Isn't that right, Nory?"

"I told him that," Anora said. " 'Cept he didn't see fit to believe me."

"Got an eyewitness places you at Smithy's the same time thirty head of his cattle disappeared."

Ben struck a cocky pose. "Maybe your witness ought to get his eyesight checked. 'Cause you got another eyewitness says I was here with her."

Jesse let his glance stray from Ben to Anora and back to Ben. "You got any objections if I look inside the barn?"

"Not a one."

Jesse heard Anora's sharply indrawn breath. "I think I'll just do that, then." Stepping around Anora, Jesse made his way across the yard and into the barn's shadowy recesses. The building had a stale, unused smell that matched the general air of neglect pervading the Three Boulder Ranch. As if life had given up and gone away. Jesse peered into a few rickety and unoccupied stalls, his nose assuring him that no animals had been housed in here for quite some time. And certainly not last night.

He stepped back into the sunlight and squinted against the brightness. Anora stood next to Ben, speaking in low, intense tones, words that Jesse couldn't catch. The sun behind Anora silhouetted her shapely limbs through her thin cotton gown. Seeing the two of them together Jesse couldn't help but shake his head at the unlikeliness of the match. The one good thing, far as he could see, was that Anora didn't have a passel of whining, hungry brats pulling at her skirts. Yet. The thought of her carrying that tinhorn's child wasn't something he cared to contemplate. Neither was the disquiet that lodged in his gut at the thought.

Approaching them he extended his hand to Ben who pretended not to notice. " 'Preciate your cooperation, folks."

"Anytime, Marshal." Jesse got the sense that King was somehow goading him, while Anora seemed awfully intent on the parched, dusty ground beneath her feet.

"You understand it's necessary I check out the validity of all reports."

"And you understand when I say I don't expect you'll have cause to be out this way again."

Jesse's eyebrows shot straight up. King's remark sounded suspiciously like a threat. He noticed the way Anora dug her nails into King's forearm. Rather than challenge the man, Jesse responded with a laconic shrug. "Never quite know where my work will take me next."

As he mounted Sully he heard the buzz of low-voiced conversation behind him. A conversation he would have given his eyeteeth to be listening in on.

"Where were you last night?" Anora turned on Ben the second Jesse was out of earshot.

"Here with you, sister dear," Ben drawled.

"We both know that's not true. I heard you ride out of here near abouts midnight. And I didn't hear you come back at all."

Ben gave her a measuring glance. "You told Quantrill I was here all night."

"Course I did. How else to keep up the facade of us being a happily married couple? Marshal couldn't help but think something strange was afoot if he knew you were out carousing till all hours." Her voice softened. "You weren't anywhere near Smithy's spread, were you?"

"Course not," Ben said.

"Did anyone see you? In town, I mean?"

"I swear. I wasn't anywhere near town last night."

Anora felt herself begin to relax. Surely things would blow over. The train would resume its schedule. Ben would get his leg fixed.

"I was afraid Jesse would spot your clothes and stuff when he was in the barn."

Anora winced inwardly at the look Ben shot her, hearing the casual way she'd used Jesse's given name.

"Everything's stored inside the trunks. He wasn't in there long enough to snoop that good. Besides, he's looking for cattle, not my socks and bedroll."

"Still, it's good he didn't suspect anything amiss."

Ben shot her another searching look. "Good for who?"

"Whom," she corrected automatically.

"Oh, by the way," Ben said, digging in his pants pocket. "I got something for you." After turning her hand palm-up, he placed twenty dollars in her palm and curled her fingers around it so it didn't fall.

Anora felt cold dread squeeze her insides. "Wouldn't those men take this on account?"

"We worked ourselves out a different arrangement," Ben said. "One that suits all of us better."

"Ben King, I swear, if you get yourself into trouble—"

"Hush, Nory. I'm not getting into trouble. I swear. I got me an honest-to-goodness job. Settle down and I'll tell you all about it."

6

Anora stacked her hands beneath her head and stared up at the ceiling. The curtain swayed slightly in the breeze, causing shadows and light to chase each other across the rough-hewn beams. Beneath the scratchy sheet she shifted her legs restlessly. Normally by this time she'd have been up for hours, with fresh bread already baked for her lunches.

Giving a weighty sigh she pushed the sheet back and forced her uncooperative legs over the side of the cot. Nothing to be gained from lying abed all day, even if the thought was a tempting one. Once she was up and moving she'd be forced to face things she'd prefer to leave alone. Things like the railway strike, and Ben's new "job." She'd have to think about the money she needed to send Ben to

Boston and pay the surgeon and hospital. And she'd have to contemplate Jesse Quantrill.

She poured a measure of water into her wash-bowl and splashed some onto her face, recoiling from the sensation. Unfortunately her actions only succeeded in reminding her of the day Jesse carried her to the creek and dipped her foot into the icy cold water.

Resolutely she pushed the marshal from her mind and concentrated on getting herself dressed and into town. With any luck the strike would be over and she could collect yesterday's lunches from Lettie's icebox to sell at a reduced rate.

The minute she set foot onto Station Street she knew the strike hadn't ended. An uneasy quiet hung in the air. Folks milled about idly or gathered in little clusters to talk amongst themselves, low-voiced. Anora couldn't predict the effect the strike would have, but folks in Boulder Springs were used to seeing a seemingly inexhaustible supply of goods. It didn't take much to foresee a rise in prices as feed and supplies grew scarce. If crime increased, Jesse would have his hands full.

She gave herself a mental shake. How'd that happen? She'd promised herself she wouldn't think about him anymore, yet he'd gone and crept right back into her thoughts. Something that had to stop.

Sam and Lettie's store was packed, as was the boardwalk out front. Inside, Anora made her way amongst the clamoring customers and went around back of the counter. Lettie was racing back and forth in a manner Anora had never seen before, little wisps of hair pulled free from her bun and flapping in her eyes.

"Need a hand?" Anora asked.

"You angel." Grabbing an apron, Lettie tossed it toward Anora, who caught the garment in midair. Lettie lowered her voice, so no one but Anora could hear her. "There's a run on sugar and coffee. No more than half a pound each per customer. Some of them'd stockpile it if we let 'em. Anyone wants a sack of flour or beans it's cash only. Most important, convince 'em we got lots of everything. The strike won't last forever and we got enough of most things to see us through. Leastways we do so long as everyone just buys as much as they need."

Anora tended the customers and took her cue from Lettie's firm, no-nonsense tones, telling folks there was no need to panic. Hadn't Lettie and Sam settled here long before the railway line came through? And hadn't they managed just fine back then?

It was well past midday before the crowd thinned to a trickle. Anora fetched one of her sandwiches from out back and had just taken a bite when she grew aware of a ruckus outside.

"Wonder what that's all about?"

She followed Lettie and Sam out front of the store.

"I don't much care for the looks of this," Lettie murmured.

Anora got prickles up and down the back of her neck seeing the street aswarm with lines of men on foot, marching shoulder to shoulder in the direction of the railway station. There looked to be hundreds of them. More than the entire male population of Boulder Springs.

"Who are all those men? Where are they going?"

Lettie turned to her husband. "Sam, go fetch your shotgun."

"Honeybun, do you really think that's necessary?"

"These here boys aren't locals." Lettie crossed her arms over her ample bosom. "Someone's sent in a group to stir things up. Don't rightly know whose side they're on in the strike, and don't much care to find out."

Lettie turned to Anora. "You'd best hightail it home, sweetcheeks. Things here could get ugly."

"But—"

"No buts," Lettie said firmly, tugging the apron over Anora's head. "Do as I say. There's a good girl."

The sight of Sam hustling back with a loaded shotgun stabbed a chill of foreboding through Anora as she grabbed her shawl and set off at a half run. A scant half block from the store she heard the sounds of the mob increase in intensity behind her, and thought of Penny over at the schoolhouse. Her friend might have no way of knowing anything was amiss till it was too late.

Dark gray clouds hung overhead, blanketing the town in oppressive heat, and Anora wondered if they were in for a thundershower. By the time she burst into the schoolhouse, hot and sticky and breathing heavily, she knew she must look a sight. Penny stopped talking midsentence. Desks creaked as the students, one by one, craned their necks in curiosity to watch Penny make her way to Anora's side.

"What's wrong?" Penny asked, in a low voice.

"I'm not rightly sure," she said. "But you might want to dismiss early. There's a group of men gathering down by the station. Out-of-towners. Looks as if they're here to stir things up with the strike. Lettie had Sam fetch his gun."

"Lordy, I can't send the kids out in that. What'll I do?"

Anora thought for a minute. "Why don't I go fetch the marshal? He'll make sure the kids get home safe."

"Good idea. I'll keep them busy here till you get back. Anora?"

Anora glanced back at her friend.

"Thanks. And you be careful."

"Course."

Outside the wind had risen some, but rather than cooling things off it stirred up the hot and humid air, making the heat even more oppressive. Behind her Anora heard the noise of the crowd increase in tempo, punctuated by the occasional shout and muffled curse. She was drenched in perspiration by the time she reached Jesse's office, only to find the office unoccupied, the door locked.

"I should have known," Anora muttered. It wasn't Jesse's style to wait for a problem to occur. Likely he was on the scene, right in the thick of the action. Best she return to the schoolhouse and help Penny keep the kids occupied till it was safe to dismiss them.

Moments later she heard the hubbub behind her, like a swarm of angry bees. Glancing back she saw them. Several hundred men marched shoulder to shoulder, heading her way.

For several precious seconds she stood frozen in place, certain she'd be trampled. Then the sea of faces moving her way jolted her into action. Picking up her skirts she ran to the side of the road and pressed herself as tightly as she could against the wall of the building.

The crowd advanced. Anora sucked in her breath, trying to squish herself even flatter. As the first few rows of marchers brushed past, jostling against her, she firmly planted her feet to keep from getting bowled over. Anora recalled the time she and Ben had gotten lost in the middle of a cornfield. She'd pushed between the stalks, row after row, as leaves tugged at her clothing and brushed her face, and flies buzzed around her head. Today felt the same in some ways.

She jumped when a shot rang out, echoing through the muggy air. As if by a prearranged signal the men broke ranks. A horse neighed in terror.

She wasn't in a cornfield, rather in the midst of a riot, surrounded by surging, heaving bodies, the air rife with curses and shouts. When the crowd bolted Anora was swept along with it, powerless to stem the tide of movement.

She yelped in pain as someone trod upon her foot; spun about to find herself pinned in place with someone else standing on the hem of her skirt. Desperately she sucked in a breath and fought the waves of fear and dizziness that threatened to overtake her.

"Anora! What in blazes—"

Hearing her name echo over top of the crowd, she followed the source. Forced herself to focus.

Jesse, astride Sully, was making his way through the throng, grim-lipped with determination. He stopped mere inches away and extended a strong arm in her direction.

"Get on!"

"I don't—"

"I said get on!"

Her shawl fluttered to the ground behind her as she placed her hand in Jesse's hardened, callused one and made a leap for the stirrup. She missed her footing but Jesse hauled her upward as effortlessly as if she weighed no more than the breeze, settling her in front of him with her skirts hiked indecently high. She thought she heard Jesse mutter a curse as she squirmed around, seeking a position where the saddle horn wasn't digging into her leg.

"What the hell are you doing in the middle of all this?" Jesse raised his voice to be heard over the ruckus.

"Looking for you."

"This is no time to be out for a stroll."

"What's going on?"

"My deputies and I are escorting these gentlemen to the outskirts of town. We don't need their likes stirring up the locals."

"Who are they?"

"A splinter group from the Knights of Labor. They've been following the line, trying to stir up sympathy for the strikers."

"Is that bad?"

"Numbers like these aren't good. Locally there's a lot of support for labor. Yet plenty other folks hereabouts rely on having the trains run rain or shine."

"Marshal?" Eddy rode up alongside them.

"What is it?"

Anora felt Jesse's hold tighten fractionally as he spoke to his deputy.

"Word is, group of ranchers got themselves organized into an ambush position up ahead."

"What in the name of—?"

"They're already riled about the rustlers. 'Pears they decided to vent their hostility on these here boys instead."

Jesse cursed under his breath. At least she assumed it was a curse, it being an expression she hadn't heard before. Jesse jerked on the reins, guiding Sully out from among the marchers. "You stay with the men, Eddy. Charlie and I'll ride on ahead."

"What about her?"

Anora flushed at the way Eddy cocked his head in her direction. She shifted as if to get down. "I'm in the way here. I should—"

Jesse's arms tightened about her, stilling her movements. "Sit tight, Anora. You're not going anyplace till I say."

She swiveled to face him. "Who do you think you are to talk to me like that?"

He cocked her a smart-aleck grin. "Don't you know? I'm the law. What I say goes."

"Not so far as I'm concerned."

"The safety of the good citizens of Boulder Springs is my concern. Every last one of its citizens."

Before Anora could argue further Jesse touched his heels to the horse's flanks, urging Sully into a gallop, and it was all she could do to hang on. A sideways glimpse of Jesse's face confirmed her thoughts. He was enjoying every minute of being in control.

On the outskirts of town a hodgepodge of horses and wagons marked the spot where the labor activists had struck a sort of a camp. Smoke from the cooking fire curled upward in a foggy gray spiral, and the smell of simmering beans made Anora's stomach growl. Jesse heard it, too. She could tell by his easy grin.

As if by a prearranged signal he and Charlie slowed their horses to a walk and proceeded down the road past the camp before they stopped. Looking around her, Anora saw why. It was the perfect spot for an ambush. Jagged cliffs and scrub provided loads of cover, yet allowed a clear view of both the road and the camp.

"Wait here," Jesse told Charlie.

Anora couldn't quite credit the gutsy way he rode directly to the base of the cliffs. "Smithy, come down here. We need to talk." Jesse's arm tightened around her midsection. Was he using her for cover?

"We're outside of town, Marshal. You ain't got no jurisdiction."

Anora held her breath, waiting on Jesse's reply.

"I can't rightly talk to a man I can't see."

The sound of movement and the skittering of a handful of loose rocks was followed by the appearance of Anora's neighbor, Smithy. Anora shrank back against Jesse. The man facing them was unshaven, unsmiling, and, to her way of thinking, looked dangerous.

"What's all this about, Smithy?"

"Me and some of the other ranchers, now we got concerns."

"So stop by my office where we can discuss those concerns. This is no way to deal with it. You know these fellas aren't your rustlers."

Smithy grew belligerent. "Me and the others, we ain't seen any sign yet that you're anything but a lot of talk, Marshal." He narrowed his eyes, as if seeing Anora for the first time. "What are you doing with that woman?"

"Mrs. King is witness to a robbery by the same gang that rustled your cattle. She identified one of the outlaws."

Smithy spat on the ground. "Seen her old man that night with my own two eyes. Don't see you locking him up."

"You know that's not the way the law works, Smithy. I need proof. And I'll have it before long. Proof enough to land Rosco behind bars."

"Please me more to see the varmint hanging from a tree."

"That'll depend on the judge. Now why don't you and your friends head home, peaceful-like? These fellas camped here are moving right along the way I asked them. You don't need to be making trouble with them."

Anora scarcely dared to breathe, while Smithy gazed skyward, as if deliberating Jesse's words. Finally he spoke over his shoulder. "Your call, boys."

Several dozen ranchers, armed and mounted, appeared to line up alongside Smithy.

An older, grizzled fellow acted as group spokesman.

"We want your word, Marshal. Something's gotta be done."

"My word," Jesse said. "Stop by my office tomorrow, anyone who wants to."

Anora felt waves of movement from all sides as the ranchers scattered, at the same time the marchers arrived and started loading up their wagons under the watchful eyes of the two deputies.

"Everything all right?" Jesse called.

"A-okay," Eddy replied. Charlie nodded his agreement.

"Meet you back in town, then."

Anora thought Jesse'd forgotten all about her until, heaving a pent-up sigh, Jesse guided Sully in the direction of the Three Boulder Ranch.

"You were cool as a cucumber back there," Anora said admiringly. "Staved off what could have easily turned into a disaster."

"It's been my experience that any reasonable man would rather talk than shoot. Smithy's a reasonable man. He's just fed up. Can't say as I much blame him."

"I can easily walk the rest of the way," Anora said. She was starting to feel much too comfortable leaning against Jesse's broad chest, cradled in his arms.

"Sit tight," Jesse said. "You're my shield in case anybody takes a potshot at me."

Anora near choked. "That's not very chivalrous."

It took Jesse's deep-throated chuckle to let her know he was joshing. "I was kind of hoping to get you home before that storm hits." No sooner had he spoken than lightning streaked across the distant sky and his words were punctuated by a low growl of thunder. Beneath her, Anora felt Sully tense. The horse flattened back his ears.

"I know, old boy, I know." Jesse reached around Anora to pat the animal comfortingly on the neck.

"I'd guess he doesn't like thunder," Anora said.

"Can't say as how I blame him."

The sky turned from leaden gray to black in a matter of seconds. Thunder drummed from farther afield while the rain stayed behind. It seemed the heavens sprang a leak directly overhead to deluge her and Jesse with its contents. Sheet followed sheet of rain, soaking the two of them to the skin.

As suddenly as the rain hit, it receded, leaving scrub grasses bent flat from the torrent. The trees, bowed under the rainfall, continued to drip as regular as rain. Anora sneezed.

"God bless," Jesse said, sounding as if he had something stuck in his throat.

Anora glanced at her cotton frock, molded to her body like skin, every curve outlined by the clingy wet fabric. She was aware of Jesse's harsh breathing directly behind her, the way his breath rasped past her ear and tickled the side of her neck. He held himself stiffly upright, as if trying not to brush against her. Likely he was as soaking wet as she was.

"Well, I've never seen a downpour like that one," she said, the silence between them growing unbearably strained.

"Hmmph," was his only response.

"Think the rail strike will be a long one?"

"Hard to say."

"Expect those men will come back?"

"I doubt it."

Anora blew out an impatient breath. "I'm trying to start a conversation here."

"Why?"

"Why?" He had her there. Why indeed? Because she wanted to get to know Jesse Quantrill better? Learn what manner of man he was?

Bother that, she told herself firmly. It didn't matter what manner of man he was. It didn't matter to her one whit. Not so long as did his job, ensured the streets of Boulder Springs were safe for women and children.

"Do you have any kin back where you come from?" The question popped out before she could stop it, and she felt Jesse tense. Felt his momentary hesitation before he responded.

"I have a sister and a nephew. Why do you ask?"

"Just wondering. Like, I mean . . . you ever been married or anything?"

"I'm not the marrying kind," Jesse said flatly.

"Oh." *What kind of man did that make him?* Anora wondered. Made him a man just like her father and all those drifting, fortune-seeking gamblers whose company her pa sought. The kind of man who knew better than to take a woman to wife, or have a family.

She was relieved when the Three Boulders was visible ahead. Somehow it felt as if she'd been on the longest ride of her life. As they reached the fallen-over posts that marked the rutted entrance to the ranch she tugged on Jesse's sleeve.

"Could you just leave me off here? In case . . . you know."

"You'd rather your husband didn't see me bring you home."

"That's it," Anora said. "Ben's kind of funny about some things."

Jesse pulled Sully up short, dismounted, then reached up to lift Anora down. His hands closed around her waist with the heat of a branding iron, searing through her wet gown and underpinnings clear to her skin. Anora felt dizzy and rested her hands atop his shoulders for support. Time slowed to a standstill. It felt as if Jesse were lifting her down in slow motion. Her skin prickled in the most unusual places; the sensitive inner curve of her elbow, the back of her knee, while something else stirred deep in her belly.

Anora wasn't sure if it was deliberate or not, the way Jesse slowly dragged her down along his length.

It seemed to Anora that he deliberately pressed her against him, hipbone to hipbone, so she could feel his male hardness. But then he stepped back, leaving her to wonder if she hadn't perhaps imagined the entire incident. She still hadn't quite caught her breath by the time he'd remounted and headed back to town.

7

Jesse stomped into his office like a man beset by demons. It had been one hell of a day. One hell of a day indeed. He still didn't know what had possessed him to pluck Anora up off the simmering street like some kind of fairy-tale knight in those books she read. He'd had his hands full with a riot waiting to happen. He didn't need his hands full of Anora, too, but that was exactly what he'd gotten. Boulder Springs was a small town and he'd no doubt set every gossipy tongue to wagging but good today. Still, at the sight of her jostled about, all small and defenseless, every one of his protective instincts had risen to the fore in a rush that left him as shaken up as Anora looked.

Damn, he planned to sweet-talk his way into her

confidence, not her bed. Or was that strictly true? He recalled the way she'd looked, the shimmery fabric of her wet gown clinging to every sweet-smelling inch of her. He'd been unable to resist rubbing up against her like some randy stud horse. And she hadn't exactly backed away, either.

She's a married woman, he reminded himself for what felt like the hundredth time in as many hours. *Her no-good husband's linked in with Rosco and you're going to use that. Use Anora's trusting way, to bust the whole pack of them. That's all.*

The door burst open abruptly. Miss Spencer, the schoolmarm, her hat askew, breathing heavily, flung herself across the room toward him.

"Marshal, Marshal. Something terrible's happened to Anora King."

Jesse felt his heart leap into his throat before he got a firm hold on himself. Hadn't he just seen Anora to the ranch himself? Taking a breath, he forced himself to speak calmly.

"What makes you say that, Miss Spencer?"

"She came by the schoolhouse hours ago, to tell me about the assemblage. She left to get you and bring you back, but she never showed up. There's no way she wouldn't have returned unless something awful happened."

Something awful did happen, Jesse thought wryly. Anora had got herself plucked up off the street and carried away by him.

He rounded his desk and took Miss Spencer's arm in a firm grip. "I'm happy to report your friend is just fine. I saw her home safe myself."

"You did?" The schoolteacher looked up at him

with wide, admiring eyes and Jesse dropped her arm like a stone. Wouldn't do to have some smitten maid dogging his every step here in Boulder Springs.

"I did indeed. And Mrs. King is mighty lucky to have a friend such as yourself concerned about her well-being. Now if you'll excuse me, I've got one pile of work to see to."

"I'm so glad you're seeing after Nory." The young woman folded herself onto a nearby bench. Obviously, she didn't intend on taking her leave just yet. " 'Cause that Ben King . . . I'm so afraid . . ."

"So afraid what, Miss Spencer?" Even as he ordered himself to mind his own business, Jesse hunkered down alongside her, their eyes on a level, and encouraged her to continue.

Miss Spencer passed him a troubled glance before staring at her hands, which she clenched and unclenched in her lap.

"Ben doesn't treat Anora the way a husband ought to treat his wife. Cherished-like."

Jesse wondered what stories Miss Spencer had been reading in the schoolroom. *Since when did a husband cherish a wife?* None that Jesse knew. *Course that doesn't give a man cause to mistreat a woman, either. Is that what she meant?* Jesse felt his gut tighten. He couldn't abide men who hit on their womenfolk. "Go on."

"Anora's . . ." She sighed. "She's way too trusting for her own good. I hear things. Ben King losing his temper and the like. Drinking too much. One of these days he's going to lose his temper with Anora, and she'll have no idea how to to defend herself. Why, she thinks Ben's harmless as a fly." Miss

Spencer slanted Jesse a serious look. "You and I, Marshal, we both know different."

Didn't they just!

Jesse rose and assisted the schoolmarm to her feet. "I want to thank you, Miss Spencer, for taking the time to come by and talk frankly about your concerns."

"Anytime, Marshal," she said, batting her blue eyes in a way that told him all he had to do was crook his little finger and she was his.

"Good day to you, ma'am."

Jesse closed the door behind her with an aggravated sigh. Damn, but womenfolk could surely be a pile of trouble a man didn't need. Miss Spencer was no doubt a well-intentioned schoolmarm. Too bad she had that desperate old-maid look to her. A look he'd come to recognize more than a mile off.

Jesse returned to his desk, but couldn't steer his mind to the work at hand, especially after Charlie and Eddy came back from seeing the Labor Knights on their way. Miss Spencer's words kept bashing about in his brain. *One of these days Ben's going to lose his temper with Anora, and she'll have no idea how to defend herself.*

As the strike continued, it appeared tempers everywhere were short and breaking. Jesse broke up more than the usual number of barroom brawls, locked away more than the usual number of surly drunks, had a talk with local ranchers, and still he couldn't stop thinking about Anora King. He hadn't seen her in town since the day of the riot. He also couldn't forget the schoolmarm's words. Just what was Ben King up to?

Rosco's boys hadn't been seen anywhere nearby either, another fact that concerned Jesse, bringing to mind as it did the calm before the storm.

He told himself it was part of his job to check up on Ben King, and Anora was merely the means to the end. At least that was the excuse he used to head on out to the Three Boulders. The fact that he brought along a dainty little pistol he'd once bought for Rose, who'd refused it, was incidental. After all, a lady in these parts ought to be able to defend herself, especially living out of town a spell the way Anora did. He was only doing his job, really. Especially if the situation arose where she needed to—

He was still down the road a piece from the Three Boulders when he heard the unexpected sound of a woman singing, the notes so pure and clear, it was hard to pinpoint their origin. Jesse stopped and cocked his head, noticing with some amusement that Sully did likewise.

The animal slanted Jesse a knowing look, then directed his attention to where a newly trampled path led through the brush edging the hard-packed dirt road. A ways through the brush Jesse spotted a flash of color amid the green, and shook his head ruefully. All alone out here and Anora hadn't even heard him coming. The old schoolmarm was right. Anora was far too trusting for her own good.

The song wasn't any Jesse'd heard before and he suspected she might be making it up as she went along. Her singing was underscored by a rustle in the bushes. Seconds later Anora appeared. She caught sight of him and the song died in her throat.

Jesse dismounted and tipped his hat. "Don't let me interrupt. I was finding the concert right enjoyable." As he replaced his Stetson he allowed himself a leisurely perusal of the woman before him. Not barefoot this time, he was happy to note, but every bit as unconventionally dressed in what appeared to be a shirt of her husband's, red in color and ridiculously large on her slender frame despite the fact that she had folded the sleeves back. He grinned. As if the shirt weren't masculine enough, Anora was also wearing a pair of Ben King's britches. Jesse allowed himself the observation that the pants looked a hell of a lot better on her than on her old man. Perched jauntily atop her head was a battered felt hat. Her hair flowed loose about her shoulders and Jesse could see the rainbow hue of colors the sun spiked through the cinnamon strands.

Anora felt herself flush as Jesse's eyes took her measure, and unconsciously she straightened. Jesse Quantrill. She'd thought of him so many times these past days it was almost as if she had conjured him out of thin air. Except he looked real enough to her. Big and powerful and handsome in the sunlight.

And look at her. Last time he'd seen her she'd been half-drowned and nearly trampled in the riot. Today she should have known she was asking for trouble, scampering about in Ben's old clothes he'd outgrown. But her gowns were all wearing thin and she didn't want to risk tearing them on the bushes as she filled her pail with wild huckleberries. Truth be told, Ben's old clothes were a damn sight more comfortable than her own. But if she'd had even an inkling Jesse would show up . . .

"I didn't know anybody was around."

"Nobody was." Jesse continued to smile at her in such a way that it was impossible not to smile back. Lord, the man could charm the birds down from the trees if he set his mind to it. When he stepped up to her and wrested the pail from her hand she could smell his unique male scent, warm clean skin, leather, and something woodsy that she couldn't quite identify. Something that sent funny hot and cold tingles down inside her nether regions.

"Any word on the strike?"

" 'Fraid not." He peered inside the pail. "Huckle-berries." He gave her another look that warmed her insides. "I bet you make a huckleberry pie every bit as good as your famous sandwiches."

"Better," Anora said thoughtfully. If Jesse hadn't brought her news, why, was he here?

"It's been years since I tasted homemade huckle-berry pie."

He sounded so much like a little boy with his nose pressed to the candy store window that Anora found herself speaking before she thought about it. "I've got some at the house. Baked first thing this morning. Why don't you come up and I'll cut you a wedge?"

"I can't think of anything I'd like better."

Immediately Anora regretted her impulsive offer. Sooner or later Jesse'd get suspicious that she didn't ask him inside the cabin. She liked it better when he stayed in town where he belonged.

Instead, he took her berry pail in one hand and

Sully's reins in the other to fall into step beside her, shortening his stride to match hers as if he'd been doing it all his life. She wanted to ask him the reason for his visit but every time she opened her mouth it seemed to shut again all by itself. Obviously the silence wasn't bothering him one whit.

Alongside Jesse, Anora grew newly conscious of many things. The warmth of the sun against her bare skin at the open vee of her shirt. The weight of her unbound hair as it brushed against the nape of her neck. The ripe, summer smell of the air. But better than all those things was the fact that she no longer felt lonely. The warmth of Jesse's presence was like the friendly hugs she exchanged with Lettie and Penny.

"Haven't seen you in town these past days," Jesse said, as they started down the rutted drive to the shack.

Anora's heart slowed a beat, then speeded right up. Dare she think that meant he'd looked out for her? Missed her even?

"I've been making a point of staying on the ranch," she said slowly. "What with Ben being away and all."

"Away for long, is he?"

"I don't rightly know. Besides, if I went into town Lettie'd put me to work in the store."

"You got something against working in the store?" Jesse tethered Sully near a clump of sweet grass for the horse to graze on.

"I like it fine. It's just that Lettie doesn't really need my help. She's only being nice. Offering me something to do to keep busy."

"Something wrong with folks treating you nice?"

Anora studied him seriously. It was a good question, and one she didn't have a ready answer for. She shrugged. "Where I come from no one treated anyone else nice. I guess maybe I'm not used to it."

"Hmmph," Jesse said. "Back where I come from, it would be considered an insult to Lettie and your friendship not to take her up on her generosity."

Anora pondered his words as they reached the stairs to the cabin. Obviously Jesse Quantrill had had a different upbringing from hers. "Why don't you make yourself comfortable on the porch?" she said. "I'll go get you that pie. Maybe I'll get changed first."

"Don't you dare. Wearing those britches, you're the most fetching sight I've seen in a long time. I mean it."

"Really?" Anora felt herself blushing at the compliment.

"Believe it. Folks in town catch sight of you dressed like that, why, you're bound to start a whole new style, instant-like."

"Now I know you're funning me."

"Anyway, britches are better for what I've got in mind." As he spoke Jesse reached into his waistband and drew out a small silver-colored pistol.

Anora stared at the dainty firearm. "What's that gun for?"

Jesse snapped open the gun and loaded it. "I brought it for you."

"For me? You know I can't shoot. You told me so yourself."

"Something that's about to change. Let's go out in the field past the barn. I'll set up some targets for you to practice. What's the matter?"

Anora knew her disappointment must show on her face. "Ben won't like it," she said flatly. "Him and Pa. I asked them both to teach me, but they wouldn't."

"Folks make mistakes, Anora. Even folks who care about a body. Living out here the way you do, you just said yourself your husband was away, well, you need to have some sort of protection. It's just plain foolish not to."

Anora gazed from Jesse to the gun and back to Jesse, indecision sweeping through her. She valued her independence, true. But lessons drummed into her over the years were hard to let go.

"You know what I said about Lettie? Same goes here. It'd be a real insult if you turned down my offer."

His words helped Anora make up her mind. Jesse was right. It was high time she knew how to shoot. Just too bad her own brother hadn't seen fit to teach her.

"What do we need?" She set her pail of berries on the stairs and turned to Jesse.

"Some empty tin cans or bottles would be good."

"There's lots out in the barn. Ben—" She hoped Jesse hadn't noticed her slip, but he was watching her, waiting for her to continue.

"Ben—?" he repeated.

Ben lives on canned beans, she'd been about to say. But she didn't want Jesse to know she and Ben didn't eat together, much less live together.

"Ben stashes them out there," she said breezily. "Lord only knows what for."

Her and Jesse's steps flattened the brittle stalks of knee-high field grasses behind the barn. Jesse set an empty can on a reasonably straight fence post whose side railings had long since crumbled to dust.

"Forget everything you think you know about guns," Jesse said. "This here is called a 'muff pistol,' because ladies can easily tuck it into a muff or a bag. Only fires one shot, so you want to make good and sure you don't miss." Jesse backed four paces from the post, turned, and fired. The can bounced into the air, then hit the ground with a hollow clatter.

He passed her the unloaded gun, handle first. "See how it feels? Fits in your hand nice." His lean, callused fingers curled over hers and directed her grip. "Not too tight. That's right. There's your sight. Front and rear. You just take a breath, line them up to your target, and squeeze."

The gun felt cold and unfamiliar. In fact her entire hand felt cold the second Jesse released it, which she knew was ridiculous on such a sweltering hot day. She could feel rivulets of perspiration snake their way between her breasts and dampen the britches' waistband where she'd cinched it tight with Ben's old belt. She tugged at the belt and wished she had on a pretty dress. Something really feminine with flounces and lace.

She took aim at the fence post, gritted her teeth, and squeezed. The chamber clicked hollowly. "Doesn't feel too hard."

"Believe me. It feels a whole lot different when you're standing close enough to look into someone's eyes." He retrieved the gun from her. "Worst mistake folks make is they panic and fire too soon. If you're too far away you lose all accuracy."

"So on that day Rosco stopped me," she said. "Say I'd had the gun with me. What would I have done?"

"Well now," Jesse said. "They were four, right? Best thing would be get close up to Rosco."

He grinned when Anora wrinkled her nose in distaste. "I know. But aim the gun to his temple and tell the others to throw down their weapons. That would be your best move. Remember, one shot. Make it count." As he spoke he set another tin can atop the fence post.

"Weren't you scared the other day when those ranchers were all stirred up? Carrying rifles and six-shooters."

"Those boys weren't really looking to kill anybody. Came in my office the next day and we had us a long talk."

"What about?"

"Smithy and his neighbors are thinking on hiring themselves a pair of 'cattle detectives' they heard about. I convinced them to save their money."

Anora's brow wrinkled. "What are cattle detectives?"

"Hired guns that watch the herds. It's about the best pay a sharpshooter can make for himself." He loaded the pistol and passed it back to her. "Here. Try this."

Anora raised a brow. "Shoot at it? For real?"

"Don't just shoot at it. Hit it."

Anora took aim and fired. The gun jerked, a

sensation she felt clean up to her shoulder. The can didn't move.

"I didn't even hit the post," she complained.

Jesse reloaded the gun, handed it back and positioned himself directly behind, his hand atop hers. Anora could feel the way he molded himself to her. His breath stirred the damp tendrils of her hair. She could feel the slow, steady beat of his heart against her backbone. Her hand shook. Her entire body was trembling so badly, Anora was afraid she might out-and-out swoon. She couldn't breathe. Her throat was parched. Swallowing was impossible.

"Relax," Jesse said, the warmth of his words tickling her ear. "Take a deep breath. Now another. Feel better?"

She'd never felt better or worse in her entire life. Jesse's arms wrapped around her, the feel of his lean length spooned against her backside was far and away the most exciting sensation she'd ever experienced.

"Take aim."

Schooling herself to forget about Jesse and concentrate on the shot, she did as she was told. Jesse let go. She squeezed the trigger. The can flew into the air.

"I did it!"

Delighted, she spun about to face Jesse. It seemed only natural that his arms would close around her. That his hold would tighten as he lifted her off the ground and swung her in a dizzying circle. It seemed all too soon before he set her back on both feet. Was she dizzy from being spun around? Or from being caught and held close to Jesse?

Slowly the world stopped spinning, leaving in its

wake an overwhelming stillness. A stillness where the heat of the barely moving air coupled with the burning heat of Jesse's gaze. She could hear the overloud pounding of her heart. Her fingers on Jesse's forearms clenched reflectively. She swayed toward him.

"Do tell. Isn't this a cozy sight?"

"Ben!" Guiltily Anora sprang away from Jesse. "I didn't expect you back this soon."

"So it would seem."

8

Reluctantly Jesse allowed his hands to drop from Anora's waist. His eyes narrowed as he stepped back and observed the interaction between the two Kings. Something was amiss. Something he couldn't quite put his finger on. And there was nothing Jesse hated more than when things didn't fit neatly into place.

As he watched Anora bite her lip and twist her hands together in obvious agitation, it struck him that she didn't care to have him and Ben King anywhere near each other.

What was she hiding?

Something big.

"Brought you home a little surprise." King limped up and passed Anora a grubby length of rope with a weary-looking pregnant cow tied to one end. "Time we got started building up that herd you been nagging about."

"I hear tell you've been away," Jesse said, crossing his arms over his chest.

"That's right."

Jesse's eyes never left the other man's face. He had a gift for smelling guilt, and King out-and-out reeked of it.

"Right neighborly of you to look in on Anora while I'm gone." King limped up to Anora and flopped an arm across her shoulders. "What's a fella have to do to get a little welcome-home kiss?"

"We have company," Anora said pointedly.

King cocked a look in his direction. "I imagine the marshal has seen a husband and wife share a little kiss before? Ain't that right, Marshal?"

"I have to go." Jesse turned away. Aware that his hands had clenched into fists, he forced his fingers to uncurl.

His heart pounded in his chest like a stampeding herd. He took three steps, stopped, and turned, just in time to see Anora rubbing furiously at one cheek with the heel of her hand.

"I expect you've got a bill of sale for that cow."

"Sure thing." King reached into his vest pocket and pulled out a dirty scrap of paper, which he waved in the air between them. "Take my word for it?"

Jesse hated being baited. He closed the space between them and plucked the paper from King's fingers. "I don't think so." He scanned the letters scrawled across the page. "I never heard of a rancher in these parts named Ross Jackson."

"That's cuz he's not from around here," King said. "He was passing through, heading due north. Driving his herd up to Montana. Old Millie ain't doing so well, given her condition, so he was fair happy to get rid of her. Give me a good price."

"Unusual," Jesse remarked, refolding the paper and passing it back. "Don't oftentimes hear of a fella selling a cow that's near about ready to birth."

"Just in the right place at the right time."

"So it would seem."

Anora spoke up, as if anxious to dispel the tension. "Marshal, I didn't get you that pie I promised."

"Some other time," Jesse said shortly. "I best be getting back to town." Behind him he heard King's grating voice.

"I seen you been out picking huckleberries again, Nory. Marshal, only a fool'd pass up a treat like Anora's huckleberry pie."

Jesse kept on walking and acted as though he didn't hear. From behind him came the sounds of someone dogging his steps and he reached Sully just ahead of King.

"You forgot something."

"What's that?" Reluctantly Jesse turned to face the other man, wondering for the umpteenth time why Anora'd up and married him. Out of pity, perhaps. She didn't love him. He'd swear she didn't.

He caught himself. Reminded himself songwriting love didn't exist.

"Your barking iron." Metal glinted silver in the sun as King held the pistol toward him.

"I gave that to your wife. Woman living out here ought to have some means of protection."

King flushed dull red. "If and when I decide Nory needs a gun, I'll be the one supplying it. We don't want your charity. You got that, Mister Lawman?"

"Sure thing." Jesse took the pistol and tucked it inside his saddlebag before he mounted. As soon as he was astride, Sully gave an impatient little crow hop, as if the animal was as anxious as he was to get away from King. "You best register that brand your cow's wearing, so's folks hereabouts know she's yours."

"And dissuade those rustlers roaming these parts."

Jesse gave him a measuring look. "Somehow I doubt you have any worries on that score." Heels to Sully's flanks, he left King choking on his dust.

"What the hell'd he mean by that?" Ben stared at Jesse's retreating back.

"I didn't hear what he said." Anora approached, cow in tow. "Don't you ever pull a stunt like that again, you hear?"

"Like what?" Ben pulled his innocent little-boy face, but Anora wasn't having it.

"You know very well what I'm talking about. Kissing me in front of the marshal."

"For crying out loud. I come along and find the two of you making calf's eyes at each other. 'Magine if I'd been five minutes later."

Anora stepped forward and slapped Ben, feeling a satisfying sting as her hand connected with his cheek. When he stumbled back a step she saw the red outline of her fingers and she gasped softly. What on earth had come over her? Ben looked as shocked as she felt.

"Ben, I'm sorry. I didn't mean—"

"Remember, playing this little married act was all your idea. Shame if it suddenly cramps your style."

"Wait a minute," Anora said, her voice low. "Where have you been these past days?"

"I told you. Working." He pulled a handful of money from his pocket and waved it in her face. "Got the cash to prove it, too."

"Working where?"

"Damn, Nory. You're set to drive me batty with your nagging. North of here."

"I want to know what you were doing."

"Why? So's you can report it back to your marshal buddy? You know all you need to know. Now I'm going down to the creek and get washed up. Had all I can take of your caterwaulin'."

Jesse edged forward in his chair. He'd forgotten just how much he hated the political end of law enforcement. Sure, he believed in justice, probably more than the average man. For certain he liked things nice and neat and orderly. What he didn't appreciate was a situation such as the one in hand, where Smithy and half a dozen neighboring ranchers crowded inside his office, telling him how to do his job.

"So we heard a rumor Tom Horn's available. For the right price."

"I thought we got through this the other day. Which one of you fellas is willing to put up the two hundred and fifty dollars a month Horn charges to baby-sit your cattle?"

"You're just sore 'cause that's five times what you make."

Jesse leaned forward abruptly. His palms hit the top of his desk with a thump. "Y'all listen up. I am not "sore." I know Horn. I know he earned his reputation when he was deputy sheriff in these parts. I also know he prides himself on killing being his specialty."

"We're sick of having our cattle stole out from under our noses," said one man with a nasal-sounding voice.

"That's right," chimed a second. "I say cattle thieves is no better than coyotes. Ain't nothing if we shoot a coyote sniffing around our herds."

Jesse heaved a weary sigh, wondering one more time just why he'd let Ricki cajole him into this job. Knowing the answer even before he asked the question. Because he was arrogant enough to think he could make a difference. And unlike his daddy and his brothers, he prided himself on doing the right thing. The same right thing that included ensuring the ranchers kept well out of the way while he set a trap for Rosco.

Voice lowered conspiratorially, Jesse adopted his "just one of the boys" pose. "Just so happens I've got a plan." The men leaned forward as one body.

"What kind of plan, Marshal?"

"Can't give you all the details right now. On account of I can't be putting it into action until the railway strike's over. But if you'll give me till then, give me your word on waiting, I'll put a stop to Rosco once and for all. If I don't, if Rosco or anyone else is doing wrong by you boys, then go ahead and hire anyone you want. I'll gladly look the other way."

"I don't cotton having to wait," said a heavyset rancher at the rear.

Jesse held his breath. The silence stretched interminably.

"Horn wants a lot of money," Smithy said finally. "I say we give the marshal a chance to do his job."

The room resounded with a series of grunt, nods, and mumbles before the men started to move. Smithy reached across the desk and extended his hand.

"Till after the strike."

"Agreed." Their handshake signaled the end of the meeting. Jesse stood and watched as, one by one, the men filed out.

Eddy was leaning against the back wall watching, his boyish face puckered in confusion.

"Something eating you?" Jesse asked shortly.

"Maybe." Eddy transferred the toothpick from one side of his mouth to the other.

"Too bad," Jesse said shortly.

"You don't countenance killing. How you aiming to look the other way if they bring in Tom Horn?"

"Sounds as if you expect Rosco to outfox me."

"Never said nothin' like that. It's just that the last marshal before you—"

"Wasn't me," Jesse said. "You ought to realize by now I've got my own way of doing things."

"I guess." Eddy ambled to the hat stand and plopped his Stetson onto his head. He opened the door and stepped outside, mumbling a greeting to someone coming in.

Jesse glanced to the open door impatiently. *Now what?*

His insides snapped to attention the instant Anora King, looking perkier than he'd seen her of late, stepped inside the office. She glanced up at him with a big, bright smile.

"Morning, Marshal."

"Mrs. King," he returned cautiously. She had a basket over her arm and the tip of a red-and-white-checkered tea towel hung over the edge. As she drew near, his mouth started to water at the delicious smells coming from inside the basket.

"Brought you a fresh-made huckleberry pie," she said, her face pinkening up as she spoke. "Seeing as how you didn't get any the other day."

"You didn't have to do that." Matter of fact, he quite wished she hadn't. Seemed every time he'd managed to tell himself he was doing a fine job of keeping her at arm's length, she turned up on his doorstep looking prettier than a picture. Tugging at all his protective male instincts the way no one had since Rose. And in a fashion far more disturbing to his peace of mind.

"Aren't you the one said to me, just the other day, what's wrong with a body being nice?"

"Guilty as charged." Jesse allowed himself to relax ever so slightly. "Sure does smell like a little slice of heaven. You care to sit?"

"I wouldn't want to keep you from your work." She perched daintily on the edge of the straight-backed chair across from his desk, still warm from Smithy's backside, Jesse reckoned. "I'm on my way over to Lettie's." At his questioning look, she lowered her gaze. "I thought lots about what you said after you left the other day and decided you were right. Who's to say we ought not give a body the chance to feel good?" She brightened. "Besides, Penny's fixing up a back corner of the store with some picture books, to encourage the youngsters to read over the summer. A lending library, she called it. I'm helping her get it set up."

"That's good." It would get her off the ranch and keep her away from that stooge of a husband. Even as the thought surfaced, Jesse asked himself if he was more bothered by the fact that Anora was married or the man she'd chosen to make a life with.

Jesse sat down and leaned way back in his chair, laid one boot-clad ankle across the opposite knee, and pressed the tips of his fingers together like a church spire.

"How you been keeping?"

Anora seemed surprised by his asking. "Me? Never better. Why do you ask?"

Jesse chose his words carefully. "I was worried the other day. 'Fraid your husband might have got the wrong idea about what we were doing. Me teaching you to shoot."

They both knew it wasn't the shooting they were talking about. It was the way they'd been together, and clearly liking it.

Anora glanced at her lap where her hands were folded, prayerlike. "Ben means well. He just isn't too good at expressing it, is all." Something danger-ous twisted into a big old knot deep inside Jesse as he listened to Anora defend a man they both knew wasn't worth defending. What was it about womenfolk? Such fools where men were concerned. Then he recalled his brothers; men could act just as big of fools as anybody, over a woman who wasn't worth the time of day. He recalled the school-marm's concerns about King's temper.

"He didn't . . . hit you or anything, did he?"

Anora bit back a smile. "Truth be told, I'm the one who slapped him."

"Did you now?"

"Yes. He made an improper suggestion about the nature of you and I together. And he's sorry."

I bet he is!

Deciding it was time to change the subject, Jesse leaned forward abruptly and peered under the tea towel in the basket. "Sure does look as good as it smells."

Her smile was as bright as a rainbow after a storm. "Well, I'd best not keep you any longer."

"Let me get that door for you." As he rounded the desk, Jesse brushed past her, so close he could feel the heat emanating from her, smell the fresh-ness of her skin and her hair. A dozen unnamed feel-ings shot through him, so strong he saw his hand tremble as he reached to open the door. He turned back to her.

"Anora?"

"Yes, Jesse?"

She stood alongside him, all big-eyed and moist pink lips. Close enough to touch. And, Lord, he wanted to touch her. He balled his hands into fists at his side to help resist the impulse as he cocked her his famous devil-may-care grin. "I kind of miss your dungarees."

"Oh, you." She made to give his arm a playful swat when, watching her face, he saw something shift. Something powerful. Seconds later she clutched his forearm with a strength he hadn't thought her capable of. "Jesse. There's something I need to tell you."

Jesse caught his breath. Behind him he could hear the clock on the wall tick off the seconds as he watched Anora worry her bottom lip. Before she could speak the door flew open, catching him on the shoulder and knocking Anora's hand from his arm.

"Hey, Marshal." Jake from the telegraph office waved a paper aloft. "Good news. Strike's over. Come tomorrow old iron Bessie'll be stopping at the station, right on schedule."

9

All day long, as folks came and went from the store, it seemed all anyone could talk about was the strike being over. Anora, for her part, was relieved. Maybe now things would get back to normal around here. Normal, like she'd get back to work. Between her and Ben, they'd save enough for his operation sooner than a body could shake a stick.

Best of all, she'd be too busy to notice this powerful urge to spend time around Jesse Quantrill. Just to see him. His charm-the-knees-off-the-bees smile. The way his eyes crinkled at the corners, then darkened with slow, molasses-melting want when his gaze met hers.

Seeing him wasn't enough anymore. These days she had the most unsettling urge to reach out, to touch him. Like back in his office. Lord a'mighty, she'd been on the brink of blurting out her newest fears. That Ben was riding with Rosco's gang. That the money her brother was suddenly throwing around had come from pulling holdups.

She wasn't proud of her actions, but after he went out yesterday she'd snooped through Ben's things in the barn. To her dismay she'd found a lady's ring with some kind of shiny blue stone and a gold locket in the shape of a heart. Where else would Ben have gotten these things, if not from thieving?

Lucky for her, Jake had interrupted her with Jesse. She had swallowed her concerns and, during the pandemonium that broke out up and down the street as news spread of the end of the strike, she'd been able to melt away, to lose herself in the bustle of Lettie and Sam's store. She frowned slightly as she concentrated on standing the books side-by-side A-to-Z, the way Penny had shown her.

"Anora. Anora. Did you hear?" Penny bounded into the store and skidded to a stop alongside her.

"That the strike's over? Nobody's been talking about anything else all day."

"Not the strike. That's old news. The dance."

"What dance?" Her friend was acting mighty strange, hopping from foot to foot and wringing her hands with excitement.

"Tonight. Down on Station Street. They're already building a wooden dance floor raised up off the street. Oh, you simply must come. Everybody'll be there. Nothing like an excuse for a party."

Anora picked up another book. "I don't feel much in the mood for partying right now. I believe I—"

"Oh, but you have to come. Doesn't she, Lettie?" Penny turned to Lettie and, from the way the two women were eyeballing her, as if she were some kind of specimen under glass in one of those museums back east, Anora knew she wouldn't get a moment's peace until she agreed.

"I'll have to make sure it's okay with Ben first." She sighed inwardly at the way her two friends exchanged looks. Too late to wish she'd never started this charade. Ben as her brother was one thing. A gal couldn't rightly help who she was kin to. But pretending Ben was her husband was beginning to wear right thin with her.

For one mad, impulsive moment she considered dropping the truth into the conversation, casual-like. *Oh, by the way. Seems everyone has a slightly wrong impression. Ben and me, we aren't married. Lord, no, brother and sister is all.*

Wouldn't that cause a stir!

Her mother had lectured her and Ben long and loud on the evils of deceit. How a body got trapped into a lie, telling more and more falsehoods trying to defend the first lie. And hadn't Ma been right? She didn't see any way out from under this whopper.

"There. It's settled. You're coming." Penny clapped her hands together and sent Lettie another look, this one so plumb full of meaning Anora started to feel left out.

"What is it?" she asked, shifting her gaze from one woman to the other. "Come on. Out with it. What's the big secret?"

"Out back." Lettie took Anora's arm and

shepherded her through the crowded storefront to
the back storeroom.

"What about the customers?"

"Most of them's more interested in jawing than
buying," Lettie said. " 'Sides, Sam can handle things
for a couple minutes."

The storeroom was even more cluttered than the
front of the store, but Lettie didn't let up her pace as
she propelled Anora, Penny at their heels, through a
maze of barrels, sacks, tools, and tin cans of every
size. When Lettie stopped abruptly, Anora plowed
right into her.

"Ta da!" Lettie waved an arm toward the far wall
where, draped on its very own wood hanger, floated
a delicate harvest-colored muslin gown. Cinnamon-
colored ribbons edged the bodice and dangled from
puffy gathers halfway down each sleeve.

"What? I don't—" Lettie and Penny grinned at
her like two cats in the cream pail.

Lettie lifted the gown down and held it against
Anora. "Perfect," she told Penny. "Didn't I tell you
those colors were made for Anora?"

Anora fondled the soft folds of the fabric.
Breathed deeply the new-fabric smell. She'd never
owned a brand-new gown, always somebody's leav-
ings or hand-me-downs. Reluctantly she released
the garment.

"I can't possibly accept it," she said. "Something
so fine."

"What?" Lettie stiffened as if she'd just told her
the moon was made of green cheese. "I never heard
such nonsense."

"I can't pay for it. And I can't accept your charity."

"Land sakes, girl. Since when does a body go calling a gift charity? That's a downright insult, it is."

"But—"

"Anora, just listen," Penny said. "The yard goods came in with a big flaw and Lettie had to send them back."

" 'Cept one little piece that went missing," Lettie said with a shrug. "Can't rightly say how that happened."

"You know I love to sew," Penny continued. "Gives me something to do in the evenings. I had fun. We both did. Planning the surprise. So don't take that away from us. Please."

Anora's heart swelled full to the point of bursting and she feared she was about to embarrass herself by busting out in tears. Stretching out her arms, she drew her two friends close. "I don't deserve friends like you."

"No one does," Lettie said briskly, "but you got us anyway. Now we expect to see you at the party tonight, dancing yourself silly in this new frock. Do I make myself clear?"

"As mud," Anora said, with a shaky grin.

"Good. Now, I best get back out there before that husband of mine gives away the store," Lettie muttered. Raising her voice, she called, "Just hold your horses, man. I'm coming."

As Penny watched Lettie depart she heaved a heartfelt sigh. "Don't you wish you had what they have together? Oh." She flushed. "I didn't mean—"

Anora patted her friend's arm; at the same time she resisted the urge to tell her the truth. "It's all right, Penny. Ben and I have a different kind of . . . arrangement than Sam and Lettie."

Penny nodded, obviously eager to change the subject. "You like the dress?"

"I think it's the most beautiful gown I've ever seen."

"So try it on. Let's make sure it fits."

"Right here? Right now?"

"Why not?"

"Why not, indeed?"

A short distance west of town, Jesse rode alongside his two deputies, Eddy and Charlie, their mounts cutting a close line next to the railway tracks.

"You sound pretty sure about this, Marshal." Old Charlie removed his hat and scratched his grizzled head.

"I am," Jesse said shortly.

"How come you're so sure?" Eddy asked. No mistaking the challenge in his voice.

Jesse didn't bother answering. Too difficult to explain to a lummox like Eddy the value of gut instinct, coupled with experience. Jesse couldn't say how he knew for certain Rosco and his gang would try to sabotage the rail lines. He just knew. The same way he knew Rosco had been playing close to his chest since Jesse's arrival; even going so far as to move his base of operations.

Whatever cat-and-mouse game Rosco had taken to playing wouldn't last. And it wouldn't be long now before the outlaw became once more highly visible in Boulder Springs, flaunting his misdeeds.

He was the type who couldn't resist a little show-manship. Jesse wasn't worried. He'd tangled with far more cunning minds than Rosco's. And he'd never been bested yet.

Ricki always said it was on account of him having a natural born outlaw's mind; lucky for folks he chose to wear a star. To use his cunning to uphold the law instead of breaking it, in the way of his pa and his two brothers. He'd talk to Ricki again tonight.

"I swear, Jess. Sit down before you wear a hole in my carpet."

"Sorry. I didn't realize I was pacing." Jesse turned from the window to face Ricki. She'd lit a thin brown cigar, and the pungent smell of tobacco smoke streamed toward him as she exhaled. Behind him, through the open window, the sounds of music and laughter drifted over from Station Street.

"Looks like the whole damn town turned out for the dance tonight."

"Near 'bouts," Ricki said. "We both know why I'm not down there. What's your excuse?"

Jesse raked a hand through his already rumpled hair. "I don't belong there any more than you do."

"Balderdash!" Ricki shot back at him. "If you really believed that, you wouldn't be so restless. You'd be stripped down and having it on with me or one of the girls." Her eyes moved suggestively down the length of his body. "Ain't healthy for a man like you to be going without."

Jesse laughed humorlessly. "Save it for the paying

customers, Ricki. I've gone without before. I know it won't kill me."

"Might kill you, though, to admit you're sweet on some little town gal. Gal who happens to be already spoken for."

Jesse kept his features impassive. "You mean Anora King. I feel sorry for her's all. She kind of reminds me a little bit of Rose."

"Another delicate flower in need of your protecting?"

"Don't remind me about that." He turned his back on Ricki and the insipid pink room. It had been a mistake to come here tonight. He'd known that the second he set foot inside Ricki's salon. But it had been impossible to remain in the boardinghouse with so much merrymaking going on almost right outside his window.

Behind him he heard Ricki approach. Heard the whisper of air against her gossamer sheer gown, seconds before he felt her arms snake around his waist. She laid her cheek against his back.

"You trying to seduce me, Ricki?"

"You know I'm not. I'm trying to be a friend. Got a funny feeling you could use one about now."

"I have to go." Gently he disentangled himself from her arms.

"That clinches it," Ricki said, picking up her cigar from the ashtray and taking another puff. "Anytime a body probes a little too close to the bone you bolt. Predictable as hell, you are, Quantrill."

"I'll try and make a point of remembering that." Jesse picked up his hat from the table near the door and jammed it on his head. Downstairs the front parlor was unusually silent, but the second he set foot outside the door, sounds of the celebration danced clearly in the still-warm nighttime air. Without any prompting from Jesse, Sully made his way to Station Street.

The entire street was damn near unrecognizable. On the platform outside the station half a dozen citizens of Boulder Springs had formed a musical group, and what they lacked in skill they more than made up for in enthusiasm. At one end of the makeshift dance hall two kegs of beer were a magnet for the celebrators, and Jesse felt certain the harder stuff was being tapped off somewhere nearby.

He stood in the shadowed overhang of the station house, hands in his pockets, eyes on the dancers. A wood platform stretched from one side of the street to the other for about thirty feet, with steps at one end. The edges of the temporary dance floor were strung with bobbing lanterns, while up and down the street dozens more lanterns hung from gutters and makeshift posts, keeping the night at bay and rendering the street almost as bright as the noontime sun. The sidelines were ringed with makeshift benches, where mams and grams held sleeping babies while school-age youngsters took part in their own version of the dance. Someone had scattered a bundle of straw to help keep down the dust.

Jesse's gaze returned to the temporary dance floor, where a bevy of partners dipped, twirled, stomped, and spun. He told himself he was merely watching, not seeking out anyone in particular. Deep down he knew he was watching for the light to hit a cascade of cinnamon-colored curls. Several minutes marched by without him spotting Anora among those present, yet his instincts told him she was out there someplace.

Abruptly his attention shifted and he straightened as he made out the furtive movements of a shadowy figure slinking away from around back of the musicians. He'd just started after the first man to go have a look-see when he felt a hand lock around his elbow. He had his gun out of his holster before he recognized the stumbling gait of Charlie, his deputy.

"What's the matter with you?" Jesse said.

"Sorry, Marshal. I seen Ben King sneak off and thought I'd follow him."

"You do that," Jesse said, holstering his gun. "Just don't go sneaking up on him like you did me. He's likely to blow your head off. Don't let him catch sight of you. Just watch where he goes."

"He's been drinking hard these past hours," Charlie said cheerfully. "Like as not the entire cavalry could trail him and he wouldn't notice."

Jesse watched King mount his swaybacked gray and ride in the opposite direction of Three Boulders. A short time later he saw Charlie's shadowy form in pursuit. Behind him the revelry and partying continued. Curious as he was to Ben King's destination, Jesse couldn't help but think how his departure meant Anora was here on her own.

"How come I haven't seen you and Ben out on the dance floor yet?" Penny asked breathlessly, fanning herself with her hand as the musicians took a well-deserved break.

"Ben doesn't dance," Anora said. "You know. His leg."

"What about you? There's loads of single fellas who'd dearly love to give you a twirl. All they need is an encouraging smile." As she spoke Penny ladled herself a glass of punch.

"Wouldn't seem right." Anora deliberately changed the subject. "Who's that long, tall drink of water I noticed monopolizing you most of the evening?"

Penny colored slightly. "Beau Brown. Kind of cute, isn't he? He's a couple of years younger than me."

"Can't rightly say as how that appears to be bothering him any."

"Me either." When Penny giggled it was impossible for Anora not to join in. She felt as young and carefree as a schoolgirl. And the good Lord knew she'd not felt that way before. Earlier tonight she'd been walking on eggs, aware of Ben hanging around imbibing freely from the cask of whiskey. She'd been secretly relieved to see him mount up and leave.

"What'd Ben say about your new dress?" Penny asked.

Anora smoothed the gathered skirt of the garment in question. She knew she looked her best and, darn it all, she wished there were someone around to acknowledge it. She envied Penny the flattering attentions of her young man. No one had ever made Anora feel attractive and feminine and special.

"Didn't even notice, did he?"

"Doesn't mean he didn't like it. He never notices what I wear."

Penny gave her a pitying look. "Well, there's plenty other fellas here giving you more than a casual notice, if you get what I mean. Come on. It's high time you had yourself some fun." Penny took her arm and started toward the dance floor just as the musicians picked up their instruments.

Anora planted her feet firmly but Penny was bigger and stronger and the straw underfoot was slippery. What a sight they must look, Anora thought, Penny plowing ahead, dragging a plainly reluctant Anora behind her.

"Evening, ladies." Anora froze, and Penny with her, as the marshal stepped toward them from the shadows. Jesse included them both in his greeting, but to Anora it felt as if he had eyes for her alone. The approving way he looked at her made her feel beautiful. More than beautiful. Desirable. She heard Penny open her mouth and draw in a breath and knew that if her friend uttered even one word, the spell would be ruined. She gave Penny a subtle kick on the shin. Then another. Penny's mouth closed with a snap. Her friend gazed from Anora to Jesse then back to Anora. With a tiny, smug smile she turned and melted in the direction of the music and lights.

"I owe you a debt of thanks." Anora clasped and unclasped her hands in front of her and wished she had a fan or something, anything, to hold on to. "I do believe that's the second time you've saved me from being trampled."

"How so?" One corner of his mouth quirked upward in amusement. His gaze was riveted on hers. Anora felt certain there must be music being played, but its melody had faded insignificantly into the background.

"She had some buck she was fixing to have swing me about on the dance floor."

"Wouldn't your husband object?"

Anora forced a laugh. "I guess I was safe so long as Ben was here. But now he's not and so I . . ." Her voice trailed away as Jesse took a step closer. Followed by a second.

His voice was a low rumble in his throat. "Now you're not safe?"

Definitely not!

"Why, I should be, now, shouldn't I? You being the marshal and all."

"I imagine that depends." His breath wafted through the warm evening air and fanned the tendrils of hair she'd artfully arranged across her forehead. She was taken aback to smell the faint odor of whiskey on his breath, which didn't still the strong urge she had to step into his arms. "Where'd your husband light off to?"

"He said something about a game."

"I hear he's been luckier lately at the card tables."

"Where'd you hear that?"

"It's my job to hear. Hear he's been flashing a roll of bills, too. He buy you that frock?"

Anora glanced down, hiding a smile. He'd noticed the dress. "This? No. Lettie and Penny gave me this."

"Still. You must be relieved your husband has a . . . job."

"I guess." Anora focused on where the toe of her boot peeked out from beneath the hem of her gown.

"I trust it's a legitimate venture?"

"A what?"

"On the up-and-up."

"Course," Anora said quickly. A little too quickly.

"Where is it again that he's working?"

"Some place north. I don't rightly know the name of it."

"Ah, yes. The mysterious northern connection."

Anora heard the sarcasm in his voice. They both knew neither of them was fooling the other. "Why did you come here tonight?"

"What do you mean?"

"I looked for you earlier on. You weren't here. Naturally I assumed . . ."

"Assumed . . . ?"

"That you had someone . . . something else to keep you entertained this evening."

He laughed, a rich, amused rumble in the dusky air. "Maybe I did. Looking for me, were you?"

Anora bit her lower lip, aghast at her bumbling. "I only meant—"

"I know what you meant. Come on. Let's go try out that dance floor, shall we?"

Anora was torn between a longing to feel Jesse's arms around her and her sense of what was proper. "Do you think we should? I mean, if you and me go up there and share a dance, folks are bound to talk."

Jesse tilted his head to one side. "Does that bother you? Folks talking about you?"

"I guess. A little."

"Well, I respect your position. And I wouldn't dream of doing anythi—" His words were interrupted by the loud crash of shattering glass.

10

"What was that?" Anora instinctively stepped closer to Jesse.

"Sounded like it came from the street in back of us."

They both spoke at once.

"The office."

"Your office."

Anora half ran alongside Jesse as he strode through the alley that joined Station Street with Front Street. Sure enough, as they reached the other end, a shimmer of silver moonlight glinted on the shards of broken glass in front of the marshal's office and outlined the jagged hole in the plate-glass window.

Anora stood rooted to the spot as Jesse went over

and unlocked the door. Who would do such a thing? In spite of herself she recalled Ben's cocksure swagger as he hitched his pants and took himself off from the dance earlier. She squeezed her eyes shut in silent prayer. *Please don't let it have been Ben.*

She heard the crunch of boot heels against broken glass as Jesse crossed the darkened office. Anora opened her eyes in time to see him light a lantern. The sudden flare of lamplight illuminated his face, accentuating his pronounced cheekbones and square-edged jaw and stabbing deep mysterious shadows beneath his eyes.

"Watch yourself," he warned as she reached the open doorway. "There's glass everywhere."

He held the lantern aloft to reveal a brick in the middle of the floor with a crumpled note attached by a hunk of twine. After setting the lantern atop his desk he stooped to retrieve the brick. She watched the way his strong, capable fingers untied the note and smoothed the paper flat so he could read it.

" 'Mind yer own biznez— er els.' Not much for originality."

Anora moved toward him. "You're hurt!"

Jesse followed her gaze to the smear of blood edging the hastily scrawled note. He turned his palm up. "It's just a scratch."

Blood pooled in his upturned palm, leaked between his fingers, and landed in glistening dark drops on the desktop.

"You're losing a fair bit of blood for a scratch." Anora snatched up his hand and examined it closely. "Hold still. I think there's glass in it."

She whipped out her hankie and wrapped it around the tips of her fingers before slowly easing a sliver of blood-soaked glass from Jesse's palm.

She knew it had to smart like the dickens, yet Jesse didn't even flinch. Acted as unconcerned as if she were brushing a crumb of toast from his hand. "Where's the salve?"

"Hell, I don't know. Try the desk."

Anora reached across the desk and opened each of the drawers in turn. "Nope. Where else?"

Jesse didn't seem to notice as blood continued to ooze from the center of his palm and splash the scarred wooden desktop.

"Oh, for pity's sake!" She wrenched the velvet ribbon from one sleeve of her gown, knotted the ribbon across his forearm, then picked up a pencil and stuck it through, tightening the whole thing tourniquet-style. "Raise your hand above your head and hold it there."

"When did you get so bossy?"

"When'd you get so careless?" Her fingers clasped his elbow, as if she didn't trust him to keep his hand elevated. "You could have sliced off a finger on that glass."

"You're right." Fathomless brown eyes, as deeply shadowed as the room around them, glittered at her in the half light, dark and dangerous. "I was a mite distracted."

"Well, I wouldn't go around making a habit of it," she said, tilting her head at him.

"How long are you planning to keep my arm waving in the air?"

"Till the bleeding stops."

"Generally speaking, I'm not much of one for standing still."

"Somehow that doesn't surprise me." She tightened her grip, aware of the warmth of his skin seeping through the linen fabric, and the comfortable intimacy of their stance. The soft rise and fall of their breathing, backgrounded by the softer strains of music from the station.

"Listen," Jesse said. "Can you hear that?"

"Hear what?" Anora felt as if every one of her five senses were suddenly heightened. She couldn't just hear the music; its strains seemed intent on filling her. She couldn't merely smell Jesse, the musky, male scent of his skin; she was overtaken by him. She didn't just feel the heat of his skin; it surrounded her, feeding her. And her sense of taste. Excitement danced across her tongue. Followed by anticipation.

The total newness of these sensations was not only exhilarating, it was unsettling. She didn't know where to look. What to do.

"They're playing 'I'll Take You Home Again, Kathleen.'" Jesse started humming the familiar tune and before she knew how it happened he had placed his free hand on her waist, her arm landed on his shoulder's and they were dancing, sort of. Moving to the music the best one can with one's partner's arm arrow-straight in the air.

As Jesse crooned the words in a credible Irish lilt, his breath stirred the hairs on the back of Anora's neck and her insides felt funny. All soft and mushy. Soon her limbs felt mushy as well. Her hand wandered from Jesse's elbow to his shoulder, following the ridges and slopes of hard-banded muscle beneath the impossibly soft linen of his shirt.

His skin was warm and the heat seeped through the tips of his fingers and settled into the indentation of her waist. Anora shivered, nothing to do with the air temperature. Every inch of her flesh was chased in goose bumps, atingle in a way she'd never felt before. Her fingers gripped and released Jesse's shoulders as she stared straight ahead, eyes level with the open collar of his shirt. Crisp black hair curled into sight where the top button was undone.

As if of their own accord her hands slid from his shoulders to rest, flat-palmed, against his chest. She could feel the accelerated beat of his heart, drumming through her fingertips. Tilting her head back ever so slightly she studied his jaw. Its square masculine shape was edged in shadow where his whiskers had grown in during the day. If she shifted her gaze even slightly she'd be able to see his lips.

She didn't dare.

Didn't dare stare at his mouth.

Didn't know how she could possibly resist the temptation to press her lips to his.

She heard his breath catch. Could it be he was plucking the very thoughts from her head and spicing them up with a few of his own? Her heart skipped a beat, then raced ahead, leaving her feeling flushed and breathless. Vaguely aware the music had stopped.

"I think it's stopped," Jesse said. His voice was low, husky, sending little sparks of awareness skittering up her neck to her ear.

"The bleeding," he added, when she failed to respond.

The bleeding!

"Let's see." Anora spoke briskly as she took his hand in hers. She probed his palm and saw him wince.

"The edges are starting to close," she said. "Doesn't even look like you'll need a stitch." She glanced around for something to wrap across his palm and keep the wound clean. "I expect it'll smart some when you ride. It's cut right on the crease."

"It's a scratch," Jesse said. "I won't even feel it by tomorrow."

Anora disagreed but didn't contradict him. "Do you have something here that I can make a bandage from?"

"There's some clean sheeting out back near the cells." He started back there and Anora trailed after him. The corridor was full of shadows that deepened to a soft darkness till Jesse paused to light a lantern. The flare of light accentuated the room's gloomy corners and the bleakness of the two unoccupied cells, each with a single narrow cot.

Inside the first cell Anora spotted a white sheet folded on the end of the cot. "You're certain this is clean? You wouldn't want to risk infection."

"Just back from the laundry," Jesse said. He sounded shaky, and when she looked up she noticed he looked a trifle pale.

"You best sit down." Anora picked up the sheet, bit it between her teeth, then tore a two-inch strip from end to end. "I don't want you passing out on me."

"Don't tell me you think I'm a weakling?"

"No. I think you lost more blood than either of us realized at the time. Hold your hand out straight." He flopped down onto the cot and set the lantern on the floor next to him. As he held his injured hand toward her, palm up, she couldn't help but be aware of the way his long legs splayed forward, one on either side of her.

Her mouth went dry. Her hands shook slightly as she wound the white cotton strip around and around his palm, split the end with her teeth, and knotted it tight. "There. That ought to hold. You should get the doc to dress it properly tomorrow."

"It's fine the way you did it."

She shot him a wary glance. His words sounded a trifle slurred. Impossible to tell in the lamp light if his color was off. "You feeling okay?"

"Never better."

Inch by inch his legs slowly closed together, trapping her between his thighs. Anora's balance faltered and she planted her hands on his shoulders to steady herself. He turned his head and placed a searing kiss on the inside of her bare forearm. The heat from his lips ricocheted through her like a shooting star. Slowly she sank down in front of him, aware of every sinew of strength where his powerful legs gripped her tight.

She swayed toward him, fingers plowing through his hair where it brushed the back of his collar. She wet her lips, parted them slightly. The wait seemed forever before he captured her mouth beneath his.

As their lips touched, they groaned in unison. The kiss deepened. This time Anora knew to part her lips. To expect the delicious sensation of Jesse's tongue wrapping itself around hers. Sweeping the inside of her mouth in a way that turned her bones to liquid.

Jesse's arms closed around her and crushed her against him. She could feel her nipples tingle as they met the hard wall of his chest. His hands roamed possessively across her back from the base of her spine to just above her shoulders, then back again, lower this time. He cupped her bottom in a shockingly delightful way, urging her hips closer against the juncture of his legs. Anora felt the manly stirring of him; evidence of his arousal that swept her away on a dangerous, uncharted current of excitement.

She murmured in disappointment as his lips left hers, then sighed in pleasure as his plundering mouth found the sensitive hollow between her shoulder and neck. She arched her spine, her head lolling back as his lips wrought their magic on the sensitized skin of her neck.

She stiffened slightly as she felt his fingers wriggle down inside the neckline of her gown beneath her underpinnings, but when he brushed the nipple of one breast a sensation so exquisite shot through her, she jerked taut in his arms. Her mouth formed a round O of surprise, before he once again claimed it for his own. Jockeying himself into a reclining position, he tugged her prone atop him.

Sprawled across Jesse, Anora was frustrated anew by the layers of clothing between them. She managed to unfasten the buttons fronting his shirt and allow herself the pleasure of touching his chest. How his flat, masculine nipples hardened when she grazed them with her thumbnail. His breath caught as she ran her palms lingeringly through the crisp black vee of hair peppering his breastbone. Daringly she edged her fingers down near his navel, dangerously close to the fastening of his pants. All the while his mouth and tongue were teaching her new and wonderful ways a man and woman kissed.

She felt the insistent pressure as he ground his hips against hers, and she accommodatingly rolled her hips in return, a move that elicited a groan of pure masculine pleasure. He grabbed a handful of her skirt and pushed it up out of the way. His fingers snaked their way past her stocking tops, branding the bare skin at the top of her thigh.

Oh, my lord! she thought.

"I can't!"

With a startled exclamation Anora pushed herself up and onto her feet. Her chest rose and fell as she wrapped her trembling arms around her waist and fought for breath. Everything he did to her, every place he touched felt so good, too darn good; she just wanted the touching to go on and on forever.

What he must think of her, a supposedly married woman, groping and breathing heavily here in the dark with him. Hot, stinging tears of shame and frustration burned against her lids. When she opened her eyes he was lying ever so still on the cot, arms wishboned beneath his head, nothing moving except his chest and his eyes. Wary, watching eyes.

With one economic move he rolled to his feet and retrieved his hat, which had fallen to the floor. He dusted it against his thigh and the movement sent his shirtfront flapping.

"Don't look at me as if you're afraid," he said. "I heard you."

"But you don't know why."

"I don't need to know why, now do I? A lady says no, I respect that." He rammed his hat on his head, picked up the lantern, and brushed past her, back to the front office, leaving her alone in the dark. Part of her wished he'd lock the cell door after him. Give her a ready excuse to curl up on the cot and not have to face anyone ever again.

Anora didn't know how long she stood there before she became aware of sounds in the outer office. The steady swish of a broom as someone swept up broken glass. The outside door opened and shut, followed by a low, masculine curse. Shoulders straight, head high, Anora marched out front to see Charlie, face-to-face in earnest discussion with Jesse.

Charlie looked over at her and his jaw dropped.

Anora cleared her throat. "I finished refolding that sheet we used to bandage your hand, Marshal. I hope you'll have the doc take a look at it."

Jesse responded with a noncommittal grunt.

"Enjoying the dance, Charlie?" Anora asked pleasantly, as if the sight of her coming out of the jail cells was an everyday occurrence.

"Indeed I am, ma'am." Belatedly Charlie dragged his hat from his head and pressed it to his chest.

"Well," Anora said pleasantly. "Now that the excitement here's all through, I believe I'll take myself back to my friends at the dance."

She reached the door and grabbed hold of the knob as if her life depended on it. Turning back, a ready smile on her lips, she said, "Evening, gentlemen."

Her smile faltered. Across the dimly lit room she saw Jesse's shirt still unfastened, his chest criss-crossed with faint red welts from her nails.

His eyes met hers above Charlie's head. She tore her gaze from his and fled.

Anora ran the entire length of the alley and didn't stop until she reached Station Street, where only a few stragglers remained. A handful of men gathered around the beer kegs, seeming intent on draining them dry. The musicians had packed up their instruments. Most of the lanterns had been put out.

"There you are!"

She swung about in relief as she recognized Penny's voice.

"Where have you been? Lord, girl, you had us worried. Mrs. Graft said she and her husband had offered you a lift home, but they couldn't find you. Figured you musta left already. I didn't think you'd go without saying good-bye. What happened?"

Penny stepped close, touched a streak of dried blood near Anora's wrist, the spot on her sleeve where the velvet ribbon had fluttered earlier. "Are you hurt?"

Anora shook her head vehemently, aware of the way Penny's Beau hovered nearby. "Just tired. I'll tell you later."

"You look tired," Penny said critically. "Beau and me, we'll take you home."

"You don't have to—"

"Save the argument. I won't have you walk home alone in the dark. Lord only knows where those out-laws are lurking about."

Beau and Penny swayed from side to side on the

wagon's wooden bench, singing off-key some of the songs Anora guessed they'd danced to earlier tonight. She stared up at the cloudless backdrop of the night sky, ablaze with hundreds of stars. It was a familiar sight, one she'd witnessed countless times before on the trip west, but tonight she felt the heavens had taken on an extra shine. Even the half moon seemed more intense than she recalled.

Was she changed for life? A few kisses. The brush of skin against skin. The simple magic of sharing another's heartbeat.

She didn't know which was worse. To want Jesse and know he wanted her, yet not give in to temptation. Or to have him think her a woman of loose morals, plenty eager for him to warm her bed when Ben wasn't around.

What a tangle! She glanced enviously at Beau and Penny. Noted the way his arm circled Penny's shoulder and curled her up tight alongside him. How lucky they were. How simple their enjoyment in each other's company.

"I really appreciate the lift," Anora said as Beau drew his team to a halt near the front porch.

"No, problem, ma'am. You want for me to go in with you? Make sure everything's in order?"

Anora gave Penny's hand a squeeze and mouthed the words, "He's sweet."

"No thank you, Beau. I'm just going to splash some water on my face and fall right into bed. Like as not I'll be asleep before my head even touches the pillow."

Penny gave her a quick hug, long enough to speak directly into her ear. "I want to hear *everything*. I do mean *everything*." She drew back. "Night, Anora," she said in normal tones. "Sweet dreams."

"Night, you two." Anora stood on the front porch and watched the wagon slowly make its way toward town, Penny and Beau a shadowy lump that could have been one person rather than two. With one final glance at the heavens she turned and went inside.

11

All was in readiness.

Jesse, crouched low in the saddle, leaned over and patted Sully's sweaty neck. It had taken him several days of intense concentration, thinking with the criminal part of his brain, along with watching and waiting. Eventually his nose had led him to the tunnel a few miles west of town and a cache of dynamite, which he had carefully dismantled.

He glanced at his watch. Anytime now the noon train would scream into Boulder Springs. A few minutes later it would snake its way west toward the tunnel's entrance.

A barren and inhospitable stretch of land with barely a scrap of green fronted the tunnel, and Jesse knew the risks he and his deputies were taking. In all likelihood Rosco had the surrounding hillside staked out with gang members, witnesses to his latest misdeed.

Charlie wiped a sheen of perspiration from his upper lip and slipped a plug of tobacco into his mouth. "Gotta tell ya. Sure am relieved you knew which wires to pull, boss."

Jesse cocked him a wry grin. "You hope."

Charlie's only answer was a snort, which turned into a startled exclamation.

"Hey!" Charlie pointed with a crooked index finger. "Ain't that Ben King? What's he doing?"

Jesse felt his insides recoil as if a lead ball had landed in his belly. "Son of a bitch! Don't tell me Rosco sent a boy to do a man's job."

King, astride his swaybacked gray, was picking his way gingerly along the tracks toward the tunnel. Every now and again he'd pause, look over his shoulder, then up into the foothills, almost as if he could feel their eyes upon him.

"Ain't he wandering a damn sight near where the dynamite was set?" Charlie asked.

"I wonder," Jesse murmured, more to himself. "Could it be Rosco's intention to get King out of the way? Permanent-like?"

"You think Rosco's that black-hearted?"

Before Jesse could respond, Sully sidestepped. The horse's big hooves started to slide on a loose patch of rubble and sent a shower of rocks skittering down toward King. Even from this distance Jesse could see the look that crossed the other man's face.

Abruptly King wheeled his mount about-face and headed for the hills. Jesse turned to his deputies.

"He's mine. Charlie, you and Eddy circle around behind. Whatever you do, don't spook him."

That said, he took off after King, confident his mount could easily outrun the gray.

Up ahead, King abruptly vanished and Jesse hesitated. Now what? Was he being set up? About to ride straight into an ambush around the next bend?

He shook his head. Could it be he'd underestimated Rosco? The prospect didn't feel good. As he watched the surrounding hills for movement he finally caught a glimpse of King, making better time than Jesse would have thought possible. Just then he heard the train's whistle and prayed he'd effectively dismantled the dynamite charge. He turned and watched. As the train passed through the tunnel without incident he breathed a silent prayer of relief. Passengers and crew would never know how close they'd come to being Rosco's next victims.

King left a trail behind him a mile wide and Jesse slowed right down, letting caution be his guide, as he listened to his inner voice that insisted there was no need to rush. The hair on the back of his neck prickled a warning as King's trail led him to a parched plateau. It felt quiet. Too quiet!

He scanned the surrounding countryside and finally spotted a weathered gray shack that blended so perfectly with its surroundings it would have been easy to miss, if it had not been for the sight of King, who dismounted out front and hobbled inside.

Jesse paused. Something smelled bad all ways around. Why would King deliberately lead him to the gang's hideout? Unless—

An explosion ripped the air and the shack disintegrated in front of his eyes. Whatever pieces didn't blow sky-high were devoured by flames. King's horse bolted. By the time Jesse reached the demolished structure he couldn't help but think that if he'd followed more closely on King's heels, could be he'd have been caught inside as well. Was that Rosco's plan? To take both of them out at once? Didn't make a whole lick of sense to Jesse. The town would just up and hire a new marshal. Eliminating him didn't do much more than buy Rosco time. Time for what?

The flames burned out as fast as they flared up, and he ventured close enough to see the booted feet of a man's charred remains just inside what used to be the door. Jesse removed his hat and bowed his head.

He'd seen death in all its many guises; young ones, oldsters, and every age in between. Over the years he'd schooled himself to save his pity for those the victim left behind. In this case, Anora King was the real victim. And she wouldn't take kindly to his pity. Jesse knew that. Just as he knew he had to work clear of it before he broke the news to her.

Ben King's death left Anora King a widow. Jesse chased away the thought the second it took shape. What kind of man was he? To even think of moving in on a widow whose husband's body lay still warm?

Anora's money pouch was satisfyingly full and her lunch barrow empty, as she made her way to Lettie's store. Lord, but it felt good to once more find herself a woman of means. Tonight she'd sit right down and have a heart-to-heart talk with Ben. Make him listen. Convince him that whatever he'd got himself involved in, his "job" wasn't worth the risk.

She had just about reached the store when she heard it. A rumble in the distance that sounded almost like thunder. She felt it too, a tremor so slight that if she hadn't stopped walking to listen, she would have missed it. A tremor that began in the soles of her feet and rippled faintly up her legs.

She shaded her eyes and gazed skyward. No storm in the offing, at least not evidenced by today's cloudless blue sky. She listened, but the sound wasn't repeated. Not on the way to the store, or later as she made her way homeward.

The shack was sweltering hot, what with the stove blasting away, even though she'd left the door wide open in an attempt to have a little fresh air pass through the room. Anora opened the oven and dipped her basting spoon into the nice fat drippings from the plump roasting hen she'd prepared for dinner. The bird was browning nicely. She turned the pan and thought about mashed potatoes. Gravy. Fresh ears of corn. The kind of meal she hadn't cooked for Ben. Not ever.

Mostly 'cause he was never around at the meal hour; not from any reluctance on her part to prepare the food. It just seemed a waste given that Ben didn't seem to care or appreciate her efforts. She'd gotten used to making do. A leftover sandwich. An egg fetched from the chickens. When Ben did eat, it was like as not cold beans straight from the tin.

But not tonight. Tonight they'd share a real meal,

complete with napkins, candles, and fresh flowers on the table. They'd have a long talk, the kind they ought to have been having all along, ever since their pa was killed. She'd tell him about those doctors in Boston. Her plans for their future. Together they'd start to feel like a real family. The thought sent warm flutters through her, and at the sound of horse and rider out front she pasted a welcoming smile on her lips, turned to the door, and froze.

"Afternoon, Anora." Jesse Quantrill stood in the doorway. He swept his hat from his head and ducked slightly as he came right on in, as if he had every right in the world to be there.

She was incensed by his intrusion, but not so riled that she missed the uneasy way he fingered the rim of his hat. She'd never seen Jesse act this way. Kind of tentative-like. Unsure of himself.

"Marshal."

He sniffed appreciatively. "Something sure smells good."

She knotted her hands in her apron, wondering if Ben was in trouble. "Is this a social call? 'Cause as you can see I'm just about to serve the meal. Mine and Ben's," she added.

Jesse cleared his throat. "Actually, that's the reason why I'm here."

The sober tone of his voice warned her to prepare for the worst. "I'm afraid I don't understand."

"Why don't you have a seat?" He pulled out one of the crude wooden chairs alongside the table. She saw the way his eyes briefly flickered over the candles. The jelly jar of wildflowers. The colorful napkins she'd just finished hemming.

"I prefer to stand, if it's all the same to you." Anora clung to the ridiculous notion that if she remained standing before Jesse, he wouldn't be able to see the bed. The narrow cot that was barely wide enough for her and all too obviously did not accommodate a husband and wife.

"Mind if I sit?"

She opened her mouth to say yes, she did, in fact, mind, but she was too late. Jesse had already lowered himself into a chair, which responded with a protesting groan. Setting his hat on the table he turned to look at her and the expression in his eyes struck terror into Anora's heart. It was a look that apologized in advance for what he was about to say, and she resisted the childish urge to press her hands to her ears and block out his message.

She forced her gaze to remain fixed on his.

"Ben's dead."

Not until she heard the words did she realize she'd been holding her breath. It left her lungs in a whoosh at the exact same time her knees buckled, and she would have fallen flat if Jesse hadn't jumped up and grabbed her.

Being caught and held in Jesse's arms was the last place she wanted to be. It was also the only place she wanted to be. The one fortress designed to offer safe haven, to buffer the pain of hurt and loss that clawed at her insides.

Ben is dead!

Jesse clasped Anora tight against him and tried to absorb some of the shudders racking her small frame. Knowing even then that there was nothing he could do to lessen the impact of his news.

She didn't attempt to deny his words, or rail at him for details. She asked neither how nor why, just quietly burrowed against him and accepted the small measure of his comfort as he rubbed his hands lightly, soothingly across her back. He didn't murmur platitudes of how it was all right. How things would eventually be better. He knew firsthand how empty words held little solace at a moment such as this.

As he held her and rocked her, Jesse wished for the power to make it better. To chase away the pain. When he felt a wet warmth dampening his shirtfront he was glad to be there, blotting her tears. Even in grief Anora didn't wail or cry, just leaned against him and let the healing river flow.

His mind wandered back in time to the blackest day of his life, when he'd broken similar news to his sister Rose. Rose had accepted his words in the same dignified way as Anora. She'd accepted his quiet strength, his comfort; all the while Jesse'd felt consumed by guilt, aware of the part he'd played in Cameron's demise. Much like today, with Ben King. Why hadn't he overtaken the other man in time to stop him from going into the shack?

Gritting his teeth, Jesse wished he were anyplace other than here; at the same time he knew he'd never leave Anora alone to face her empty future. As he stroked and rocked and petted her, his eyes lighted on the table. Bitterly he wondered what manner of celebration she'd been planning. Surely Ben King, for all his faults, must have had some redeeming features. Been worthy of the love of a woman like Anora King.

Love! Hah! Look what love did. It took a sensible

woman like Anora and turned her into a victim. It was sadder still to see her shed tears over a man who, in Jesse's opinion, wasn't worth it.

He tried to find a gentle way to extricate himself. To leave Anora alone with her memories. Alone with her grief.

As if sensing his need to pull away, Anora took a step back, flashed him a tremulous smile, and wiped her tearstained face with a corner of her apron. "Thank you," she said, "for coming here personally."

Jesse felt as if she'd just twisted a knife in his gut. Although she knew, they both knew, he could have sent someone else, Charlie, Lettie, or the school-marm, to break the news.

Lord, he hoped she didn't ask for the details. At the same time he schooled himself to recite the facts exactly as they'd happened, sparing neither himself nor her. But she didn't ask.

"I know Ben had his faults," Anora said quietly, her voice not quite steady. "But he was all the family I had."

Jesse knew firsthand how it felt to be alone. Schooled himself against the wash of sympathy that threatened to shatter his professional detachment. Now was not the time to be anything other than the local lawmaker, the bearer of unfortunate news.

"Well," he said, his voice unnecessarily loud in the emotion-racked interior of the shabby one-room cabin. What kind of future did she have? A woman on her own out here? "I'd best be getting back to town. His, um, his remains will be at the undertaker's. Whenever you feel up to making some decisions."

"Decisions." She looked blank and Jesse cursed the fact that while he longed to get away, his conscience wouldn't allow him to just up and leave.

"You know. A service. A burial."

"Oh," Anora said quietly. "When ma and pa died we just, buried 'em. You know. Right there where it happened."

"It's different here in town. Folks will be looking to pay their respects and the like."

She sounded surprised. "They will?"

"I expect." The open doorway beckoned, precious freedom, mocking him from across the room. Finally he could stand it no longer. "You haven't asked what happened."

"No." Anora sank bonelessly into the chair. "I know it was cowardly of me. Somehow, by not knowing, I can imagine it was gentle and peaceful-like." She leaned forward and blew out the candles, the soft hiss of her breath sounding over loud in the silence. Then she turned to Jesse. "It wasn't, was it? Gentle and peaceful-like?"

"No," Jesse said. He decided in that instant to spare her as much as he could. "He was just in the wrong place at the wrong time."

She nodded as if to herself. "That was Ben. All his life, it seemed. Wrong place and time."

Jesse fought the urge to approach her, to lay a comforting hand upon her shoulder. Instead, he hovered near the doorway, hat in hand, unable to shake the feeling that he was letting both of them down. "If you need anything, anything at all, you just give a holler."

He wasn't sure if she heard or not, but he took

her silence as dismissal. Outside Sully cropped a clump of sweet grass, and angled his head up as Jesse approached. Was that reproach in the animal's liquid brown eyes? In that instant it seemed to Jesse that Sully, with his infinite animal wisdom, cottoned more than he, a mere man, ever would. For slowly and very deliberately the animal turned his back on Jesse. *Go back*, he seemed to be saying. *You're not through here yet.*

Jesse balled his hands into fists and glanced beseechingly at a sky doing its best to release the daylight to night. Then he turned and retraced his steps, each one more difficult than the last.

12

The labored rise and fall of Jesse's breath was the only sound that penetrated the velvet evening air till he reached the teetery wooden steps, where his boot heels rang an appropriately hollow sound like a death march. The cabin door stood open, just the way he'd left it, the room beyond in semidarkness.

Why was he going back?

Because he'd walked out on Rose when she needed him most. And she'd almost lost her baby, his nephew, because of it.

Anora was strong. She'd recover. But if he didn't know for certain he'd done everything he could, *he* might not.

She wasn't where he'd left her at the table and it

took his eyes a minute to adjust, to discern her among the room's lengthening shadows.

He heard a soft, pitiful sound coming from the bed and followed it with his eyes. She was so slight he could barely make out her form, curled up tight in a ball.

She sounded scared! Scared and alone. Attuned to her as he was Jesse could feel her fear, her aloneness, as audibly as if she'd shouted it to the heavens. But of course she didn't say a word. He didn't know if she was aware of him even after he'd moved to her side.

"Anora." His voice was low, aquiver with some emotion he neither recognized nor acknowledged. His hand, as he reached to smooth the tear-damp tangle of hair from her face, trembled slightly, only gaining confidence as he culled warmth from her skin to his.

"Jesse." His name was a breathy sigh on her lips, a whisper of salvation as she turned to him. When she scooted over it seemed only natural that he settle next to her in the narrow space. Only natural that he thread his fingers through hers and squeeze tightly, offering support.

Her hand was so small he feared the slightest pressure would crush it. Yet the way she slid her fingers into his signaled complete and total trust.

Lord, he didn't deserve her trust. Not when he'd used her and her husband to get at Rosco. Hell, it could even be his fault Ben King was dead.

"Thank you," she said, her words so low he had to strain his ears to catch them. "I couldn't face being alone right now."

"You're not alone." She sounded so frail, so defenseless. In spite of himself he kicked off his boots and stretched out next to her, then shifted to gather her against him. He felt a tremor ripple through her, starting with her toes. Lord, the soft rise and fall of her chest against his. The sweet warmth of her breath bathing his face.

"This feels nice." Her voice sounded hollow, as if it came from underwater or far away. "No one's ever held me like this before."

No one?

Such an admission should have been enough to send him bolting once more for the door. Instead he smoothed a tangle of red-gold curls from her forehead, cupped her face between his callused palms and offered her the only comfort he was capable of, as his lips brushed the soft, dewy skin of her forehead, her cheeks, her eyelids, and finally her mouth.

She parted her lips beneath his as if his kiss was the most natural thing in the world. Immediately he felt the embrace get out of control. All guise of comfort evaporated, leaving in its stead the heated need of man for woman and woman for man; a need as old as time itself.

He pulled away.

She followed, her mouth seeking the comfort of his, her hands betraying her need to hold someone, something, as she gripped him with a suddenly awesome strength.

"Don't," she murmured against his lips, when he tried to resist. Tried to sit up and away. To straighten clothing that had suddenly become loosened.

"I have to," he said. "You won't thank me tomorrow if we—"

"I don't care about tomorrow." Kneeling above him she began the slow, fumbling act of unfastening her shirtwaist. Jesse licked his lips, unable to tear his gaze from the silken shadows and planes slowly, tantalizingly revealed to him in the room's half-light, as she removed first her blouse, then her chemise.

Her breasts fell free, forbidden fruit within his reach. Pale white skin, too soft and translucent to touch. Rosy nipples that even as he stared, begged for his touch. Craved the moist warmth of his kiss.

He felt her small, nimble fingers on the buttons of his shirtfront before she pushed both shirt and vest off his shoulders. He sucked in his breath at the scalding moisture of her tongue as she dipped it across one nipple, pressed her lips to the crisp, dark hair matting his breastbone. Then fastened her mouth atop his.

Her breasts flattened against his chest before she dragged them slowly across him, and Jesse's resistance shattered. Blood drummed through his veins as he recalled each and every time he'd seen Anora. Been with her. Wanted her. Touched her, knowing even as he did that he couldn't have her. That she belonged to another.

Now she was with him, begging to be his. And Lord help him, he would have her. Even knowing as he took her that he didn't have the right.

He eased her skirt down past her hips, inch by tormenting inch. He felt the gentle curve of smooth, pale thighs, softer than any skin he'd ever touched.

Except for her breasts. Surely such softness didn't really exist.

Hooking a finger under the waistband of her pantalets he skimmed them off. Soon Anora was totally naked. Totally his. With a speed he didn't know he was capable of, he shucked off his clothes and gathered her against him, feeling a rightness that shocked even him. He felt her indrawn breath as every inch of her skin met every inch of his.

He squeezed his eyes shut and silently begged for her to touch him, but she didn't. When he opened his eyes she was still watching. Obviously waiting for him to take the aggressor's hand. Some switch, considering she'd practically stripped him naked. He was accustomed to bedding women whose enthusiasm and aggression matched his. Anora, he suspected, needed to be gently coaxed. His loins tightened at the challenge.

"You're not . . . changing your mind?" It just about killed him but he had to ask, knowing he could stop now only if he had to. After that . . .

She shook her head, took his face between her hands, and whispered, "Make love to me, Jesse." The sweetest words he'd ever heard. He responded by allowing himself the liberty of touching her. Everywhere.

She lay beneath him soft and submissive, her little sighs and breathy moans telling him she approved what he was doing, the way he touched her; gently here, rougher there. A damp, open-mouthed kiss here, the gentle heat of his breath across her dewy skin. Her breathing quickened as his touch grew bolder. As he watched her eyes glaze over with passion as bright as sunlit emeralds, he felt a possessive sureness.

He was the one! Anora's response was for him and him alone. He pushed from his mind the memory of her dead husband. Nothing existed save the here and now. Himself and Anora. Spinning through time in a seamless cobweb of light. No before. No after. Only now.

Her limbs trembled with need, her breath caught in ragged gasps, and still she hadn't touched him. Taking her hand in his Jesse guided it from his chest, across his stomach, and lower, to the part of him that craved her touch more than life itself.

"Oh!" She gave a startled gasp, whether at the boldness of his actions or the size of him he didn't know. All he knew as he closed his eyes and savored the sensation of her tentative fingers exploring his length, was that he'd never before experienced such powerful intensity in a woman's touch.

He coaxed her legs apart, knees bent alongside him, and angled himself against her. As he swooped down for one more kiss before their joining, he felt her tremble as her arms gripped his shoulders and her knees clung to his hips. His kiss was as urgent as his need of her and he entered her smoothly, only to stop, half-embedded.

Surely she wasn't that small; too small to fully accommodate him. He pushed harder. Saw her biting on her lower lip. She looked up, their gazes met, and in that second he knew.

Knowledge hit too late as his body, acting on pure instinct, tore through her maidenhead and possessed her fully.

He knew that he'd hurt her. Too late now. All he could do was try to make sure she got as much pleasure as possible from their coupling.

With every fiber of self-control he could muster he withdrew despite her small, half-protesting cry. Poised above her he lavished kisses on her breasts, her stomach, her hipbone, until he felt the tension slowly seep from her, felt her begin to tremble anew with need.

He dipped his tongue into the salt-sweet skin of her navel, then skimmed lower, through the downy cinnamon curls, to kiss her precious femininity in apology for earlier hurts. He heard her indrawn breath as his tongue located the tiny pearl of sensation buried deep inside her womanly petals. Slowly he laved the tiny bud as he felt a new and different tension grip her limbs.

Almost at the bursting point, he entered her smoothly, heard her deep, rewarding moan of pleasure as he increased the pressure, stroking her with gentle, heated precision that pushed her up and over the pleasure plateau.

His own release followed with a draining, mind-numbing, shattering intensity. As he crashed back to earth atop her, Jesse knew he'd just experienced everything heaven had to offer. And was about to enter hell.

"You were a virgin." The first words out of his mouth and they weren't exactly loverlike. As Anora touched the harsh line of his jaw and his unsmiling lips she wasn't worried. Could the man who'd just made love to her the way Jesse had be anything other than patient and understanding?

Unless . . . She'd heard some men didn't enjoy bedding a virgin. Preferred a woman with more experience. Was Jesse one of those?

"Was it . . ." She angled her head toward his. They were lying on their sides, facing each other, the only way they could both recline on the narrow cot. "Was it awful for you?"

Jesse gave a short, barking laugh. "Awful? No, I wouldn't say that."

"I'm glad." She snuggled against him, enjoying the hair-roughened length of his leg where it rubbed against hers.

"Anora. You're avoiding the issue."

"Issue?" She gazed at him, puzzled.

"Your marriage wasn't a normal one. Why not?"

"Oh, that."

"Yes, that."

"Ben." For a short time in Jesse's arms she'd managed to forget Ben was never coming home. "Ben was injured as a youngster. He couldn't . . . You know . . . claim his husbandly rights." Anora didn't know how such a lie popped glibly to her lips. It was just . . . After what she and Jesse had just shared she couldn't bear for him to think badly of her. That she'd deceived him all this time.

"He what?" Jesse bolted upright as if he'd been branded with a cattle iron.

"Don't make me say it again," Anora pleaded.

"So that's why you were always giving me the come-hither?"

"It's not like that. Not between you and me."

Jesse rose and commenced pulling on his clothes. She hadn't really looked at him before. But now a crescent of moonlight filtered through the cabin's only window and gave her rather an enticing view of his male anatomy. Sleek buttocks. Tapered hips and waist. Flat, hair-downed stomach. A chest deep-walled with muscle. She felt her body respond as she looked at him, if such a thing were possible.

"I don't sleep with virgins."

"Only widows?" she said, stung by the abrupt change in him. "You needn't worry. I'm not about to go tattling, to brand Jesse Quantrill the despoiler of a woman's virtue." Watching a dull red flush creep up his neck to his cheekbones she sensed she'd gone too far.

With Jesse fully dressed, Anora was doubly conscious of her nakedness as he leaned over and brought his face to a level with hers. "I don't like being used."

"I didn't—"

"Oh, yes, you did. You could have told me the truth. And what you really wanted."

Anora grabbed the sheet and tucked it around her nakedness. "I didn't want anything," she said. Her words were hollow and lacked conviction. She had wanted Jesse. Wanted him to notice and desire her. Now she'd gotten her wish.

"Nothing except the chance to lure me into your bed under false pretenses?"

"Oh, you . . . you know nothing. Not one single thing of how it feels to be young and female and all alone."

Jesse's eyes were mired with an emotion she didn't fully understand. "I've got a pretty fair idea," he said. Then he left.

He'd worked Sully into a terrible lather by the time he reached the livery, and he felt a new twinge of guilt. Seemed he was abusing everyone who crossed his path tonight, including his poor horse.

"Sorry, old boy," he said as he removed the saddle and briskly rubbed the animal down. "I guess she kind of made me crazy. Women."

Sully gave him one of his long, soulful looks, as if he knew exactly what Jesse meant.

Anora's last words continued to hammer around and around in his head. *You know nothing . . . of how it feels to be young and female and alone.* His baby sister Rose had said the same thing, right after she'd admitted it was Cameron who'd gotten her in a family way. Adding, candidly, the unfairness of a world where it was perfectly fine for Jesse to sleep with whomever he chose. Yet not all right for her, 'specially now she was with child. For his part, Jesse'd tried to do his best by his sister. Convince Cameron to take her to wife.

Look how that had turned out!

As for the Kings. Jesse couldn't sleep that night for one relentless question circling his brain. Could he have ridden harder, reached Ben King sooner? He knew it was more than likely the explosion had been triggered by the shack door opening. Still and all, if King hadn't run in there, maybe he'd still be alive.

13

It was the smallest funeral service Jesse had ever attended. Only he didn't actually attend. He more like skulked in the background, telling himself he just wanted to make sure Anora was holding up all right. Except he might as well have saved himself the bother. He didn't catch even a glimpse of her face behind the concealing black veil. Lettie hovered over her like a mother hen, while the schoolmarm defended her from the other side. There were few other townsfolk in attendance, no one Jesse recognized.

He also hadn't seen hide nor hair of Rosco. In deference to Anora, Jesse had his deputies keep their knowledge of Ben's dealings with Rosco to themselves. All the townsfolk knew was that there'd been an explosion and Ben King had been in the wrong place at the wrong time.

Lettie had come around his office, taking up a collection to bury King, stating in her no-nonsense way that Anora didn't have the means. Jesse knew that he'd made far too generous a contribution. He kind of figured, seeing the way Lettie widened her eyes and gave him a scrutinizing look, that she'd keep the fact to herself.

The service was blessedly short, the casket lowered into the ground, with Jesse backing up out of range of vision a split second too late. The schoolmarm spotted him. He was too far away to hear what was said, but he knew, from the way Anora angled her gaze directly at him, that it concerned him. The others in attendance followed her lead.

Nothing for it, Jesse knew, but to offer the widow his condolences. Removing his hat, he faced the approaching group and waited.

"Sorry for your loss, Mrs. King." Even to him the words sounded stiff, as if his throat had rusted shut.

Anora bobbed her head curtly as if they were nothing more than strangers, her eyes unreadable behind the black veil.

"If you need anything . . ."

Anora turned to Penny. "Kindly tell the marshal that should I have need of anything, he's the last person on earth I'd go to."

Jesse winced at the coldness in her tone.

"Anora says—"

"I heard her," he said shortly. "Loud and clear." Wheeling about, he headed to where Sully stood waiting.

After the funeral Jesse fell into his more familiar role as an outsider. It struck him how folks seemed to look at him from the corner of their eyes, not straight on; he swore he could hear the buzz of conversation behind him the second he was out of earshot. Were they speculating about him and Anora? Wondering what he had to do with King's getting killed?

Jesse knew he was making mountains out of molehills, yet was powerless to control his thoughts as summer's gauzy heat gave way to autumn's riotous colors. The days cooled, the nights grew longer, and Boulder Springs saw little in the way of new developments. It seemed as if Rosco had ceased to exist.

Days melted into weeks and Jesse chafed at the lack of action. He packed and unpacked his bags a half a dozen times, telling himself that while Boulder Springs held nothing for him, he'd come here to do a job. His sense of honor demanded he see it through. Sooner or later Rosco would tip his hand, and when he did Jesse would be waiting.

It was late September when it struck Jesse that he hadn't seen Anora in town lately. Her usual spot on the railway platform had remained conspicuously empty for at least three or four days. He considered asking Lettie or Penny Spencer if they'd seen her, but in the end decided to make a quiet visit to Three Boulders himself and see if she was all right. As an afterthought he took along the pistol. He'd feel better knowing she had some sort of shooting iron for protection.

The ranch looked just as he remembered, Ben's

passing apparently having made little or no impact. And as he rode up to the cabin Jesse experienced a twinge of guilt. He ought to have checked on her before this. Maybe cut and stacked some firewood to see her through the winter.

Not, of course, that Anora was his responsibility, he assured himself quickly. But she was a woman alone. Polite society held a certain code of behavior when it came to dealings with the fairer sex.

He mounted the rickety front steps and rapped on the half-open door. No response. As he peered around the door into the unoccupied room he realized now why she'd always taken pains to keep him out of the cabin. The cabin where it was obvious she slept alone.

Maybe she was down by the creek. He'd just started down the front steps when he heard a strange noise coming from the bushes at the side of the shack.

His entire body tensed; his pace quickened. Pushing the bushes aside he nearly tripped over Anora, who was down on her hands and knees, heaving the contents of her stomach.

He froze, unsure what to do as she finished retching and slowly dragged herself to her feet and wiped her face with her apron. Lowering the apron from her face, she looked up and spotted him.

He would have sworn it was impossible for her to grow any more pale, but that was exactly what happened. Anora, whiter than bleached cotton, swayed unsteadily on her feet.

He took a hesitant half step toward her, then stopped when she held up one hand as if to ward him off. She cradled her midsection protectively with her other hand.

"What are you doing here?" Her voice was flat, as lackluster as her skin and her hair.

"I hadn't seen you in town lately." His tone softened. "I'm sorry you're not well." Up close, he realized she must have been sick for a time. The skin around her eyes was puffy and bruised-looking. He suspected she'd been crying. "Are you in a lot of pain?"

She shook her head and moved past him in the direction of the cabin.

"How long have you been sick?"

"Not long. It'll pass." She reached the steps and turned. "You've seen me. A little worse for wear, but hardly at death's door. You can go now."

As she spoke the wind picked up, bringing with it the sickly sweet smell of overripe berries and chicken droppings. Anora's eyes widened; she swallowed convulsively, tripping in her rush to escape inside the cabin.

Jesse caught her before she hit the ground, shocked by how thin she felt beneath her voluminous gown. He could feel every rib. The sharp outline of her hipbones. His palms cupped her belly.

He stiffened.

The overly rounded curve of her belly.

His thoughts flew backward in time to Rose and the sickness she'd experienced when carrying his nephew. A sickness triggered unexpectedly by sharp odors.

When Anora tried to wriggle from his grasp, his grip automatically tightened. She glared up at him, clearly too spent to fight.

He stared at her, hardly daring to allow his suspicions to surface. His thoughts must have been clearly written on his face, because suddenly she averted her gaze. When he felt the fight go out of her he knew for sure. Recognized the unmistakable instinct of a mother protecting her unborn.

Jesse released her so abruptly she stumbled before catching her balance. As he turned away he felt the self-loathing rise up in his throat and threaten to choke him.

He forced himself back around to face her. "Why didn't you tell me?"

She raised her chin a notch and straightened her shoulders. "Nothing to tell."

The rise of emotions was blinding and knocked him nearly senseless. She faced him all proud and defiant, the same way Rose had. Except with Rose he'd been the aggrieved brother defending his baby sister's virtue. In Anora's case he'd been the despoiler of that virtue. The lowest of the low. A cad of all times. And the man who ought to be calling him out for his actions lay dead and buried.

With a muffled exclamation of self-disgust Jesse turned and stumbled blindly toward Sully. It took every ounce of his strength to pull himself into the saddle. Once mounted, he rode away without a backward glance.

Anora watched him go, arms folded protectively across her abdomen, her emotions in a tangled knot. She'd never seen Jesse look so down on himself. For a minute there she thought he'd cottoned on to her condition, but then the strangest thing had happened. She'd watched the bluster ooze clear out of him. Wherever that reprieve came from, it had bought her some badly needed time, a fact for which Anora was profoundly grateful. Either that, or he'd guessed the truth, and was hightailing to town, where he'd pack his bags and be on the next train.

"Good riddance," Anora muttered as she turned to go inside, wishing with all her might that she meant it.

Something moved near Jesse, and the ripples of pain that split his skull were unbearable. He groaned and squeezed his eyes tightly shut. The movement increased, as did the pain, knifelike shards through which he recognized a woman's voice.

" 'Nuff of this nonsense, Jesse Quantrill," Ricki said. "You lie here much longer I'm gonna charge you rent."

"Leave m'lone." His tongue was an uncooperative hunk of dry flannel, his words almost incoherent.

"I've left you alone long enough," Ricki retorted. "Watched you fair try an' kill yourself with alcohol poisoning. 'Fraid I've had about all I'm prepared to put up with."

Jesse tried to move but the pain was too intense. "I'm dying."

"You wish," Ricki said. "Fact of the matter is, you got about the worst hangover I ever seen. And I don't feel sorry for you one whit."

Jesse squeezed one eye open a slit. "What happened?"

"You tell me. All I got outta you was a lot of babbling about Rose and Anora."

Anora! Memory came flooding back, despite his best efforts to keep it at bay. "How long I been out?"

"Two days. A record for you, far's I know." As she spoke Ricki pressed a glass into his hand. "Drink this and I'll get you some coffee."

Jesse didn't dare sniff at the contents, just tossed the drink back and hoped his stomach didn't empty itself all over him. His innards lurched sourly; he clamped his lips tightly together, swallowed the bile, and felt a faint settling.

"I'm not even going to ask what that was."

"Best not to," Ricki said as she took the empty glass. "Think you can sit up?"

"Do I have to?"

"Uh-huh. Nice and slow. You'll feel dizzy at first."

Dizzy wasn't the half of it. Sweat beaded his forehead. His entire body shook like a wet dog. Gritting his teeth, he swung his uncooperative legs to the floor one at a time, only to have the floor rush up to meet him.

He felt Ricki's arm around his shoulders holding him upright. As his breathing slowed closer to normal he met her gaze.

"You gonna tell me what happened to send you off like this?"

He tried to shake his head and winced at the pain. "Can't."

"Sure you can, soldier. This is Ricki, remember. You can tell me anything." Her voice dropped an octave. "Like you have in the past."

"Remember when Rose was in a family way? And Cameron refused to do the honorable thing?"

He thought he detected a faint wariness in her

eyes, but it passed so quickly he decided he must have imagined it.

"You tried talking to him and things went bad."

Jesse exhaled heavily. "Real bad. For a while there I wanted to take him apart, limb by limb, for what he'd done. But I never wanted him to die."

"I know that. Rose knows that, too."

"I've done the same thing."

Ricki frowned. "What same thing?" She paused. "You don't mean you and some girl . . . Here? In Boulder Springs? Who on earth . . . ?" Her voice fell flat. "Not that Anora King."

" 'Fraid so."

Ricki clucked her tongue against the roof of her mouth thoughtfully. "You sure it's yours? I don't mean to be crude, but sometimes . . ."

"Not a shred of doubt."

"Well then." Ricki rose and poured him a cup of steaming black coffee. "I suppose the two of you'll be getting hitched."

"What makes you say that?"

" 'Cause I know you. Honorable to a fault."

Jesse snorted. "Anora hates me."

Ricki cocked her head to one side. "They say love walks a fair close line next to hate. 'Sides which, I've seen the way she looks at you. Matter of fact, I've seen the way you look at her. Which, I expect, is how you got yourself into this fix."

"We both know I'm not husband material."

"Oh, well then," Ricki said airily. "In that case I'd best come by and help you pack. Train goes through at noon. You can just hightail it straight out of town and away from your responsibilities."

Jesse drained his coffee cup with a noisy slurp. "You got a real talent for knowing just the right thing to say."

"I try," Ricki said, with a smile. "I do my almighty best."

14

Jesse wouldn't call it luck, exactly, but as he watched Anora cross the street and go inside the church, he admitted it was an opportunity. For, while he'd been chafing to have a word with her in private, he was reluctant to go back to the ranch, feeling unsure of his welcome.

Unsure? Hell. In her place, he'd as soon blow his head off as talk civilly. But surely if he came upon her in the house of the Lord . . .

Swiftly Jesse crossed the road. As he climbed the steps to the church and reached to remove his hat he scowled, realizing his palms were damp with sweat. He felt as nervous as a schoolboy at his first dance. And he didn't much cotton to the fact of Anora having that kind of effect on him.

Inside he paused and allowed his eyes to adjust to the dim light. He hoped he wouldn't find Anora cloistered with the preacher, confessing to having engaged in the act of procreation outside of the marriage bed.

He spotted her standing alone up near the statue of the Blessed Mother. As he watched she leaned forward and touched her taper to a candle. The flame flared as the second candle took light and Anora sank to her knees. Noiselessly Jesse started toward her, before he had time to change his mind.

He reached her side and stood, scarcely daring to breathe. Anora's head was bowed, her eyes closed, as her lips moved in silent prayer. He drew a deep breath and filled his nostrils with the smell of her. Country blossoms, fresh clean air. Scented soap. His heart pounded so loud behind his ribs surely she could hear it, but if she did she didn't let on.

Eyes raised to the statue before him, he added his own particular version of prayer, then dropped to his knees alongside Anora. She started. Her eyes flew open wide and she sucked in her breath at the sight of him, kind of a soundless gasp.

"Wouldn't have taken you for one to set much store in the Lord," Jesse mumbled, not knowing what else to say. He turned his hat round and round in his hands as he spoke.

"There's plenty you don't know about me, Jesse Quantrill," she retorted. "By that same token, what brings you here?"

"I followed you in."

"Why?"

When he spoke, his voice was unsteady. "Why didn't you tell me?"

"Tell you what?" She appeared inordinately interested in the flickering candles near the statue's feet.

Emotions welled through him furiously strong and fast. Anger. Uncertainty. Guilt. "We'll be married." The words came out terse and clipped, not at all the way he'd meant to ask her.

Her head snapped back as if he'd struck her. "I beg your pardon?" Her voice was a harsh whisper in that holy place and he lowered his own accordingly, leaned instinctively close, to where he could feel the warmth of her breath and watch the sudden activity of a small vein pulsing near her throat.

"I said we'll be married. I'll not have any bastard running around wondering who his daddy is and why he didn't stick around long enough to give his mama his name."

"I'll see you in hell before I marry the likes of you."

At least she didn't bother to deny it. "You carry my child."

Her eyes on his were unemotional. He only wished he could be as stalwart as she. But she'd had a longer time to get used to the idea. To formulate her moves. "No one need know. They'll all think it's Ben's."

"Over my dead body."

Color flowed into her face, making her look strong and spirited. "I made the mistake of playing at marriage before. I won't be party to it a second time."

"Don't expect me to sit back and watch my child passed off as another's."

"You know what you can do about that, don't you?"

"What's that?"

"Leave. We both know you never intended to stay in Boulder Springs."

Jesse inhaled sharply. "Things change."

"Do they? Do they really, Jesse? You walked out on me, full of self-righteous fury at what you saw as my duplicity." She paused for breath, her eyes searching his face. "For us to marry would be to live another lie."

"I did you wrong," Jesse said stiffly. "I believe in honoring my obligations."

Anora got to her feet and studied him, the way he vibrated with barely suppressed self-righteousness. "I was not wronged. I made my choice freely. Now I live with the consequences of that choice. I'll hear no talk from you of obligations."

His lips thinned stubbornly. "I'll give you a spell to get used to the idea, if that's what you need."

"There's naught to get used to," Anora said. "I'll be just another widow lady raising her child alone. Happens all the time."

Jesse rose and ran a hand through his hair. "There's no point putting me off, 'cause I won't be."

Anora cocked her head thoughtfully. He sounded as if he meant every word. But hadn't she heard other men sound sincere as the preacher one minute, forgetting a gal's name the next?

"This kind of thing happen to you before?"

"Nope."

But she saw the shadow momentarily darken his eyes and knew something was buried in his past. "Well," she said with false brightness. "I'll think on what you said." As she spoke, her mind leapt ahead. Did she have enough money to disappear for a while? Someplace Jesse wouldn't find her. She thought about the ranch. The only home she'd ever known. Could she bear to leave it? To leave behind her two best friends, Lettie and Penny?

"Don't try it," Jesse said shortly. "I'd find you."

"I . . . I . . ." Anora bit her lower lip, nonplused. How could he have known what she was thinking? "I don't know what you mean."

"I think you do." Slowly he replaced his hat atop his head, his gaze never leaving hers, and Anora felt a deep shiver work its way from her brain to her toes. Jesse Quantrill was a man used to getting his own way.

Not this time.

She straightened her shoulders. "I appreciate your concern, Marshal. But I really shall manage just fine."

"Don't patronize me, Anora." He had hold of her almost before she saw him move; lightning fast. She heard a little squeak of protest and realized it came from her. "You got no choice. 'Cause I'll make good and sure every meddling gossip in this town knows who fathered your babe."

"No one would believe you."

"If you think that, you don't know much about human nature. Folks are always ready to believe the worst. 'Specially if they find it titillating."

Anora felt her bluster fade. "Why, Jesse?" Her

voice was the merest whisper as she appealed to his sense of decency. If he even had one. "What have I ever done to you?"

"You don't think denying me my own flesh and blood is enough?"

"Everyone knows men don't care about things like that."

He was silent so long she wondered if he'd answer her. She watched the emotions flit across his face, a gamut of them she couldn't even begin to guess at. Mighty powerful emotions, if his grip on her shoulders was any indicator.

"Haven't you figured out yet that I'm different from most men?"

"No denying that," she said softly. Even now she felt herself start to weaken. How easy it would be to nestle against him, to let him make everything come out right.

He abandoned you once! her conscience told her. *Nothing to stop him from doing it again.*

It was true!

Precisely why she determined to do this on her own, no matter how much Jesse claimed to want a part of it. She knew, despite what he said, he'd lose interest soon enough and ride off into the sunset on that splendid horse of his. Better he did it sooner than later. Before she lost every last shred of pride, and begged him to stay. Begged him to love her back.

"Well, Jesse Quantrill," she said loftily. "I believe I have considered your offer in the manner in which it was extended." She felt his grip loosen.

"Good."

"I decline. If you choose to ruin my reputation, then let it rest on your head. Along with the part you played in sending Ben to his death."

She'd scored a direct hit! Jesse released her, his face unnaturally pale beneath his tan.

"What did you say?" His words were long and drawn out, dangerously low.

"I hear the rumors. Folks figure you had it in for Ben. Maybe could have stopped him before he went inside that shack."

She had to hand it to him, he recovered fast. "Goes along with what I told you. How folks are more than willing to believe the worst."

"Is it true?"

He sucked in his breath, his color high. Now she'd gone and made him angry, and she reveled in her newfound power. To know she could lash out and wound.

"I guess that's one thing you'll always wonder about." He turned to go, then swung back around to face her. "I brought you this." He pulled the pistol from his belt and held it toward her. "I brought you bullets for it, too."

Anora looked from his face to the gun, then back to his face.

"Take it." He gripped the barrel, handle pointed her way. She reached for it. The metal was still warm from resting against his waist.

"What's it for?"

"Protection."

"Funny." She stared down at the pistol gripped in her small hand. "When the only person I need protecting from is you."

"You think on what was said here today. I'll be by later for an answer."

"I already gave you my answer."

"Then I guess it'll be up to me to change your mind."

The sickness passed as she'd known it would and she actually started to feel in a fine fettle. Lettie and Penny both commented on how much better she was looking. "Kinda glowing from the inside out," as Lettie put it. Anora, aware of the way her waistline had thickened and her bosom filled out, knew that while she was able to hide her news for now, she couldn't keep it a secret forever.

For the time being, though, she hugged her secret close as, for the first time ever, she found herself looking forward to the quiet peace of winter. Come spring she'd have her very own baby. She need never be alone again.

She'd not be alone today either, from the looks of things. For coming toward her was a strange sight indeed, Jesse guiding a runabout pulled by a splendid pair of grays.

"Whoa!" He sawed on the reins and pulled to a stop just short of the porch. Anora forced her mouth into disapproving lines.

"I told you last week I didn't want you making a habit of dropping by."

"And, I believe I told you, I'm quite accustomed to doing as I please."

He jumped lightly to the ground and plucked up a basket, which he carried into the shack.

Anora tried to ignore him, but out of the corner of her eye she spotted a tin of chocolate biscuits peeking from the basket.

"I suppose you expect me to make you coffee as well."

"Not at all." Jesse pulled a chair forward and straddled it as effortlessly as if he did it every day. "Fetch your prettiest bonnet. I'm taking you for a drive." He gave her a critical once-over. "Put some color in those cheeks. You're looking a trifle pale for my tastes."

"There's not one single thing wrong with my color," she said.

Jesse tilted the chair precariously on its rear legs and eyed her thoroughly. "I guess there's not at that. Still, some fresh air would do you and the young one good."

Her color flourished then. She felt herself flush with embarrassment at the casual way he referred to her condition. "I don't believe it's seemly for you to speak to me that way."

"I didn't think we stood on propriety, you and I."

Anora felt her cheeks grow even hotter. "If I accompany you for a drive will you promise not to speak of such matters?"

Solemnly he placed his hand over his heart. "I swear."

Jesse handed her into the buggy, then sprang up next to her and gathered the reins. She heard the protesting squeak of wheels in need of oil, and clamped one hand atop her hat as the buggy set off with a lurch. She'd not been in a rig of this sort before and she settled back in her seat, aware of how different things looked from her perch. Or was it Jesse's presence that made the autumn leaves appear more red-gold? The sky a deeper blue? Even as she detected a subtle softening in the austere landscape that seemed to flash past them in a blur.

"Where are we going?" Anora asked, as he guided the buggy away from Boulder Springs.

"Thought we'd cross the river toward Indian Springs." She could tell by the look he flashed her that he was aware of her concern at the townsfolk of Boulder Springs seeing them together, and she was grateful for his understanding.

Silence stretched between them uncomfortably and she was casting about in her mind for a way to break it when Jesse spoke. "Are you set with everything you need?"

"I don't know what you mean."

"For the ranch. Before winter has us in its grip."

"Oh. For the ranch. I should be fine."

Jesse shot her an impatient look. "You've yet to spend a winter in these parts."

"That's true enough."

"Come first snowfall you'll find yourself quite isolated."

Anora pulled her spine a little straighter. "I'll make out just fine."

Jesse gazed at her sideways. "I didn't mean to imply you wouldn't. But I'll be looking in on you regular-like just the same."

Anora stared straight ahead. "So long as you're here, you mean."

He pulled the buggy to a stop and turned to face her. Try as she might, there was no way to avoid his searching gaze. "I'm not up and going anyplace, Anora. And you know the reason why as well as I do."

Anora didn't know what to say. The remainder of their drive passed in silence that should have been uncomfortable, yet for some reason wasn't. In what felt like all too short a time Jesse dropped her back at the ranch, tipped his hat in farewell, and took his leave, with a promise to be back this way next week.

In spite of herself Anora found she looked forward to her weekly drive with Jesse. He showed up regular as clockwork, always with a thoughtful small gift such as flowers or fresh honey. Since she had no desire to be beholden she'd started to reciprocate in kind, presenting him with some fresh-laid chicken eggs or a loaf of her crusty homemade bread. It began to take on tones of a ritual, this exchange of gifts, this peaceful time together, away from town and wagging tongues.

"What's that you have there?" she asked, as he lifted what appeared to be a huge orange squash from the back of the buggy.

"Tomorrow's All Hallow's Eve." Seeing her blank look he continued. "Don't tell me you're not familiar with the legends of the restless spirits and how to appease them."

"What spirits?" Anora followed Jesse inside, where he plunked the squash on the table. To her amazement he pulled out his pocketknife and started to saw at the vegetable.

"You never heard about Jack and the trick he played on the devil?"

"No. Should I have?"

"I thought everyone had heard those old stories. Date back a thousand years or more, the way I heard tell. Pass me a bowl, would you? I'll scrape out the insides."

Anora did as he asked, unable to tear her eyes away from the corded strength in his muscular forearms, where he'd rolled his sleeves back past his elbows. As he spoke he hollowed out the center of the squash.

"Seems the devil didn't take too kindly to old Jack playing a trick on him. After Jack died he couldn't get into heaven, but the devil wouldn't let him into hell either. So he was left to roam the world with only a lump of coal and a pumpkin."

"So?"

"So?" Jesse echoed. "So nowadays folks light a candle inside a pumpkin to keep Jack and the other restless spirits away."

"What other restless spirits?"

"Samhain, the god of witches, assembles the souls of everyone who died during the past year, and puts them into the bodies of animals."

Anora eyed him skeptically. "You're making this up."

"I swear. The bigger the sinner the lowlier animal he turns into."

"I never heard such pagan nonsense. What would the preacher think if he heard you talk this way?"

Jesse made no response, just continued to scrape out the insides of the pumpkin.

"Want a scary face or a friendly one?" he asked, the tip of the knife blade flush with the pumpkin's skin.

"What's the difference?"

"Beats me," Jesse said, starting to cut. "My sister, Rose, always wanted a friendly face. She was an awful coward when she was young."

"Your sister." Anora sank into the nearest chair. "Where does she live?"

"In Philly. She has a dress shop there. Does pretty well for herself and her boy."

As he spoke Jesse cut holes in the pumpkin for eyes, a nose, and a toothy grin. Then he lowered a candle stub inside and lit it. The light glowed eerily, illuminating the maniacally grinning face, and Anora clapped her hands in delight.

"Now what?"

"Stick it in the front window tomorrow night to keep the unfriendly spirits at bay."

"I will. Thank you, Jesse." For some reason Anora had a lump in her throat. She didn't think she'd ever been given a more thoughtful gift.

"You're welcome. Now, you ready to take a spin into town with me?"

"Into town?" Anora blanched. "I don't think . . ."

"You can't hide out here all winter and show up next spring with a babe in your arms. Folks are bound to notice."

"I'm not ready," she said.

"Fine." Jesse rolled down his shirtsleeves and stabbed his arms into his jacket. She wondered what she'd done to make him so short with her. "Well, let me know when you are."

Jesse pulled into the livery and unhitched his rig. After flipping a gold piece to the boy who worked there to see to the horses, he stomped down the street in the direction of his boardinghouse, forced to admit how cold and impersonal his room was starting to feel. Shabby as Anora's shack was, she'd managed to turn it into a home. Every week he went out there it got harder to leave. Well, let her stew for a while. See just how much she enjoyed her own company.

"Whoa there, where's the war?" Ricki asked, when he would have brushed past her.

"Ricki. I didn't see you."

"Didn't see anything but red, I'd wager. How's the courting going?"

"Courting." Jesse spat out the word as if it were poison.

"Did you do like I said? Take her little gifts?"

"For all the good it's doing me."

Ricki cocked her head. "And still she's resisting your charm?" she drawled. "Who'd have thought?"

"I had all I can take of this courting nonsense. From now on, she wants something from me, let her come to me for it."

"A woman in a delicate condition needs to be handled in a delicate manner."

"Don't you have your own problems to worry about?"

Ricki's face grew thoughtful. "Matter of fact, I do. Good day, Marshal."

Two long and lonely weeks passed, during which Jesse made good his promise to stay away from the ranch. Anora staunchly told herself she didn't care.

She didn't need him or anyone else. She refused to admit just how much she'd looked forward to his visits. To their little outings together.

After making her way from the henhouse to the cabin, a disappointing four eggs in her basket, she pushed open the cabin door, stepped inside, and stopped cold.

Rosco, the man who'd robbed her last spring, sat with his filthy booted feet propped atop her clean kitchen table.

15

"I don't have any money." Anora spoke as if unconcerned, although her heart was pounding so loudly she wondered Rosco couldn't hear it. He smelled as bad as she remembered and looked even worse. Ashen-faced. She set down her egg basket at the opposite end of the table from his boots. Somehow she had to get to the sink, where the gun was stashed in an empty tin pitcher.

"Actually, missy, you're mistaken. You got a considerable swag," Rosco said. "Mine by rights."

"I don't understand."

"Me neither. How that idiot husband of yours could have pinched it out from under my nose."

Anora's mind was awhirl. Ben stole from Rosco? Keep your head, she counseled herself, even as her eye strayed to the pitcher holding her gun. Six paces, no more.

"Land sakes, I had no idea," she said. "I must say, I surely did work up a thirst. Can I get you a nice drink of cold water?"

With a calm she was far from feeling she started toward the sink. One pace. Two. Three. Mustn't let him see her eagerness.

"No water," he said, adding sarcastically, "though I surely do thank you for your hospitality. Got any whiskey?"

" 'Fraid not." She waved a hand. "Do you mind if I get myself a drink?"

"Hell, no." Rosco got to his feet and hitched his pants. "Though I was hopin' I wouldn't hafta take this shack apart board by board."

Anora grabbed the gun, whirled, and planted the barrel against the side of Rosco's head. "Hands in the air!"

He rolled his eyes to the side of his head where the pistol lodged and swallowed thickly as he slowly raised both hands.

"Don't move," she told him. "Don't breathe. Don't even blink. This pistol has a really touchy trigger."

"I hear you, Miz King."

"That's good. Now you head on out that open door, down those steps and move on down the road. If I ever see you around here again I swear I'll shoot first and ask questions second. That clear?"

Under her watchful eye Rosco edged slowly toward the door, Anora on his heels. Her right hand was trembling so badly she gripped her wrist with her other hand to try steady it. All the while she didn't take her gaze from the back of Rosco's head.

Once outside, past firing range, Rosco's bluster returned with full force. "You ain't seen the last of me yet, missy. Not till I get my hands on the booty your husband stole."

The second Rosco was out of sight, Anora collapsed on the porch. Her hand retained its deathlike grip on the gun and she had to use her free hand to unclench her fingers one at a time. The gun dropped to the floorboards with a hollow clatter.

"Thanks, Jesse," she whispered through trembling lips. Too bad he hadn't given her the bullets.

Once the shakes passed Anora was struck by the irony of her situation. Two men; each wanted something from her. And she didn't for one minute believe either of them would give up. If, as Rosco claimed, Ben had stolen from him, she had little doubt that he'd make good his threat to tear the ranch apart, board by board. Besides which, recently she'd had the creepy feeling of being watched from a distance. She'd been sleeping poorly and starting at unexpected noises outside, neither of which was good for the babe.

Sometime in the wee hours of the morning the solution to her double-edged problem struck her. Get rid of Rosco and she'd see Jesse pack up as well, having accomplished what he'd set out to do: rid Boulder Springs of the hoister. First thing tomorrow she'd stop by Jesse's office.

To her chagrin, Jesse didn't question her request for the bullets, just fetched her a boxful.

"Here you go," he said. His gaze skimmed her ripening form, taking in the subtle changes wrought by her condition. "I'm glad to see you heeding my advice to have some firepower on hand."

Anora chose her words carefully. She wanted to let him know Rosco had been at the ranch, but incidentally. Right now he probably just thought that she'd missed him and was using the bullets as an excuse to see him. "I realized you were right. A woman alone can't be too careful."

His words were low and charged with feeling. "You needn't be alone." As he spoke he caught her hand in his.

Anora closed her eyes against the flood of emotions. She could feel the strength of Jesse's fingers, clasped around hers. His skin was warm, callused. How easy it would be. One word from her and . . .

Her eyes flew open. She pulled her hand free. It was Jesse's job, damn it, to keep the countryside safe. Where was he while Rosco was out at Three Boulders? Tucked up nice and safe with his old friend, Ricki?

"You manage to trap that bandit Rosco yet?" she asked with seeming lack of concern as she tucked the bullets safely inside her bag.

"I expect to any day now."

"Good." Anora prepared to take her leave. " 'Cause it fair gave me the creeps the other day, him showing up at Three Boulders and all."

Jesse moved so fast her vision blurred. One moment he was across the desk. The next thing she knew he was disturbingly close, gripping her shoulders with his large, warm-palmed hands. "What did you say?"

She braced herself against the myriad of sensations wrought by his nearness. His familiar scent. His awesome physical strength, tempered by a gentleness she'd never before experienced in a man. "Rosco paid me a visit. Spun some yarn about Ben helping himself to money that wasn't his. Has the notion it might be at the ranch. Isn't that ridiculous?"

"Why didn't you tell me this sooner?"

Anora flashed him a look. "You led me to believe the man was as good as in jail."

Jesse rubbed a weary hand across his jaw. In spite of herself Anora found her eyes drawn to his mouth. As she recalled the feel of those firm, warm lips in all manner of intimate contact with hers, an embarrassing warmth flooded her limbs. A wanton heat that made it hard to concentrate on their conversation.

"I want you to move into town."

"What?" The one word came out as an outraged squawk.

"Stay with Miss Spencer or Lettie till Rosco's behind bars."

"I will do no such thing. Leave my home. Not at the whim of some two-bit outlaw or anyone else."

Jesse seemed to reach a decision. "If that's the way you want it, that's the way it'll have to be."

Something in the way his shadowy gaze rested on hers increased her uneasiness. Maybe this plan wasn't fully realized yet. Maybe she'd been a trifle hasty telling Jesse about Rosco's visit.

"What'll have to be?"

"If you won't move to town then you leave me no
choice but to move out to Three Boulders. We can
do it legal-like. Man and wife. Or we can live in sin.
Doesn't much matter to me which way we call it."

"I already told you no."

"You're forgetting one thing. I'm bigger and
meaner than you are."

"I will not be bullied, Jesse Quantrill. Not by you
or any other arrogant man." Doing a sharp about-
face, Anora reached for the doorknob. Strangely, it
remained just beyond her reach. The room continued to spin. She saw spots. Then darkness.

Anora awoke in a strange bed, surrounded by unfamiliar smells. A weird greenish half light filtered in
through a dark green blind. She tried to lift her head
just as the blind was snapped up and the room
flooded with light.

"Well, well, Mrs. King. Glad you could join us."

"Doc," she said weakly, as she flopped back
against the pillows. Her mouth was dry as old dust.
"Where am I?"

"The infirmary. Marshal fetched you here when
you blacked out."

"What happened?" Instinctively she reached to
clutch the slight mound of her stomach. The doctor
followed her actions with his eyes.

"I reckon the wee one's doing better than you.
You haven't been eating a whole lot of late, if I don't
miss my guess."

"At first it was hard to hold anything down," she
said, feeling her cheeks pinken.

Doc patted her hand. "There, there, now. I'm a medical man. No need to be embarrassed. Woman having a baby is a perfectly natural occurrence. Some good solid food. Plenty of rest. We'll have you right as rain before you can say 'confinement.' Right, Marshal?"

A shadow in the far corner of the room moved into the light. Jesse!

"Now, Marshal here has promised me that he'll see you get the best of care. Oh," he added as an afterthought. "Allow me to be the first to offer my congratulations."

Anora's tongue felt swollen and unwieldy. "C . . . congratulations?"

"Marshal here tells me you two are making a match."

Anora decided to ignore that last comment. "Why am I so tired?"

"Growing a youngster takes a powerful lot out of a woman. You need red meat and plenty of it, to build up your blood."

"I'll see to it, Doc." Jesse's voice was a muffled rumble from across the room. "Can I take her home?"

"In a buggy," Doc said firmly. "No more walking into town and back. And no riding either. Not till after the young one's born. Spring, I wager. That be about right?"

"That . . . that's what I figured on."

The doc paused to pat her hand. "Marshal explained how you feel. That it's too soon after Ben's passing to be getting hitched again. I wouldn't let that worry you none. More important that you and the young one are cared for, than what some old busybody considers a decent period of mourning."

Anora turned away as the doctor left the room. Jesse remained where he was.

"You tell him you're the father?"

"He didn't ask."

"And if he had?"

She heard Jesse cross the room and kept her face averted, unable to stop the one lone tear that zigzagged down her cheek.

"I was worried about you. Anyone would be, after you swooned that way. I had to tell him about your condition. And it's not something I'd know about unless we were close. When old Doc asked me how close, well, I told him we were secretly engaged."

"It won't stay much of a secret. Not in this town." Slowly she turned to face him. "That's what you wanted, isn't it?"

His face closed down as effectively as blinds drawn on an empty house. "Take your time getting up. I'll go hitch up the buggy."

Anora took a breath and tried again. "We don't love each other. What you're suggesting is all wrong."

"There's no such thing as love. And you've got a mighty peculiar sense of right and wrong."

"Me?"

"Yes, you. First you deceive the entire town about your name-only marriage. Now you're denying me the right to be a father to my own child."

His voice was filled with chastisement, and Anora felt a bleak emptiness inside. What would he say if he ever learned that Ben had actually been her brother? Jesse was honorable to a fault. He'd never understand her living a lie in the first place, let alone forgive her for continuing to deceive him. Part of it was her own stubborn pride, wanting Jesse to think well of her.

Not having an answer at the ready, Anora flopped a weary arm across her eyes and stayed that way until she heard Jesse leave. She couldn't marry Jesse. And she couldn't tell him the truth about her and Ben.

The second the door closed behind him she pushed the sheet aside and slid her feet to the floor. Slowly she stood and straightened. The earlier dizziness was gone. She felt better now. Determined. Back in control. After gathering up her things she let herself out by the infirmary's back door, into the rear alley. She had no plan beyond the moment, to flee as far from Boulder Springs as quickly as possible. The one refrain she heard over and over in her mind was Jesse's flat pronouncement. *There's no such thing as love.* How could she possibly marry a man for whom the notion of love didn't exist? Mentally crossing her fingers that she wouldn't run into Jesse, she stuck to the shadows and back alleyways as she made her way to Lettie's.

"Lettie's not here," Sam said. "Her and Penny took the train to St. Louis. Won't be back till the morrow."

Anora licked her dry lips and leaned over the counter toward him. "Lettie was . . . Lettie was holding some money for me. I . . . I need it now. Today."

"Sorry, Anora. All that greenbacks stuff's Lettie's department. 'Fraid I can't help you none."

"Sam!" Anora leaned across the counter and grabbed hold of the old man's vest. "This is an emergency. I need that money now."

Sam's eyes bulged in their sockets and he drew back a pace, the motion drawing Anora halfway across the countertop. Still she didn't release her grip. She heard the bell ring behind her as a customer entered the store, and didn't need Sam's sigh of relief to tell her who the newcomer was.

"There you are, Anora." Jesse forcibly loosened her grip on Sam's vest before setting her back on her feet. "Sorry about that, Sam." He slanted Anora an indulgent look. "I told you it didn't matter about the betrothal gift." He gave Sam a man-to-man wink. "You know how women set such store in these things."

Sam, red-faced and breathing hard, straightened his vest. "No harm done. Lord knows, ain't no one gets more excitable than my Lettie when it comes to certain matters." He dusted his shirtfront, then looked up abruptly at Jesse and Anora.

"Betrothal, you say?"

"That's right," Jesse said. "Anora King and I are getting hitched just as soon as we can."

As Jesse hustled her out of the store, she heard Sam call after them, his voice puzzled. "Ain't this a little sudden, now. Marshal and Mrs. King?"

"You see?" Anora said to Jesse. "That's what everyone will say. That and worse."

Without bothering to answer, Jesse handed her up into the seat of a charming buggy hitched to a dainty mare. "Can you drive?"

"Anything with wheels," Anora said, as she took hold of the reins.

"Good." He rubbed the mare's nose affectionately. "Her name's Penelope. She's a little on the frisky side, but I think she'll make a reliable source of transportation once the two of you get each other's measure."

Anora's eyes widened at his words. "Who does she belong to?"

Jesse moved around the buggy to where Sully waited, and mounted his stallion in one fluid movment. "You. Happy betrothal." Heels to Sully's flanks, he set the big black in motion and Penelope eagerly fell in behind.

He pulled to a stop outside the boardinghouse, and dismounted. "I'll just be a minute. I expect you'll be here when I come out?"

Anora gave her head a single, jerky nod. Where else would she be? Penniless and all. Even she knew that to take Penelope and try to outrun Jesse would be both childish and futile. Besides, surely she'd be able to make Jesse listen to reason. To see that their marrying was unnecessary. Maybe she could name him as the baby's godfather. She nodded to herself. Such was only one possible solution. Surely there were others.

16

Anora found the small cabin's interior, by turns, a comfort and a confinement. As she stared bleakly at the familiar four walls of her home and wondered why certain mishaps befell her, her thoughts were fractured by the incessant sound of Jesse on the front steps as he whittled a piece of wood. She clenched her teeth. The sound was a nagging reminder of Jesse's constant presence, the ceaseless rasp of knife blade against wood akin to fingernails against slate.

Beyond the ranch the last of the autumn sun disappeared from sight, staining the sky the color of ripe plum jelly. The night air encompassed her, still and fragrant, and somehow coaxed her to settle onto the porch bench, despite Jesse's presence.

"Jesse, I've been thinking." She thought she heard him chuckle, and it was the last reaction she'd have expected.

"Strikes me, anytime a woman starts a conversation with 'I've been thinking,' it bodes ill for the poor fellow who's trapped in her thoughts."

Hmmph. Thought he was mighty funny, Jesse did. Anora cleared her throat. Schooled herself to keep her tone reasonable, not to let him get to her. "We want different things, you and I. This idea of yours, us getting hitched. It'll never work."

He glanced around at her. "Know what you want, do you, Anora?"

"I surely do. And strikes me as how it's totally at odds with what you want."

"Fire." He set down his whittling and gave her his full attention.

Anora launched into her oft-rehearsed argument against their marrying. "I have a need to feel settled, permanent-like. It's something I've never had and always wanted. Someplace that's mine."

"Appears to me you got that right here. Leastways you will have once Rosco's under lock and key."

Anora felt vexed. He was deliberately misunderstanding her. "A husband just doesn't fit in with my plans. I have a need to be independent. Make it on my own."

With an exaggerated sigh Jesse folded his pocketknife and slipped it into his vest pocket, then propped his whittling board against the bottom step. "Strikes me the thing most women look out for is to have a man come along and make things rosy."

Anora glared at him. "You see any man here-abouts making my life all soft and nice? Every man I've ever met has done little else but make things worse 'n they already were. And that includes you, Jesse Quantrill."

Jesse stood and stretched. "Think I'll take a little stroll before I turn in." He paused and passed her a long, thoughtful look. "I'll sleep in the barn till we're wed."

"You'll sleep in the barn after we're wed as well." Anora rose and stomped inside, slamming the door behind her.

Jesse stared a spell at the worn and blistered door, then stuffed his hands inside his pockets and set off toward the creek. At least she'd acknowledged that there would be an exchange of vows. He'd known all she needed was a little time to get used to the idea.

He stood at the bank of the winding black ribbon that marked the creek, its sound at once both familiar and unsettling. Couldn't much blame Anora for having her doubts. Not when he'd had his share, as well. He'd never thought of himself as the marrying kind. Never given much truck to the idea of having kids, either.

Still, if anyone knew the difference between right and wrong, Jesse Quantrill did. Wrong would be him lighting out of here, with Anora in the family way. Went against every single solid thing he believed in. Wrong, as well, would be leaving her on her own at the ranch, knowing full well that Rosco was out there, up to no good.

Jesse squatted, cupped his palm, dipped it into the cool creek water, and took a long drink. Wrong, too, would be for Anora to go getting any too fond of him. Any woman he knew who took a foolish notion into her head, fancied herself in love, ended up in a mess, one way or another. Better for them both if Anora kept him at arm's length. So far, that looked to be the one area where there wouldn't be any problems.

He watched the moon's leisurely ascent as he made his way over to the barn. As its gentle illumination revealed the surrounding landscape, he made mental notes of all the things that needed doing to batten down the ranch in readiness for winter.

Anora carefully wound the tea towel around the hot handles of her canning kettle before she lifted the cumbersome pot off the stove top. As she carried it to the table one of the jars inside tipped over and splashed boiling water onto the back of her hand.

"Dash it all!" Anora bit her lower lip against the stinging burn as she lowered the heavy kettle to the table. A red welt was starting to show and she reached for the butter dish, only to find Jesse's hand atop hers, stilling the movement.

"What happened?" Was that concern in his voice as he cradled her burned hand, tilting it toward the light for closer examination?

"Nothing." Anora tried to pull her hand back, but he tightened his grip.

"Doesn't look like nothing. I'll get you a piece of ice. Do you have any salve?"

"I was going to put butter on it."

"Ice is better. Take the sting right out of it."

By the time Jesse returned with a hunk of ice from the in-ground icebox he'd built out back, her hand had begun to throb something fierce. As Jesse settled her into a chair and pressed the chip of ice against her burn, she gave a sigh. Instant relief.

Jesse pulled the other chair around to face her and straddled it backward. The thing she'd noticed about him, right from the first, was that for a man his touch was exceedingly gentle. "Why didn't you call me to lift that heavy kettle for you?"

Anora blew out an impatient breath. They'd had this conversation several times previously. Jesse seemed to think that ever since they'd exchanged their vows she'd turned into some sort of an invalid, unable to do for herself the simple tasks she'd been performing her entire life.

As her gaze met his something inside of her gave a funny little hiccup. She could have sworn his concern was genuine.

"Wouldn't do for me to go getting used to having you at my beck and call, now would it? Might forget how to do for myself."

He slanted her his easy, cowpoke grin. The same grin that turned her bones to mush and made it impossible to stay cross with him. "What are you making?"

"Apple jelly," she said shortly.

Jesse released her and rolled back the sleeves of his black linen shirt. "I'll help. Tell me what to do."

Anora shook her head. "You've done so much already. Looks like a whole different ranch where you cleared away those dead trees. What with chopping wood and mending fences, it isn't seemly for you to be doing the canning and preserving as well."

"Who says?"

"I do."

"That a fact?" As the last of the ice chip melted he inspected her injured hand. "Where's the salve?"

"In that tin alongside the sink."

He pried off the lid and took a sniff, wrinkling his nose. "Smells like something gone bad. You make it yourself?"

Anora nodded. "An old Indian woman showed me how, long time ago. Back when my ma was sick. She was some sort of a medicine woman, I guess. Only one around who helped me tend Ma when she died."

"How old were you?"

Anora shifted on her seat, uncomfortable with the turn of the conversation. "Twelve. Thirteen. Something like that."

"Where was your pa?"

"I don't know. After Ma got too weak to travel he left her behind." She pressed her lips together, her mind's eye recalling that long-ago scene. Ma lying there so pale and still, Anora'd thought she was already gone. Except for the tears slowly filling her faded and weary eyes, as her mother realized she was going to die without seeing her man one last time.

Anora glanced up to find Jesse watching her closely. Too closely for comfort. The stillness in the cabin seemed to stretch on forever before he claimed her hand and spread the burned spot with a layer of greasy salve.

She flinched against the unsettling pressure of his fingertips grazing her skin.

"That hurt?"

"Not bad."

"Your pa ever come back?" he asked, casual-like.

"Sure. A couple of days after Ma was buried. Made a big show, falling face-first on top of her grave, shedding a river full of tears. Couldn't hardly see the grave for the flowers he brought."

She gave Jesse a telling look. "After that I kind of thought he might mend his ways. At least a little."

"I take it nothing much changed."

"Well, me and Ben never got left behind anymore."

Jesse gave her a sharp look. "You've known Ben for that long?"

Anora thought fast. She'd almost let the cat out of the bag. "We grew up together," she said at last. That much, at least, was the truth.

"Whereabouts did you go?"

"Everywhere. Pa was always convinced the next town, the next game, would be the one that made him rich. Then Uncle Dan died and deeded him this place."

"But he didn't come with you?"

Anora shook her head. "Pa had his faults. One of them was not knowing when a man he called a friend would turn on him, accuse him of cheating, and shoot him dead."

"I'm sorry."

Anora pushed herself briskly to her feet. It felt like the minutes hung suspended while Jesse stared, his eyes at a level with her blossoming waistline, made more obvious by the apron's slight bulge over her stomach. Slowly he rose as well. "No more lifting heavy stuff. That's what I'm here for. These jars ready for the jelly?"

She nodded. "I just need to melt some paraffin wax to seal them."

"How about you ladle the jelly, and I pour the wax on top?"

"I don't think—"

"It'll go faster with the two of us. Then we can go for that buggy ride we talked about."

"*You* talked about."

"Anora." Jesse blew out an impatient breath. "By now it's pretty obvious to Rosco that I'm a permanent fixture around here. Now, the man might be dumb, but even Rosco isn't dumb enough to show up while I'm here. Once we leave he'll think the coast looks clear. He doesn't know about Charlie and Eddy up yonder keeping watch."

Anora didn't hear most of what he said beyond the words "permanent fixture." Whose eyes was he trying to pull the wool over? He was no more a permanent fixture in her life than anyone else whose way had intersected briefly with hers.

As she ladled hot jelly into glass jars, which she passed to Jesse to add a thin seal of melted wax, she sneaked a sideways look at him. A week had passed since they'd stood before the preacher and said their vows. A week during which, to her immense relief, he'd continued to sleep in the barn. Still, he hadn't once gone into town without insisting she go, too. Anora wasn't used to having someone checking on her whereabouts every second of every day, and she'd started feeling downright edgy from all the attention.

Once the jelly jars were filled and cooling on the sideboard, pale amber contents glowing through the clear glass, she came upon an idea.

"I've got something you might be interested in." Drying her hands on her apron, she crossed the room to her bedside bureau. She took out a pair of stockings and unrolled them, then shoved her hand down inside the toe of one to pull out the ring and locket she'd found among Ben's things.

"What's that you've got?" Jesse asked, when she tipped the jewelry into his palm.

"I found them with Ben's things. Before he . . . you know. Got killed."

"You think they're stolen?"

Anora wrapped her arms protectively around her waist. "I never saw them before. He could have won them in a game, I guess. But why hide them?"

"I don't suppose these might be what Rosco's after?"

"Maybe. But he did say 'swag' loud and clear. That's money."

Jesse held the ring up to the light for closer examination.

"Maybe we're going about this all wrong," she went on. "Maybe we should be out looking for the stolen loot ourselves. Beat Rosco to the punch."

"Funny, you saying that. 'Cause I'd be willing to bet that's exactly what Rosco's counting on. Us doing all the work so he just waltzes in here slick as you please, and pockets the spoils."

"How would he know if we found anything?"

"He's got somebody keeping a lookout. Don't think that he hasn't."

"But I haven't seen anyone. Not since that day he was here."

"Anora. I don't mean to alarm you, but he's close by. Rosco's not skilled enough to pass through this way without leaving some sign."

"He's not rustling any more cattle, is he?"

"No. That's another thing lets me know he's fixed his sights on bigger game." Jesse tucked the stolen jewelry into his pocket. "I'll deal with this stuff later. Right now, think back on Ben's doings the last few weeks. Anything he might have said or done, some clue about what he was up to."

Anora's brow furrowed in concentration. She looked up at him and shook her head.

"Was he doing any work around the ranch? Mending fences. Digging holes. Anything like that?"

"He wasn't hardly ever here. Stayed away days at a time. When he did come home, it was mostly only to change his clothes before he went into town."

"Speaking of town, I'll hitch up the buggy now."

"Jesse, please." Anora laid a restraining hand on his arm. "Don't make me go with you."

He frowned. "What's the matter? I thought you liked visiting Lettie and Penny."

"Penny's at school." She sighed. "If I go over to the store . . ." She paused. "Everyone's talking about us. Staring at me. I'm starting to show. They all wonder . . ."

"Wonder what?"

"I'm sure they all wonder why the hasty marriage. Ben not even cold in the ground, and all."

Not to mention that their uneasy friendship while Ben was alive hadn't been overlooked by the town's wagging tongues, either.

"I don't like leaving you here alone."

"You've got no choice in the matter. You came to Boulder Springs to be a lawman. Besides, I've got that pistol you gave me."

Jesse pulled a face. "You and I both know you couldn't hit the broad side of a barn from three paces back."

"Jesse, I've been taking care of myself for most of my life."

Jesse felt his throat seize up from some unnamed emotion, making it hard to talk. Damn, she looked so fine and feisty, standing there. "There's two of you now."

"All the more reason for me to take good care, wouldn't you say?"

He reached out to smooth back a strand of hair that had sprung free and curled against her damp forehead, then caught himself. "You're right," he said gruffly. "I've got work to do."

He allowed himself only one backward glance as he rode away. Anora stood where he left her on the sagging front porch, one hand resting against the post, the other raised in farewell. The perfect picture of domesticity with her apron billowing out in front of her.

Jesse gave his head a shake as if to clear it. What was happening to him? Getting soft, he was, spinning himself pictures of a snowy future, slippers by the hearth. The little woman fixing him a hot meal.

He had to concentrate on one thing at a time. Get Rosco behind bars. Convince Anora to leave Boulder Springs. Maybe she'd move back to Philly with him. He could set her up with a nice hat shop or something. That ought to satisfy her need for what she called independence. He could see to it that she and the child had whatever they needed. Jesse nodded to himself. It was a highly workable plan. Satisfaction thrummed through him. It felt good having goals to focus on.

He hadn't gone far before he heard the sound of approaching hoofbeats and pulled up, waiting for Charlie to reach his side.

"We got us a problem, Marshal. Fact is, we got a whole passel of them."

"Where's Eddy?"

"Keeping watch over the Three B. That's one of the problems."

"Why's that?" Jesse resumed his pace in the direction of town and Charlie rode abreast.

"Folks in town is complaining how they can't find a lawman when they need one. All of us been out this way all week."

Jesse nodded curtly. It was a fact. He'd been neglecting his other duties. "What else?"

"There was a murder across the river in Indian Springs last night."

"What's that got to do with us?"

"A working gal was strangled, her body dumped in the river. Fella from town took his kids fishing. Found her early this morning."

"Like I said, what's that got to do with us?"

"She was seen talking to a man late last night. Fella who matches Rosco's description."

Jesse's hands tightened reflexively on the reins. "What else?"

Charlie exhaled heavily. "This last is kinda touchy, but needs being said."

"Then what are you waiting for? Spit it out."

"Eddy and me went for a drink last night. I reckon he had more'n his share."

Jesse cocked him a look. "Only Eddy?"

"I was stone cold-sober. Good thing, too, given what he was telling me about being over to Ricki's the other night. You know how thin them walls is."

"Get to the point," Jesse drawled. "I'm not much interested in Eddy's sex life."

"Well, the rooms were all taken, so him and his gal took themselves into some sorta closet for a little slap and tickle. Turned out they were next door to Ricki's room and he heard Ricki in there with a fellow. Pretty angry with each other they were. Lots of cussing and name-calling."

"Ricki's more than capable of looking after herself."

"Eddy knows that. Which is why he didn't pay too much attention till your name came up."

"My name?"

"Yeah. Heard Ricki say she was sorry she'd ever had anything to do with bringing you to Boulder Springs. Fella musta punched her or something, 'cause she let out a cry. Then he says, get this, that once he's settled his score with you, won't be enough pieces to scrape together to bury."

"I didn't realize I'd made any enemies in the short time I was here." Instinctively Jesse rubbed his left shoulder as he pondered on who might be bearing him a grudge. The wound on his shoulder was long since healed, his only reminder a thin white scar.

"Yeah, well, get this. Eddy thinks the fella's voice sounds kinda familiar. So he cranks open the closet door a crack. And guess who he sees coming out of Ricki's room?"

"Who?"

"Eddy swears it was Rosco."

Jesse pulled his horse up short, and turned to face Charlie.

"That doesn't make a lick of sense. I've never had any run-ins with Rosco. I never even heard his name before I came to Boulder Springs."

"Well, he sure in hell heard of you. Was it Ricki's doing that brought you here?"

"That's common knowledge around town."

Charlie shrugged. "I'm just the messenger, boss."

"Hold the fort till I get back." As he spoke, Jesse urged Sully into a gallop.

"Where you going?"

"Check a few facts. Then I'm heading into Indian Springs. I'll have a little chin-wag with the marshal there about their murder."

Try as he might, Jesse couldn't dismiss Charlie's version of Eddy's drunken ramblings. If there was any truth to it at all, Anora was in more danger than ever. Especially now that she was married to him.

17

Jesse burst up the stairs and into Ricki's room without bothering to knock. Ricki lay buried under a heap of satin comforters with only the top of her head visible. As he snapped up the blind and flooded the room with daylight he heard a low, protesting groan from beneath the covers.

"Get up, Ricki."

The red satin coverlet shifted. "Y'all know I never get up before noon."

"It is noon." Unceremoniously Jesse ripped an armful of coverings from the bed and dumped them on the floor. Ricki lay there naked, yesterday's face paint smeared across her eyes and lips like something gone bad. She rubbed her eyes with the heel of her hand.

"Jesse, my love," she drawled, shifting her legs suggestively. "See anything you like?"

"All I see," Jesse ground out, "is your lying face. Why, Ricki?" Taking hold of her arm, he pulled her to a sitting position. "What's Rosco's beef with me?"

Ricki's hand trembled slightly as she reached to her bedstead and sloshed a couple of inches of liquor from an open bottle into a glass. She tossed back the drink in a single swallow. Looking more composed, she plumped the pillows against the headboard and arranged herself in an artful pose as she smoothed her hair back from her face with both hands.

"Who says Rosco has a beef with you?"

Jesse reached over and turned her right cheek toward him. Makeup couldn't camouflage the purplish bruise across her cheekbone that marred her otherwise flawless skin.

"You know how I feel about a man who hits a woman. You also know how I feel about being lied to."

Ricki pulled back, buried her face in her hands for a moment, then slowly looked up, her gaze meeting his.

"I guess, sooner or later, our past comes back to haunt each and every one of us."

"Meaning?"

"Remember Rose's beau, Cameron?"

Jesse swore. "How could I forget? To this day Rose hasn't forgiven me."

"Maybe she would. If you ever figured a way to forgive yourself."

He didn't bother to acknowledge the truth in her words. "Why bring him up now?"

"Cameron was Rosco's half brother."

Jesse bolted to attention. "Are you certain?"

"Sure as I'm lying here. When Rosco found out where I came from he started asking me, you know, who I knew back home. Had ourselves a nice little chat about Rose and her boy. Kind of ironic, isn't it? You and Rosco both being the boy's uncle."

Jesse shook his head in disbelief. "You knew all along. Yet you never said a word?"

Ricki poured herself another shot of bourbon. "Rosco was the only one hereabouts who'd front me the money to buy this house."

"Some two-bit outlaw fronted you a loan?"

Ricki extended one manicured index finger toward Jesse. "That's where you fouled up. You believed what you'd been told. That Rosco was small-time. That you could bring him down easy."

"What are you talking about? He is small-time."

Ricki shook her head. "That's just a part he's playing. Deep down, he's smart. Smartest man I ever met. 'Cept for maybe you, Jess."

"So why'd he pull off a series of small-time heists?"

"To build a reputation. Then he used me to bring you out here."

"Son of a bitch." Jesse smacked his palm with a balled fist. How could he have missed seeing such a setup? "That bastard's been playing me like a violin."

"Not just you, Jess. Rosco's been playing all of us. I've got enough to pay him back, but he won't take it. I expect he enjoys knowing he could put me on the street tomorrow."

Jesse started to leave, then paused at the doorway.

"You and the girls be careful. Word is he killed one last night in Indian Springs."

Ricki just nodded. "He's got a nasty temper, that one. You take care, yourself."

By the time Jesse returned from Indian Springs he was in a right royal stew. Now he knew how a puppet felt. He'd been dancing to Rosco's tune all the way along, and it wasn't a good feeling. Besides which, he'd viewed firsthand the way Rosco had misused the whore from Indian Springs. The thought of the man putting so much as a hand upon Anora made his skin crawl.

First up, he had to toss out every preconceived notion he'd ever had about Rosco and how to deal with him. Here and now he was starting right from scratch.

Shame it was too late to undo his marriage.

The thought tumbled through his brain, shocking him with its directness.

It was the God-sworn truth. He did his best work with only himself to think about. Throwing Anora into the equation just complicated things all the way around. Not to mention gifting Rosco with a vulnerable spot for attack.

All because you couldn't keep your britches fastened.

Jesse shook his head. Hadn't he prided himself on being smarter than that? Truth told, he was no better than the next man. Or any man who'd made his share of mistakes.

There was no sign of Anora in or near the cabin, and the rush of emotion he felt at her absence was one more reminder of his past misdeeds. The way they all came back to haunt him.

Instinct led him along the path to the creek and for now his instinct held him in good stead. For there stood his wife, stripped down to her unmentionables, waist-deep in the narrow, fastest-running bend of the creek.

When he stepped out from behind the bushes and into view he watched a look of surprise cross her face.

"You startled me," she said. "I didn't know you were back already."

As Jesse approached the creek bank, anger that had been building steadily all day found a ready outlet.

"How dare you place my child in danger?"

Her eyes widened. When she didn't move he splashed into the water, boots and all, grabbed hold of her, and jerked her to shore.

"Rosco killed a woman last night. Mostly I expect because he's pissed at me. You got an urge to be next?"

"You're not making one lick of sense."

He watched the way goose bumps surfaced across her exposed flesh. The thin lawn of her chemise clung to the lush roundness of her breasts and outlined the dark circlets of her nipples. Harshly Jesse reminded himself that this physical attraction was what got him into this situation in the first place.

"I expected you'd have the sense to at least stay inside."

Anora rubbed her arms as if in an effort to warm herself.

"Where are your clothes?"

"Over there."

He grabbed her gown off a branch and draped it across her shoulders like a cape though it didn't cover much of her. Her legs, sheathed in wetly transparent pantalets, were clearly outlined, long and slender, and his gaze wandered to the apex of her thighs and the shadow of her woman's triangle. Shifting his eyes near her waist he saw the softly swelling evidence of his lust. In that second something changed in him forever. A child grew there. His child. He felt a powerful unleashing of possessiveness, the likes of which he'd never before experienced, an emotion so strong it all but took his breath.

"What if I'd been Rosco stepping forward right then? What then?"

She gave him a wide-eyed, innocent look. "You said your deputy was keeping watch."

Jesse felt an unreasonable jolt of jealousy. Had Eddy viewed her the way he had? Wet and clinging unmentionables plastered to her skin. "Exactly. I don't want you coming down here to bathe anymore."

She gave him a speculative look from those smoky, thick-lashed eyes of hers. "Give another week or two and it'll be too cold anyhow."

Jesse exhaled sharply. No meek and retiring woman, this one he'd taken to wife. Even as the thought surfaced, he had to admit meek and retiring women had never held much fascination for him. "When I get the chance I'll try to rig up a way to bring the creek water closer to the house."

"You'd do that for me?"

"I don't want you hauling heavy water buckets in your condition."

Anora only laughed. "Jesse Quantrill, if you have your way I'll be not only fat, but lazy to boot." Jesse couldn't believe it. She'd laughed at him. Worse yet, he could tell from the glint in her eyes she was enjoying every minute of their sparring.

When they reached the porch she gave him a saucy grin. "Lettie and Penny came by for a visit. Penny's still miffed she didn't get to be the bride's attendant."

"Anora. I've been thinking."

She gave him a cheeky grin. "Does that bode ill for me?"

He ignored the playful way she flung his earlier words at him. "You ever been to Philly? 'Cause my sister's there and—"

"How can you even think about leaving right now? You've got that horrid old outlaw to stick behind bars."

"I didn't mean the two of us. I meant you. Taking a trip would give you the chance for a change of scene. Before the babe comes and all."

Anora placed her hands on her soggy hips and faced him down. "I swear, Jesse Quantrill. You are the most frustrating man alive. First you practically drag me to the altar. Now you're trying to railroad me out of town."

"Ours is hardly a normal set of circumstances."

"And whose fault might that be?" She marched inside and gave the door a resounding slam behind her.

Jesse stared hard at that door for a good two or

three minutes before, mind made up, he took the steps two at a time. He flung the door open and was greeted by the sight of Anora, stripped to her skin.

At Jesse's intrusion Anora jerked the coverlet from the bed and tucked it around herself, too angry to feel embarrassed. "I suppose a closed door means nothing where you were raised."

Jesse leaned against the wall, just inside the room, one booted ankle crossed over the other. "I don't recollect as we had any doors. Myself, I'm getting mighty tired of having this one slammed in my face every time I turn around."

"You get what you deserve," Anora snapped back. "Make up your mind what you want from me, Jesse. Because I've had a bellyful of your teeter-totter moods. One minute you're sweet and caring. Next thing you're hopping mad, and no special reason to it, far as I can see."

"You're right," he said, surprising her with his admission. "How come you stopped taking lunches into the train station?"

"I thought . . ." Anora paused, searching for the right words.

"You thought what?"

"That you wouldn't approve of your wife doing that kind of work."

"You never bothered to ask?"

She shrugged. "Could you please leave so I can get dressed?"

"Why certainly," he said, with a compliance that instantly put her on her guard. "I'll just go fetch my stuff out of the barn while you get changed."

"What stuff?"

"From now on I'm sleeping inside with you."

He didn't give her a chance to respond. The second the door closed behind him, Anora scrambled into dry clothes with hands that trembled, even as she tried to hurry.

Sleeping inside with her! Did that mean Jesse would be demanding his rights to the marriage bed? Or that he was staying in here to protect her from Rosco? They hadn't really talked about anything beyond the fact of their getting hitched. When he'd stayed out in the barn this past week she'd inwardly heaved a huge sigh of relief. She had enough new things to be getting used to, what with Jesse underfoot all the time and a new life growing inside of her.

As she glanced around the tiny cabin, Anora was beset by a rise of emotionalism. Her home, her safe haven, was about to be invaded and there wasn't a single thing she could do about it. And no place she could go where she'd ever feel safe. Unless . . .

She jumped when she heard a knock on the door. Followed by Jesse's voice. "Is it okay if I come in?"

No!

"Yes," she called with a tired sigh. She'd thought her decision to take each day as it came was a workable plan. That was before she knew Jesse intended to sleep inside. She wondered if he blamed her for getting in the family way so he'd feel duty-bound to offer marriage. She'd heard tell men didn't appreciate being forced to the altar.

Yet, he was the one who'd insisted that they wed!

Anora shook her head. *Men*. Her mother had been right. Every last one of them was a selfish son of a bitch. Which didn't stop a girl from loosing her drawers when the right one came around. Ma had followed Pa until she got too weak from the sickness that came after that snakebite. Even then she'd pined for him every single day they were apart, right up until the day she died.

She glanced over her shoulder to where Jesse was banging a nail in the wall to hang his jacket on. Sure looked to her like he was fixing to make himself right at home.

As if feeling her eyes upon his back he slowly turned to face her. "I've been giving a few things some serious thought the last couple of days. Seems to me maybe I ought to turn in my badge."

"Turn in your badge? You can't do that. Why, you're the best marshal Boulder Springs ever had. Everyone says so."

"Oh, they do, do they?"

"Yes, indeed. In the store I heard all about how you handled those ranchers when they wanted to hire those "cattle detectives." Don't rightly know what they are, but the townsfolk didn't seem to figure they were a good thing." She took a breath. "And those strikers when they were here. You got them away without anyone getting hurt."

Jesse interrupted her impatiently. "Rosco's after me personally. Not just whoever happens to be Boulder Springs' marshal."

"Why's Rosco after you?"

"It's a long story."

And one he clearly wasn't fixing to share, Anora gathered. Which only meant the man had his secrets, same way she had hers.

18

Anora woke to the muffled sounds of stealthy movement in the cabin. Moonlight shone through the window and illuminated Jesse near the door, pulling on his heavy jacket.

"What is it?" she whispered, as she sat up.

Jesse stepped over his bedroll and hunkered down alongside the cot. "I heard something outside. I'm just going out to have a quick look around."

Anora pushed back the coverlet. "I'll come with you."

His hands against her shoulders anchored her in place. "No, you won't. Stay here. Go back to sleep."

Anora gave him a disbelieving look. Go back to sleep? While he was prowling around, his life in possible danger?

"I'll be back soon as I can." His grip gentled. He leaned toward her and for one heart-stopping moment she thought he was going to kiss her, but he settled instead for stroking her cheek with the tip of one gloved finger. She clasped his hand in both of hers.

"Jesse?"

"Yeah?"

"You be careful."

"Always."

Anora slid from bed and locked the door behind him. It was chilly in the cabin and she pulled on her wrapper and poked a few sticks into the dying fire. Then she fetched her pistol and placed it within easy reach of the rocking chair as she settled down to make hot chocolate and wait.

At some point she must have dozed off. Next thing she knew she heard the sound of gunfire. Two sharp shots in rapid succession cracked through the valley.

Jesse!

She grabbed her pistol and raced out onto the porch, where she could hear the faint echo of the shots. Dead ahead frost gilded the roof of the barn, causing it to shimmer silver in the moonlight. She sucked in a mouthful of the still night air. The last echo faded, leaving only the sound of her own breathing, plus the overloud pounding of her heart as her eyes scanned the deeply shadowed landscape. Was that a stealthy movement she spotted from the corner of her eye?

A twig snapped nearby, sounding like a third rifle shot in the quiet night. She whirled toward the sound, gun pointed, her grip unwavering.

"One step closer and you're a dead man."

"Don't shoot, Mrs. King. I mean Quantrill. It's me, Eddy."

"Eddy." Her shoulders sagged with relief. "You about scared me to death. What were those shots I heard?"

"Don't rightly know. Came from somewhere over the ridge."

"Who's over there? Is Jesse . . . ?"

"I'm here, Anora."

She spun toward the welcome sound of his voice. "Thank God." As he joined her on the porch it was all she could do not to fling herself into his arms. She settled for moving a step closer. Her gaze slid over him, inch by inch, while she reassured herself he was indeed unharmed.

"Whoever it was got away clean. Meet me here in the morning, Eddy. See if we can't pick up his trail."

"Whatever you say, Marshal. Night, ma'am."

Jesse herded Anora inside and slammed the cabin door harder than necessary. "I thought I told you to stay put."

"I heard shots."

"So you decided to rush right out into the middle of the fracas?" As he spoke he shrugged out of his jacket and pegged it on the back of the door. His movements were jerky, as if he held his anger tightly leashed.

"I made you hot chocolate."

She watched him struggle to keep his expression stern.

"Damn it, Anora. I've got enough on my mind without—"

"Don't tell me no one ever worried about you before?" As she spoke she closed the distance between them. His chest rose and fell with agitation. He didn't seem to know where to look. Gently she reached up and pushed a springy lock of hair back from his forehead. His skin was cool beneath her fingertips.

From there, the temptation was too great. She stroked his cheek with the back of her hand, as if her gentle touch could erase the deeply grooved frown lines bracketing his mouth. His jaw was rough with a night's beard growth, and the thrill of feeling such raw masculinity beneath her fingertips sent a tingle clear up her arm.

When she started to trace his upper lip with her index finger he yanked her hand away, fingers manacling her wrist so tight it stole her breath.

"Just what do you think you're doing?"

Anora dampened her lips with her tongue. "What do you mean?"

The sound of his harshly indrawn breath hung suspended between them as he released her. "Maybe you don't recall. You're the one who ordered me to sleep out in the barn."

She turned away. "Maybe you should have stayed there."

Jesse caught her arm, drew her back around, his grip gentle this time. "So help me, Anora. I've never been married before. I don't know what you want from me."

Anora raised her chin a notch and stared him in the eye. "I want a real husband this time. Not just a father for my babe. I want someone I can love, who'll love me back proper."

He dropped her arm like a hot brick. "That's the one thing I don't have to give."

"Then why are you here?"

He lowered his eyes to her middle. "We both know why."

Anora wrapped her arms protectively across her midriff. "That's not good enough, Jesse. Not for me. And it won't be for her, either."

His jaw dropped. "Her? How do you know it's a 'her'?"

"I don't for sure. Just a feeling. Sometimes when she's moving—"

"She moves? You feel her?"

"Course I feel her move."

His eyes remained riveted to her belly. "What's it like?"

"Kind of like a butterfly bashing at my insides. She's moving now. I think you woke her."

Not knowing where the impulse came from, Anora took Jesse's hand and pressed it, flat-palmed, beneath her wrap. "Feel that? Just a little swish? Like a fish swimming upstream."

The expression on Jesse's face did unsettling things to her own insides. Wonder warred with surprise and lost out to delight. When his glance shifted to her the look in his eyes warmed her clear through to the other side and she stepped willingly into his arms.

He dragged his lips across hers with hungry desperation, seconded by the needful way his hands stroked and kneaded her back, molding her frame to his. They stood like that forever, lips to lips, belly to belly, thigh to thigh. She felt his manhood stir and kindle an answering response deep inside her woman's body, a gentle warmth that exploded into sensations so strong she would have been frightened, but for Jesse.

This time he undressed her slowly, pausing to press a scalding kiss to every newly revealed inch of her skin. He hesitated when confronted with her slightly rounded stomach. "I won't hurt you, will I?"

Anora shook her head and watched with greedy eyes as he stripped off his own clothes and joined her on the narrow cot. She was not nearly so bashful this time, her hands eagerly stroking him everywhere, with no prompting on his part. He was all lean and hardened muscle. On his shoulder her questing hands discovered the puckered ridge of a long-ago-healed scar.

She was just about to question him about the scar when his fingers did something so delicious to her inner thigh that all coherent thought was driven from her mind. Joining himself to her, Jesse made such gentle, passionate love to her that Anora had to fight back the tears of emotion that burned beneath her eyelids. Once again he lifted her to that exquisite, special place reserved for the two of them, and Anora felt her heart burst open to a future full of promise.

"Anora." Jesse's voice was a soft purr in her ear. "Do you think maybe we could see about getting us a bigger bed? There's hardly room for you and your belly in here, let alone a fellow the size of me."

Anora smiled to herself as she snuggled close. "I think that's a right fine idea, Marshal."

The last thing she recalled before she fell asleep

was the feel of his big fingers smoothing her hair, and the satisfying sound of their mingled breath, rising and falling in unison.

The following day Eddy and Charlie showed up bright and early at the ranch, and Anora served the menfolk coffee and fresh-made cinnamon rolls before they went trooping out to see if they could pick up a trail from last night's intruder.

As she stepped onto the porch to see them off, Jesse gave her a long, hard look. "You stay put this time. I mean it. Keep the door locked as well."

"Don't you worry about me," she said. "I'll be sure to have a hot meal waiting when you come back."

Upon their return Anora ladled up heaping plates of chicken and dumplings, which she set in front of the three men. Old Charlie took off his gloves and blew on his hands. "Colder out there'n a witch's t . . . toe," he amended with a quick, apologetic look to Anora.

Anora kept her face impassive. "This ought to warm you up."

"Sure smells like something this side of heaven," Charlie said.

"I'll say," Eddy seconded.

Anora fetched the coffeepot and refilled the men's cups, conscious of the looks that passed between Eddy and Charlie as they ate. The cabin was silent save for the sound of their forks scraping crockery as they spooned up every last bite of their food.

"Seconds, anyone?"

She was conscious of another look being furtively exchanged. "No, thank you, ma'am." Both men spoke in unison.

"Sure was good, though."

"Thanks a heap."

"You're welcome, I'm sure." The words were barely out of her mouth before they jumped up, jammed their hats on their heads, and left, slamming the cabin door behind them.

Anora looked at Jesse, who lolled back in his chair, its front legs raised off the floor, coffee cup clasped in his large, capable hands. "Did you see that?"

"See what?"

"Your deputies were acting mighty peculiar. Both of them. Kind of like they know something's hot on their trail, so's they mustn't tarry, but keep ahead of it all the time."

"That's quite the imagination you've got there."

"It wasn't my imagination one whit." As she spoke, Anora cleared away the plates and plunged them into hot, soapy water. "The two of them were as edgy as a horse on its way to the glue factory."

Jesse rose and stretched. His shirt pulled free from the waistband of his pants and Anora averted her eyes, turning back to the sink. Lord, and wasn't there something powerfully intimate about sharing your home with a man.

Even with her back turned she felt Jesse approach, moving with that pantherlike grace of his. She pretended not to notice, intent on the bubbles in her dishpan, the little rainbow prisms of color she could stir up in a certain lamplight.

It was hard to pretend indifference when Jesse

wrapped his arms around her waist. Anora closed her eyes and leaned blissfully back against him as he pushed her hair out of the way and nuzzled the nape of her neck. The baby kicked right then and helped her ignore the nagging voice that reminded her how menfolk had a penchant for running out, just about the time a woman needed them most.

"Got me an idea," Jesse murmured against her throat.

"Uh-huh? What's that?"

"I'll finish up here. You go get changed into something pretty. The two of us'll take a little spin into town."

Anora turned in his arms. "Something's up, Jesse. What is it?"

Jesse managed to look hurt and reproachful at the same time. "Nothing's up. I thought a change of scene would do us both good, is all. I might even stop and talk to the millwright about some lumber for a new bed."

She gazed deep into his eyes. "You're not just trying to get me away from the ranch?"

"I swear." Jesse raised his right hand, as if swearing an oath.

"All right, I guess," she said finally, drying her hands on her apron. "But I'm showing now. I saw the way Charlie and Eddy wouldn't look me in the eye. We're going to start a whole new passel of gossip."

Jesse clasped both her hands in his. "I know your pa ran out on your ma when she needed him most. I'm not going to do that to you. Whatever it takes, I mean to earn your trust."

He seemed so sincere. Anora wanted to believe him, she truly did. "I want that, too."

"So go get changed. I want to have you back here before dark."

Boulder Springs seemed unnaturally quiet as they drove down Main Street. No one coming or going through the doors of the saloon. Hardly a body on the streets. Anora looked at Jesse. "It's not a holiday or something today, is it?"

"Nothing that I know of."

"Sure is quiet."

"Folks are likely hunkering in for the winter. Could see snow anytime now." As they reached the hotel, Jesse pulled the carriage to a halt.

"What are we stopped here for?"

"The day I moved out to the ranch, I left some things behind. Thought I'd go in and fetch them."

Anora gave him a suspicious glance. "You were staying in a boardinghouse before you moved out to the ranch. Not the hotel."

Jesse jumped from the carriage and busied himself wrapping the reins around the hitching post. "I left some papers in the hotel safe." He came around to Anora, and held out a hand to help her down.

She gazed at his extended hand. "Why do I have to come in?"

"Something wrong with a man wanting to show off his new wife?"

Anora crossed her arms over her chest. "I am not a possession, Jesse Quantrill. Don't you dare go treating me like one."

"Oh, Anora, for pity's sake." Catching her by

surprise, Jesse tumbled her out of her seat and into his arms.

She let out an outraged squawk, balled her hands into fists, and pushed against his chest with all her might. "Put me down this instant."

Jesse ignored her attempts to free herself, as he carried her across the boardwalk and into the hotel. Once inside the lobby he set her on her feet.

"Don't you ever—"

Her words were interrupted by a commotion behind her. Turning, she saw a crush of townsfolk spilling into the lobby, led by Lettie and Sam. "Surprise!"

She swung around to face Jesse and saw him bite his lip to keep from laughing aloud. "What's going on?"

"Seems your friends didn't appreciate our elopement, so they took it upon themselves to throw a little celebration."

"The whole town's here," she said in wonder, as folks continued to push their way toward them. Soon the entire lobby was filled to capacity and Anora was swept up in the crowd, overwhelmed by the shouts of congratulations as folks pumped her hand and clapped her on the back.

Before she had recovered from the surprise, the air vibrated with strains of music, a cue for folks to pair up and start to dance. Someone tapped the keg of ale to flowing freely. A table of goodies had been set out alongside a second table heaped high with gifts. Jesse stood an arm's length away, looking relaxed and at ease as he accepted his share of congratulations and well-wishes. As if he felt her gaze, he turned and his eyes found hers. A look of shared understanding passed between them, an intimate look that warmed Anora from her toes to her nose.

Maybe this marriage to Jesse wasn't such a bad thing after all. Perhaps together they could forge a life and a future, based on mutual trust and understanding. She could give her unborn babe the kind of security she lacked in her nomadic upbringing. Maybe Jesse would turn out to be the husband she needed, even if he didn't love her the way she loved him. Someone tapped her on the shoulder and she spun about, losing sight of Jesse.

When next she spotted him he was near the door, huddled with a man Anora didn't recall seeing before. Judging by the expression on the other man's face a serious discussion was in progress. Anora's eyes widened as Jesse took out his money belt and counted some bills into the other man's hand. Just what was going on?

At that moment Penny distracted her. Her gaze dipped pointedly to Anora's blossoming waistline. "I guess now I know the reason we haven't seen much of you lately."

Anora smoothed her jacket over her stomach. "Seems my secret's out."

Penny gave her a cool glance. "I thought we were best friends, Nory."

Anora reached to clasp her friend's hand. "You and Lettie are my best friends in the entire world."

"Really?" Penny's voice rang with hurt. "Then you've got a different idea about friendship than regular folk. And you've had yourself two husbands while I've little chance of getting even one."

"What about Beau? I thought you and he . . ."

Penny's eyes were suspiciously shiny, as if she fought back tears. "If you'd been the least bit interested, like a real friend, you wouldn't even ask me that."

Anora bit her lower lip. "If I've offended you somehow, I apologize. Believe me, I didn't set out to fall in love with Jesse. Or to marry him, for that matter."

Penny shook her head pityingly. "You've got a real talent, Anora. Gone and snagged yourself a second husband who spends all his spare time at Ricki's."

As Penny turned and walked away Jesse must have sensed her distress, for he immediately left his dealings and made his way to her side.

"What was that all about?"

"Seems I hurt Penny's feelings."

"Want me to talk to her?"

"There's no point. She's hurting bad right now. And I don't think it has anything to do with me." She looked around the room. "Where's Beau Brown?"

"You haven't heard? He up and married some widow lady over in Indian Springs. Some woman whose husband left her a sizable fortune."

"Poor Penny. I ought to have been there for her. Instead of being so caught up in my own things."

"It happens. No matter how well intended a body is, some stuff just gets past you, is all. Other folks wind up feeling let down."

"I suppose. Who was that man you were talking to?"

"What man?"

"Over near the door. You gave him some money."

"Nothing you need fret about. Just a little surprise for later."

"Another surprise?" Anora asked.

"You just wait."

19

"You're quiet," Jesse remarked as they headed back to Three Boulders. The rear of the carriage was piled high with gifts galore, from embroidered samplers to homemade relishes to a beautiful patchwork coverlet for their bed. Seated next to Jesse, Anora felt as if her heart were full to bursting, a sensation that seemed ripe for the undoing.

"You ever have a sense that things are much too good to continue on? When you just know something bad's going to happen, up around the next corner?"

Jesse muttered something unintelligible under his breath.

" 'Cause that's sure in creation the way I'm feeling. I know it's crazy and I've got no truck with feeling that way, but there it is."

"Funny way to feel as you head home from a party where you were the guest of honor."

"Isn't it just?"

They both lapsed into thoughtful silence for several miles before Anora piped up, "Jesse, what about Rosco?"

"What about him?"

"Think he might be the something bad?"

"You just quit that talk about something bad. I'm not about to let anything happen to you. Not so long as there's breath in my body."

Anora clutched his arm. "Don't say that. It's bad luck. Quick, make the sign of the cross."

"I'm not a religious man. You know that."

"Then I'll do it." Head bowed, Anora murmured a hasty prayer that nothing untoward would befall her husband. After that she immediately felt better. Strange the way it seemed as natural as breathing to think of Jesse as her husband, to fear for his safety.

When they reached the ranch and disembarked, Anora bounded ahead of Jesse, whose arms were laden with gifts. Just inside the door she screeched to a halt. For there, in the place formerly occupied by her narrow cot, stood a brand-spanking-new iron bedstead, topped with a plump feather mattress.

"Where in heaven's name . . . ?"

She heard Jesse behind her. "Remember that surprise I promised you earlier?"

"This is it?" Anora approached the bedstead and reverently ran her hands over the fancy iron footboard.

"That fellow you saw me talking to was a furniture broker. When he told me how this bed had been delivered just this morning I didn't want to take a chance on missing out, so I had him bring it out and set it up while we were still at the hotel. Shall we see how Lettie's quilt looks on it?"

Anora made her way to Jesse, took his face in both her hands, and kissed him full on the lips. Before she could step away, he dropped his packages, jerked her into his arms, and kissed her his way, long and deep, his tongue teasing hers. The kiss lasted a long, long time.

Anora felt her color rise. "My, I feel a trifle tired after all the excitement. I wonder . . ."

"Mmmm hmmm?"

"Would it be unseemly of me to have myself a little lie-down?"

"I think that's a meritorious idea. I just might have to join you." He placed one finger under Anora's chin and raised her face to his. "What's this here frown all about?"

"I feel so bad."

"Why?"

"For doubting you. I saw you talking to that man, giving him money, and . . . I don't know. I guess I got so used to Ben and my pa, frittering their money on cards and drink."

"I'm not like them, Anora."

She smiled cockily. "No, you're not. More than likely you take after your own kin."

"Dear Lord, if I thought that, I swear I'd go out to the barn and hang myself this very instant."

Anora didn't know exactly what it was she'd said wrong, but from the second the words left her lips about Jesse's kin, a change seemed to come over him. He didn't join her on their new bed that afternoon, and although they slept side by side each night, he didn't make another claim to his husbandly rights. Anora suspected he found her swelling belly unsightly and resigned herself to the fact that they likely wouldn't be together again until after the baby was born.

Yet, in spite of Jesse's distance and moodiness, Anora had never felt happier. The Yuletide season was approaching and, for the first time ever, she busied herself making gifts for her friends.

"Oh, bunk. I've dropped a stitch."

"Let me have it." Lettie reached across and took the knitting needles out of her hands. The older woman's fingers flew as she unfastened a row, picked up the dropped stitch, then added a few rows of her own to the half-knit pink sweater. "Hmmph." She checked out the garment with a critical eye. "I must say, your knitting is improving all the time."

"Practice makes perfect. And I got lots of time to practice."

"That'll end soon enough when the young one comes."

"I wish Penny had come out with you."

"She's pretty busy with the school."

Anora gave a wistful sigh. "I miss her."

Lettie leaned forward and patted Anora's hand. "She'll come around in her own time. I know the girl. She's still hurting over what happened with Beau Brown. But soon as that little one puts in an appearance, why, you won't be able to keep Penny away. Wait and see if I'm not right as always." She sat back. "Shame about that latest holdup."

"What holdup?"

Lettie gave Anora a searching look. "Lordy, sweetcheeks. You're married to the marshal. Don't the two of you talk?"

"Not about lawmaking," Anora said. "Tell me about the holdup."

"Seems Rosco's back at his old tricks. Except this time a child got killed."

Anora stifled a gasp. "How dreadful."

"That's what everyone says. A posse took off after him, but he gave them the slip near the river."

"Jesse never mentioned it to me."

"He likely doesn't want you to worry about something you got no control over. Menfolk get some strange ideas, 'specially about their women being in the family way."

Anora nodded. But she knew it wasn't her condition that had Jesse keeping quiet about Rosco's activities in the area. It was the fact that Rosco had a personal vendetta with Jesse.

Lettie rose and stretched. "Lord, it gets dark early. Sam's bunion says we're in for snow. And Sam's bunion is never wrong."

Anora smiled. "I can hardly wait. You be careful on the way back to town."

Lettie tilted her muff Anora's way, giving her a clear glimpse of the pistol tucked inside. "Any rowdy foolish enough to try messing with Lettie winds up a sorry dead man."

From the porch Anora watched her friend off, then scuttled quickly back inside. The air temperature felt to be dropping by the minute. She threw another log on the fire and bundled into an extra shawl, wishing Jesse were home safe. No one had warned her how being married to a lawman brought its own private hell of worry.

It was full dark before her straining ears caught the sound of a horse and rider and, as the newcomer climbed the porch stairs, she reached for her pistol. It wasn't Jesse, for she'd recognize his footsteps anywhere. She faced the door, pistol in one shaking hand, when she heard Charlie's voice on the other side of the door.

"It's me, ma'am. Charlie. The marshal sent me."

Ever wary of a trap, Anora opened the door a crack and peered out, making sure he was alone.

"Come in." She stepped back as he entered, then immediately locked the door behind him. Charlie went directly to the fire, pulled his gloves off with his teeth, and held his hands to the warmth.

"Where's Jesse?"

"He asked me to tell you he won't be home tonight. Sent me to bring you this note, and keep an eye out in his absence."

"You can't stay outside all night. You'll freeze."

"I'll hole up in the barn. I'll be okay. These old bones are used to this weather."

Anora unfolded the note he passed her, and held it toward the lamp, her nose wrinkling as the faint smell of cheap scent wafted toward her. The same cheap scent that seemed to have a permanent place in Ricki's wardrobe. Even the writing paper was effeminate, bordered by a line of doves with curling ribbons in their beaks.

Unlike the paper she held, there was nothing effeminate about Jesse's bold scrawl. The note stated that he'd return on the morrow and that she was to take every precaution in his absence. Anora wondered why he even bothered to write. Charlie could have relayed the message in person. Or was he looking to flaunt the fact that he was at Ricki's while she was alone at the ranch?

"He's at Ricki's, then?" she said, as if Jesse had included that information.

Charlie nodded. "Ricki and her girls are a good conduit to Rosco's comings and goings."

Anora crushed Jesse's note in her fist. "I'll rest easier when that man is behind bars." She tossed the crumpled page into the fire and set about making Charlie a hot meal. The poor fellow needed something warm and solid in his belly if he was to keep watch all through the night.

The new bed felt awfully empty without Jesse trussed up alongside of her, and Anora tossed restlessly, her ears tuned to the slightest sound outside the cabin. The baby inside her shifted, and Anora knew the sudden need to relieve herself, something that had been happening with greater frequency of late. She rose. Wrinkling her nose at the sight of the chamber pot Jesse had produced for this very purpose, she bundled up and made her way outside to the privy.

On her way back to the cabin she paused and gulped in huge lungfuls of cold air. Not a single star showed through the thick blanket of clouds in the sky. Snow clouds, if she put any stock in what others had been saying all day.

Where was Jesse? Was he outdoors, staring up at this same cloud-muffled sky and doing his best to keep warm on some lonely lawman's vigil? Or was he trussed up snug and warm, ensconced in the bed of Boulder Springs' infamous madam? Plying Ricki with the physical attentions he'd withheld from his own wife?

Some wives might be prepared to share their menfolk, to look the other way from their alley-catting. Anora wasn't one of them. A fact she'd be sure and make clear to Jesse at the first opportunity, for if that was the type of marriage arrangement he thought he'd entered into, he was in for a rude surprise.

She started as something cool and damp licked her cheek, and glanced up in time to see a snowflake drift past her face. Followed by another. And another. Silent as the night they drifted down, a scant handful to start. Then, as if by magic, she watched their numbers increase, doubling and doubling again. She stood a spell, drinking in the magic of the moment, till finally she made her way inside, aware that to take a chill would be bad for both her and the babe.

The cabin felt cozy and warm after the outdoors, and Anora had dutifully locked the door after her, when the hair on the back of her neck stood on end. She'd know that smell anywhere. Slowly she turned.

There were three of them: Rosco and two others. Each man held a gun trained directly at her.

Anora swallowed her fear. She must be brave for the sake of the baby.

"Didn't dare come alone this time, did you,

Rosco? Afraid I'd run you off the ranch the way I did before?"

She watched the sudden shift of his henchmen's eyes to their leader, as if seeking confirmation of her words.

"Sit down and shut up," Rosco said.

Moving slowly, her mind awhirl with possible means of escape, Anora did as she was told. Rosco jerked his head to one of the men, who moved forward and tied her hands behind her, lashed to the chair back.

"Good idea," Anora said pluckily. "Don't take any chances on being bested by a woman a second time."

"You two. Out," Rosco said. "I'll take care of this one alone." His beady eyes fastened on Anora's face, intercepting her anxious glances toward the door. "If you're hoping to be rescued by the old guy, you can save yourself the bother. Me and the boys already took care of him."

"I'm surprised at you," Anora said, as the other two outlaws took their leave. "I thought for a certainty you must have found whatever booty you claim Ben stole."

Rosco advanced until he stood directly in front of her, her eyes at a level with his belt buckle. She had to breathe through her mouth, the smell of him was so foul.

"You think this is about money?"

"Isn't it?"

"No, indeedy. This here is all about how the best man always wins. 'Specially when he's up against a Quantrill." He laughed unpleasantly. "I been playing that marshal for a sucker long before he blew into town."

"Pity," Anora said. "As it surely must take the fun right out of it if no one knows just how smart you are."

Rosco thumped his chest with a burly fist. "Folks'll know soon enough just who bested who." His eyes narrowed, as if seeing Anora for the first time.

"That a swollen belly you got there, girl? Quantrill didn't waste much time, from the look of things, did he? Too bad he won't be around to see his brat birthed."

"Jesse will never let you get away with whatever it is you're planning. He knows you killed that woman in Indian Springs. And that child yesterday. You'll hang for murder."

Rosco's eyes glittered with malice. "Not before Quantrill pays for the murder of my brother."

Anora tried to hide her reaction to Rosco's words. Jesse killed Rosco's brother? Not *her* Jesse. He wasn't a murderer. But he also hadn't wanted to tell her why Rosco was after him personally.

"You best get out of here," Anora said. "Jesse's due back anytime."

Rosco laughed. "I don't think so, missy. He's long gone till morning. A fact I made darn good and sure of."

Anora's mind raced. Jesse'd been at Ricki's earlier tonight. Anything could have happened. Ricki could even have slipped him a drink guaranteed to knock him out till tomorrow.

Rosco stared at her stomach. "Whose brat is it?

Not that it much matters. One's as bad as the next."
He stood. "Way I see it, I'm doing the whole of
society a favor, make sure he never gets born."

Anora tasted fear unlike anything she'd ever felt
before. She struggled to free her hands, but the
bonds were too tight. "I'm sorry I didn't shoot you
when I had the chance."

"Regular little spitfire, ain' cha? Might have even
given you a go myself at one time. Show you what a
real man's capable of."

"Right. A real man. One who picks on defenseless women and children."

Rosco's mouth twisted grimly. He grasped a handful of Anora's hair and yanked her head straight back.
Her eyes filled with tears from the sudden pain. "One
thing I hate it's a mouthy woman." Raising his other
hand he backhanded her across the mouth. Anora's
ears rang from the blow. Her mouth filled with blood.

She watched in horror as Rosco raised one
booted foot and aimed it directly at her midsection.
With both feet against the floor, she pushed with all
her might. The chair tipped, taking her with it. She
felt a searing pain in her temple. Followed by darkness.

20

Snowflakes started to fall, gently at first, then with increasing force. Jesse turned up the collar of his jacket, too late to stop the handful that had melted against his neck and trickled inside his shirt. Ahead of him rode Eddy and two other men, temporary deputies. Jesse didn't know whether Rosco had intended to kill that youngster yesterday, and he didn't much care. To his mind, they'd been playing cat and mouse too long, a game he was about to put an end to once and for all.

The wind shifted, bringing with it the acrid smell of wood smoke. Eddy dropped back to his side.

"Smell that? We got 'em dead to rights this time."

"Damn and thunderation!" Jesse reined Sully to an abrupt halt.

"What is it?" Eddy pulled up as well and turned to Jesse, a puzzled look on his face.

"Rosco won't be there." The ominous feeling that built in his gut and poured with heated urgency through his veins was too powerful to ignore. "Any man who's eluded capture this long is way too smart to have a fire going, leading us straight to him."

"Smart? Rosco?" Eddy spat a plug of tobacco on the ground.

"You and the others ride on ahead and locate that fire. With luck you'll find some of Rosco's men."

"Where you going?" Eddy called as Jesse wheeled Sully around, back in the direction of Boulder Springs.

Home.

He didn't say it out loud, but the one word pounded over and over in his head and kept time with the way Sully's hooves pounded the frozen ground beneath him. Like Anora, Jesse had never found a place that truly felt like home to him. Till now.

Home. The picture conjured up by that one word had nothing to do with the ramshackle shack where he'd been hanging his hat lately, and everything to do with a certain cinnamon-haired woman who kept the home fires burning.

He never should have listened to her; left her alone at the ranch. He should have insisted she move into town and stay with Lettie. Better yet, he ought to have bundled her onto the train himself and sent her to stay with Rose till Rosco was either dead or behind bars. Dead being his preferred choice.

Jesse'd never been much of one for formal prayer, but he raised his eyes heavenward and intoned a silent plea for Anora's safety. Hell, he would have sold his soul, what was left of it, to the devil himself if he thought it would help keep Anora safe.

He crested the ravine above the ranch at the same instant the moon peeked out from a gap in the clouds. The ranch lay spread beneath him like a fuzzy white patchwork quilt. The pristine white covering blanketed the landscape's flaws and blemishes and smoothed out the harsh lines of bleakness and neglect. No light showed from the cabin's window. Beyond it the barn lay in dark, snow-shrouded silence.

Sully whinnied softly and danced nervously in a circle as they approached the barn.

"Easy, boy." Jesse spoke low-voiced as he patted the animal's sweaty neck soothingly. He opened the barn door and urged Sully inside. The hair on the back of his neck seconded his bad feelings and cut through the pervading stillness. A stillness that ought not to be there. Charlie should have heard him by now. Should have called out.

The back of Jesse's neck positively bristled. He unholstered his Colt and dismounted. His feet made no sound as he moved across the hay-strewn barn floor. From the rear of the barn he heard the cow and her calf moo plaintively.

He discovered Charlie gagged and bound in the last stall. Jesse removed the man's gag and cut his bonds.

"Sorry, Marshal," Charlie said, as the gag was removed. "There were too many."

Jesse leapt to his feet. "Ride into town. Bring back help." He raced through the snow to the cabin, and his heart hit his knees as he reached the unlocked door. A beam of moonlight followed him in and tumbled across the empty bed. Maybe she'd made her way outside and managed to hide in the dark till Rosco left. So where was she now? Had Rosco taken her hostage? His fingers trembled as he lit the lantern. The light flared, throwing grotesque shadows on the walls and ceiling. Highlighting the still-as-death white face of his wife, lying near his feet.

He dropped to his knees. Anora's hands were lashed behind the back of an upended chair. Her eyes were closed. Lamplight reflected off the dark pool of blood staining the floor beneath her.

"Dear Lord." He pressed his fingertips to the side of her neck and probed the faintly beating pulse. She was alive. He pulled out his knife and hacked at the ropes binding her wrists. His blood boiled at the sight of her raw and bleeding flesh. How long had she struggled to get free?

"You'll pay for this, Rosco."

Gently he scooped Anora up in his arms.

There was so much blood her night robe was soaked clear through. What had that monster done to her? He laid her on the bed, relieved to see her eyelids start to flutter. She was coming to.

It wasn't long before her eyes flew open and fastened fearfully on him. He started to summon up a reassuring expression that vanished as she let out an earth-shattering scream and pulled her knees to her chest.

"Ssssh," Jesse said soothingly. "It's me, Jesse. He's gone. You're going to be all right."

She let out a second cry, a sound both numbing and bone-chilling, the likes of which he'd never heard uttered by anything human. Jesse had never felt as powerless as he did at that moment, helpless in the face of Anora's pain.

"You're bleeding bad," he murmured, leaning close. Her chest heaved as she fought for breath and struggled against the pain. "Do you know where you're hurt? Can you tell me?"

"Feels like . . . I'm being . . . split . . . in half . . . with an ax," she said, panting between the words.

Jesse laid one trembling hand upon her distended belly and felt the telltale tightening of her contraction.

"The baby." He caught one of her cold-as-death hands between both of his.

"No." It was a hopeless attempt at denial. "It's too soon." Twisted up with another spasm, she squeezed his hands so hard he bit his lip and held on till she slowly eased her grip.

Reluctantly Jesse freed his hands and reached to push a sweat-dampened hank of hair off her face. Her skin felt flushed. He rose and tugged off his jacket, then fetched a cloth and a basin of cool water. He added wood to the fire and filled the kettle, placing it to boil. After rolling up his sleeves he washed his hands thoroughly, using lots of soap and clean water, ever conscious of the torturous moans and cries from the woman on the bed. His fault. All his fault.

Anora's labor was mercifully short. Once the

birthing pains stopped she appeared to drift off to sleep. Jesse hoped it was a healing sleep. She'd need all her strength.

Their daughter, so small and perfectly formed, lay lifeless, smaller than the span of his hand as he cradled her in his palm. He washed the blood from her doll-sized body and held her for a long time, just looking at her, marveling at the perfection of her tiny limbs. The faint blue marbling of veins visible through her translucent skin.

She had no eyelashes or eyebrows, yet a crown of dark, downy fuzz covered her head. Tenderly he wrapped her fragile body in a clean towel and wondered what color her eyes would have been. Dark like his? Or green like Anora's? A vast and bitter emptiness soured his innards. He'd never see her ride or toss a ball or hear her call him Da da.

Night lifted to reveal the shadow of day as Jesse remained by Anora's side. His infant daughter hadn't lived long enough to draw her first breath, while his wife hovered between life and death. All because of Rosco.

In the powerful light of that early, empty dawn, Jesse acknowledged what he knew he had to do.

Anora slowly surfaced from the inky blackness that continued to call her back, beckoned her into a safe, warm, feelingless place, away from the light and pain she instinctively knew awaited her.

Reluctantly she raised her lids and focused. The first thing her conscious mind identified was Jesse. He sat, knees apart, with his head bowed. She heard the harsh rise and fall of his breathing. His hands were clasped in a prayerlike position, but there was nothing pious about the emotions she felt emanating from him.

Before she could open her mouth to ask him what was wrong, the night's incidents came crashing back. Rosco. The pain. Excruciating pain.

"Jesse?" Her lips felt huge and swollen, the corners cracked and dry. His name came out an unrecognizable croak, but it was enough to capture his attention. When he glanced her way through soulless eyes, Anora wished she'd never woken up.

She couldn't bear it. Not the way he grazed her cheek with his fingertips. Or his eyes, so full of bleak despair, a black and lonely pain. It was a look that surpassed all degree of the pain that had ripped through her body last night.

Such pain.

Weak and drained as she was she pressed a hand to her flat and empty abdomen, then lifted her head up off the pillow and looked around the room. "The baby?"

She didn't need to see him shake his head. She sank back weakly, closer to understanding the terrible darkness that bound Jesse in its grip. She wrapped her arms about herself and pressed her lips tightly together, rocking from side to side, in a gesture of silent, useless comfort.

Jesse rose and stood with his back to her as he stared out the window. Her arms ached to reach for him. If only they were able to share their sadness, to help each other ease the burden weighing at their souls. But he remained unreachable.

It seemed an eternity before he turned. When he did the bleakness was gone. Replaced by something far more chilling. A primitive expression devoid of feeling. As if Jesse had lost all grip on the human emotions that separate man from beast. She knew what he was going to say even before he spoke.

"I have to go."

"Jesse, leave it. What's done is done."

"Don't you see? It's not over. It'll never be over until I do what I know I have to do," Jesse said harshly.

"I lost my child. I can't bear it if I lose you, too."

"What makes you think you ever had me?"

Anora stifled a gasp at the cruelty of his words. Aching, numbing loss swept through her with the power of a flood-ravaged river, and she felt as helpless as something caught in its current, unable to fight her way free. Unable to fight with Jesse or for Jesse. She watched through pain-dulled hopelessness as he pulled on his coat.

"Charlie'll be back anytime with the doc."

Anora took in every detail of his exhausted features and killing eyes. He was right. The Jesse she loved wasn't capable of deliberate murder. Unlike the stranger before her.

"Jesse. You're not like them."

"Who?"

"Your pa and your brothers. I know all three lived and died outside of the law."

His look spoke volumes. Told her more than she wanted to know about the outlaw Quantrills. A legacy Jesse had spent his whole life fighting. Till now.

"Don't you see?" Anora made one last, futile effort. "Your going after Rosco this way makes you no better than them."

Jesse jammed his hat on his head and gave her a world-weary look. "Don't you think I know that?" Then he was gone.

Anora stared at the door, as if she could reach through those flat and peeling panels, as if the power of her love could bring Jesse back, even as she knew no power on earth could combat the dark forces roiling within him.

Her eyes burned, then boiled over with hot, salty tears. Tears for a love uprooted before given a chance to flower or bear fruit. Tears for the child she would never know. Tears for the one man she could never have.

Exhausted by grief, unable to move, Anora let her tears continue to fall. Tears for her mother. Her father. Her brother. And the empty bleakness that was now her life.

In the early morning light Jesse barely noticed the way light, powdery flakes of snow filtered down from the sky. Once the snow stopped he no longer worried about losing Rosco's tracks, for the trail, which Rosco made no effort to cover, led him and Sully over the ridge and into the next valley.

From the valley it appeared Rosco had headed for the distant hills. Intent on the other man's trail, Jesse felt a calmness and peace the likes of which he'd never before experienced, and he stopped pushing Sully to the maximum of the animal's limits. Time ceased to exist. As did cause and effect. Death and life. Nothing was real outside of the upcoming confrontation. Something Jesse now accepted to be as inevitable as drawing his next breath.

He paused and took a swig from his canteen, neither knowing nor caring how long it had been since he'd eaten or slept. Two days? Three, perhaps. It didn't matter. He was primed and ready.

The newly fallen snow masked what should have been a relatively familiar terrain. As if the clean virgin whiteness could cover up the filth and ugliness of a world gone mad. A world where vermin like Rosco got within reach of decent folks, near enough to wreak havoc in their lives.

"Last time, Rosco." Jesse spoke aloud, his words a thin white puff encircling his head, his breath warm in the snow-frosted air.

Sully treated Jesse to a knowing look, as if he understood both the words and the importance of their mission. Jesse gathered the reins more firmly and touched his heels to Sully's flanks in silent agreement.

Pictures of Anora tiptoed through his mind. Tied up and drowning in a pool of blood. The way she looked as he left, so pale and unmoving. As if she'd given up the struggle. Juxtaposed on top of that was a picture of their dead infant daughter, no bigger than a kitten in his palm.

Resolutely Jesse banished the images to the nether regions, the area he termed "silent hell," aware as he did that no matter what happened, he'd never be completely free from the haunting of his memories. Knowing he would always blame himself for what had happened.

Long ago, Jesse'd learned to trust his instincts, and

it was instinct that told him when to slow. He knew, without being able to pinpoint how, that he was close to Rosco. He sat alert, gaze combing the hibernating countryside, ears pricked for the faintest sound. Beneath him Sully stopped abruptly, flattened back his ears, and rolled his eyes.

Jesse leaned forward and stroked the horse's sweaty neck. "Exactly," he murmured under his breath. "You can smell him too, can't you, boy? Like a cornered rat."

It seemed that not a single living thing moved in the stillness. As if he and Sully were lone survivors after a terrible war. Yet Jesse knew the battle was yet to come.

He narrowed his eyes as he slowly surveyed the landscape, and forced himself to think the way Rosco did. The man knew Jesse was on his trail; therefore he'd be sure to hole up someplace where he had the best advantage.

Jesse studied the ridge of mountains that circled him on two sides. His gaze passed over the rugged contours, then backed up to hone in on a specific place in the rock face. A faint, dark shadow that seemed more pronounced than all the rest. Perhaps the opening to a cave? He headed Sully in that direction and hadn't gone more than a few yards when his mount buckled beneath him.

Grabbing his rifle, Jesse kicked his feet from the stirrups and jumped clear of the snow-covered trap. Luckily they'd been traveling slow. Sully had managed to stop on the precipice of the booby-trapped pit. If they'd been going full-out his horse would have likely broken a leg, while he wound up, ass over teakettle, buried in a snowdrift.

Sully whinnied softly at Jesse, almost a question.

" 'S okay boy. Good boy." Jesse started toward the horse, only to give a startled cry as his feet flew out from underneath him and the world turned upside down as he dangled, feet first, five feet off the ground.

21

This sudden sequence of events proved too much for Sully. The animal turned tail and galloped back the way they had come.

"So much for loyalty," Jesse murmured, as he eyed his rifle on the snow below him, about an arm's length from where he dangled like some fly caught in a spider's deadly web.

Gritting his teeth with the effort, Jesse attempted to bend at the waist, to pull himself up to a point where he could grab his legs. If he could manage to even partially right himself he could get hold of the knife sheathed at his waist and cut himself down.

To grab hold of his legs was one thing. To actually defy the laws of gravity and pull himself upright was quite another. Cold beads of sweat popped up on his face. Maybe the sweat would freeze in the frigid air and he'd dangle here till spring thaw, strung up like some damn human icicle.

The picture wasn't a pretty one. With a muttered oath he released his tenuous hold and hung gasping for breath. White vapor clouds appeared with each breath and taunted him with their fluidity. Surely the blood rushing to his brain would help him think. To figure a way down from here before Rosco arrived and smeared him with some foul-smelling concoction designed to attract every wild animal in a hundred-mile radius. It wasn't the way he'd pictured his final days.

His thoughts turned to Anora. In some ways it would be better for her if he didn't return to Boulder Springs. Jesse interrupted himself. He couldn't think about the future. He had to focus all his energies on the here and now. Remember the reason he was here in the first place.

Maybe this wasn't Rosco's trap at all. Maybe—

Jesse yelped as a shot whistled past him. Now he was being used for target practice. Not an overly comforting prospect. He held his breath and listened, knowing the shot had come too close to be anything other than deliberate.

Several long minutes passed without a repeat, and he had just redoubled his efforts to free himself when he heard the second crack of rifle fire. Seconds later he landed on his back in the snow, while the sound of the shot still echoed through the surrounding hills.

Damned if someone hadn't gone and shot him down. After he struggled to catch the wind that had been knocked out of him, he grabbed his hat in one hand, his rifle in the other and belly-crawled for cover, trying to gauge the direction of the shots. Was there one shooter or two?

He hoped one. Both his gut and his ears told him the shooter was up near the mouth of the cave where he'd been headed. His gut also told him Rosco wasn't finished with their game of cat and mouse. If all the outlaw wanted was to see Jesse dead, he'd have lowered his aim by a couple of feet. Nope, Rosco had to be looking forward to this upcoming confrontation as much as Jesse was. Adrenaline surged through his veins as he anticipated the battle of wits that lay ahead.

Hugging the tree line for cover, Jesse slowly threaded his way to where the beckoning black hole sliced through the rock.

As he approached the cave Jesse's mind fired up a picture of Anora, white-faced and bleeding alongside their tiny infant daughter. He tightened his grip on the rifle. Soon, justice would be his.

Crouched behind a boulder a scant ten feet from the entrance, Jesse plotted his strategy. He could rush Rosco and trust that the element of surprise was on his side. Or he could continue as he was, his tread silent on the snowy ground, and keep himself well hidden. His rifle rested heavy in his hands, and he patted his waist where his loaded pistol also lay within easy reach.

He leaned against the tree trunk behind him, sucked in a ragged breath, and stared up at the midafternoon sky. The cold mountain air stung his lungs. He could wait for dark, but didn't rightly know that darkness would afford him any great advantage unless Rosco grew edgy and careless. His only other choice seemed to be waiting here till curiosity got the best of Rosco. Sooner or later the other man was bound to show his murdering face. As Jesse stared at the dull gray shards of hilltops, poking through in spots where the snow had started to melt, he had another idea. A better idea.

He recalled Ricki's words. If Rosco was smarter than Jesse gave him credit for, he was too smart to hole up anyplace that only had one way in. Or out. Jesse snapped a branch from the scrubby evergreen behind him and slowly retraced his steps, taking pains to brush away all evidence of his recent passing.

Halfway down the hill he turned onto a different trail that took him up and over the hillside's natural contours to a spot over the top of the cave opening.

It was slow going. The snow's surface had crusted over in some spots and started to sog up in others. He never knew if his next step would slip or sink. Jesse judged he had a couple hours of daylight left and didn't cotton to the thought of spending the night out here. Not with Rosco nearly close enough to touch.

His instincts held him in good stead. The sloping hillside, which from a distance appeared to form a solid rock roof above the cave, was in actual fact a junction of two slopes that missed each other by about a foot and a half and left a hole big enough for a man to crawl in or out of the cave.

Jesse eased himself close enough for a look inside.

Yes, indeedy. The cave's interior was gloomy and dark, but enough light seeped through the entrance to show him that Rosco had made himself right comfortable. Jesse spied a mattress of sorts, with a bedroll atop it. A stash of supplies and ammo leaned up against one wall.

He couldn't help but think about his pa and his two brothers, who'd met their end in a similar situation. How had Anora known his kin were wanted men? Small-town talk, he guessed, for like Rosco, they'd been holed up in a cave in the hills. A posse'd tracked them down after they'd robbed a bank. He knew his kin weren't above killing in a bid for freedom, but that particular day, they'd all three got taken down together. Jesse didn't like to think about it. He believed in justice, not vengeance, and he'd fought his whole life not to be like them, not to end his days the way they had.

Anora picked listlessly at the tray of food Lettie placed across her lap. Her friend had been kindness itself, opening her home and her heart to care for Anora, and normally she suffered in good grace the older woman's cheerful chatter as she plumped pillows and straightened the coverlet.

Today, however, was different. Lettie sat opposite her in silence. As she pleated the folds of her skirt between her fingers her eyes didn't quite meet Anora's.

"Today's the day the doc said I could get up."

Lettie nodded, her mind clearly elsewhere.

"It'll feel good to be back home. Have my own bed and things around me."

That caught Lettie's attention. "You sure that's a

good idea, sweetcheeks? The place will more than likely be chock-full of bad memories."

"I have to face them sooner or later."

"Why not at least wait till Jesse comes back?"

"He's not coming back," Anora said.

Lettie paled. "What do you mean, not coming back?" She jumped up and started to fiddle about the room. Anora watched her straighten an already straight picture. Rip an imaginary thread from the hem of the drapes.

"Is he?" she asked pointedly.

Lettie glanced her way and wrung her hands. "Sam said not to say anything. That it'd only upset you, there being nothing you can do and all."

"What did Sam think would upset me?"

Lettie drew a deep breath, then spoke in a rush. "Sully showed up at the livery. Took three of the hands to calm him down enough to take off his saddle."

"Jesse loved that horse."

"Don't you dare speak of your husband in the past tense," Lettie said sharply.

"We both know if Sully's not with Jesse, it's because Jesse's dead."

"You don't know that for a fact."

"If, by some miracle, he's not dead, he might as well be," Anora said. "He won't be coming back this way anyway."

Lettie patted Anora's hand absently. "We'll all pray for Jesse's safe return."

Anora gave her friend a dark look. "Where Jesse's gone, it's too late for prayers."

*   *   *

As Jesse studied what little he could make out of the cave's interior, trying to gauge its full size and dimensions, he heard movement from below. He held his breath and waited for what seemed an eternity. He'd started to think his imagination was playing tricks on him when suddenly Rosco appeared directly beneath him. It was now or never.

Resisting the urge to let loose with a war whoop, Jesse propelled himself, feet first, through the opening. His aim was bang on. He dropped right on top of the outlaw.

Together they landed heavily, sprawled across the cold dirt floor. Before Rosco could pull his firearm, Jesse had him pinned. He straddled the outlaw's chest and slammed his rifle barrel across his throat. Leaning his weight on the gun, he pressed, hard enough to see Rosco's eyes widen, not hard enough to crush his windpipe. Not yet.

" 'Scuse me for dropping in this way," Jesse drawled. "But then, surely you were expecting me. What's the matter? Didn't have time enough to roll out the welcome mat?"

Rosco blinked furiously and tried to swallow.

Jesse leaned on the gun a little harder. "Big mistake, Rosco. You ought to have killed me while you had the chance. The same way you killed my baby. And all those others. You never gave one of them a chance to defend themselves."

A gurgling sound issued from Rosco's throat as he attempted to talk. Jesse eased up a bit. Enough to hear Rosco's painful whisper. "You murdered my brother."

"Your brother was a clumsy fool who my sister

loved in spite of that fact. I gave Cameron a chance to do the right thing. More chance than the boy deserved." His voice wavered. A flood of red anger temporarily blinded him. "More chance than you gave my wife and daughter."

While Jesse fought to control the surge of emotions ripping through him, Rosco started to laugh. A maniacal laughter that chilled Jesse to the marrow of his bones. Instinctively he darted a glance over his shoulder. What had he missed?

The laughter turned into a rattling cough and Jesse stared in horror at the bloodstained mucus and spittle Rosco produced. His suspicions sharpened. Was this a trap? A trick to have him let down his guard?

"Get off me," Rosco managed to say. "Leave me die in peace."

Jesse eased back a hair, rifle at the ready. Eyes watchful.

"Why else do you think I led you here? Shot you down out of that trap?"

"Surely not just so I could have the privilege of watching you draw your last breath?"

"Enjoy it, boy. The same way I'm going to enjoy drawing my last breath, knowing I got you dead to rights."

Jesse shifted. This wasn't going at all according to plans. "Take another look, Rosco. Who's got who?"

"I fixed you good," Rosco chortled. "Little surprise to remember old Rosco by."

The outlaw linked his fingers together across his chest and closed his eyes. Warily Jesse got to his feet. When Rosco didn't move he backed away a step, and studied his surroundings, eyes watchful, ears tuned for Rosco's slightest movement.

"What sort of surprise?"

When the outlaw didn't answer, Jesse kicked him with the toe of his boot. "Out with it, Rosco. What's my surprise?"

The other man's head lolled limply to the side.

"Won't work, Rosco. I'm not dumb enough to fall for your possum act." Still no response. "Doesn't matter," Jesse said. "You can't stay like that all night."

But Jesse was wrong. Rosco never did move. And when he finally edged back closer, Jesse was disgusted to learn he'd spent the last hour guarding a corpse. He stared in disbelief at the dead outlaw. How had Rosco pulled that off? To up and die like that, saving Jesse the trouble of killing him?

He'd set out after Rosco with killing in his blood. Now he'd never know for certain if he was made of the same stuff of his kin, or if he'd succeeded in walking his own walk. One good thing, at least. Rosco would never prey on innocent folk again.

The outlaw's horse was tethered just outside the cave, and Jesse tossed the dead man across the saddle. Only one sure way to let Boulder Springs folks know for a certainty that Rosco's days of plaguing them were over.

As Jesse started back the way he'd come he was greeted by the most glorious sunset he had ever witnessed. Slowly he felt himself refill with the wellspring of life, to emerge transformed. Reborn. Arms raised heavenward, Jesse paid homage to the incredible

feelings that surged through him. The sky was awash
with color, raggedy streaks of crimson and orange, the
brightness backlit with a purplish hue that slowly
intensified to the deepest, darkest blue he'd ever seen.
He wished Anora were here to see it. To share what
was happening to him.

He felt the blood pumping through his veins, a
celebration of life, a victory unlike anything he'd
ever experienced before. Despite the bruised and
battered state of his body, he felt more at peace,
more alive than any man had a right to. He reveled
in each and every raw sensation coming at him
from all directions. The smell of evergreen bows,
heavy with melting snow. The crunch of snow
beneath his booted feet. The renewed beating of
his own heart, overflowing with contentment and
inner peace. A rightness to his life that took away
his breath.

It lasted for what could have been mere minutes, yet felt like an entire lifetime as he drank in
the essence of life all around him. Then he turned
and started west.

He only got off track twice in the night, mostly
because of the rain, which washed away the snow
and made everything appear different. By the time
he finally reached Boulder Springs it was morning
and he was wet, cold, hungry, and more tired than
he'd ever been in his entire life.

Jesse hesitated just outside of town. While his
heart urged him in the direction of the Three
Boulders, to Anora, his head steered him differently.
Acknowledged that she had healing of her own
to do. Hell, she might not even care about the

transformation that had taken place in him. The new man he'd become.

He headed instead for Ricki's, knowing his old friend would find him a bath and a bed. Time enough tomorrow, once he was rested and cleaned up, to figure out the best way to make things right between Anora and him.

He rode down Main Street toward Ricki's as if seeing the town for the first time. The street was a river of mud, but the boardwalks were swept and clean. Nice enough little town. Not the sort of place he ever thought he'd land in permanently or anything. Still, if Anora was fixed to stay . . .

He reined in his thoughts. He was getting ahead of himself. He hadn't a clue what Anora was fixing to do. Besides, whatever they did had to be something the two of them decided together, once the time was right. The road to Ricki's took him directly past the burial park, where a small gathering of black-clad mourners clustered together on the soggy knoll, silhouetted against the sky.

Who'd died? As he drew closer he recognized Ricki, Lettie and Sam, Penny. Not until he spotted Anora standing apart from the others, alongside the smallest casket he'd ever seen, did realization sink in. He'd arrived home in time for his daughter's burial.

Pain slammed through his limbs as he dismounted and watched Charlie and Sam lower the miniature coffin into the inhospitable earth. The winter air rang with the thuds of frozen clods of dirt hitting the box. His child! He choked back a sob as he made his way to the graveside. Folks gave him a funny, sideways look and sort of melted into the background as he passed. No one spoke. He could have been a ghost. Maybe he had died, just hadn't left this earth. He could see everyone and nobody saw him. Nope. He was too bone-weary to be dead, yet not too exhausted to feel Anora's pain as he joined her before the final resting place of their child, dug before the ground froze.

Jesse removed his hat and ran a hand through his hair. Words eluded him. He sneaked a sideways glance at Anora. The look of her pierced through to his core, that haunted look of a creature in unbearable agony, waiting only for someone to come along and put her out of her misery. He'd seen that look on a calf caught in a barbed-wire fence. And a coyote with his hindquarters shot nearly clean off, dragging himself by his front legs. He'd never expected to see it on the face of his wife.

"I thought you were dead," Anora said finally, no expression in her voice. She could have been discussing the weather. "We all did. 'Specially after Sully showed up without you."

What were you expecting, Quantrill, after the way you ran out on her? A hero's welcome? Some indication that she's glad to see you alive and in one piece? Why should she be glad to see you at all?

Jesse fastened his gaze on the simple wooden cross at the head of the grave and he wondered who'd carved the marker. Etched out the name and the date. "You named her Sarah." His voice didn't sound like his own. He cleared his throat and tried again. "That's a pretty name."

"I named her after my mother. Someone else who died before her time."

Jesse clenched his jaw so tight it hurt. He prayed for the wisdom to say the right thing. If the right thing even existed. He turned his head and forced himself to meet her gaze. Her eyes were as blank as her voice.

"I'm sorry I wasn't here to help you with the arrangements."

She nodded stiffly, her lips pinched tight together.

Jesse drew a deep breath. "I know you think I ran out on you, at the time when you needed me most. It was something I just had to do."

"Always is." Anora's gaze moved past him to the bleak winter landscape and Jesse knew she was remembering her pa and Ben. Never around when she had a need of them. How could he convince her he was any different? Not just from the other men in her life, but different from the man he'd been three short days ago. Changed on the inside.

He opened his mouth to tell her as much, but no words came out. He tried again. "I have so much to tell you. I don't rightly know where to start."

"Don't bother," Anora said, turning away. "I'm through listening."

"Anora, wait. You don't mean that. You can't mean that."

She paused and gave him a glance that chilled him to the depths of his soul. Her eyes held the hollow emptiness of someone who had given up all faith. All belief. All hope. He'd done that to her. "I never meant anything more. Good-bye, Jesse."

As he watched her walk away, head high, spine

rigid, Jesse knew he wasn't the only one who'd changed.

He turned to his deputies. "I brought back Rosco's body."

Eddy and Charlie exchanged uncomfortable looks. "He's dead then?" Charlie asked.

"Yeah," Jesse said shortly. "Didn't even get the privilege of doing him in myself."

"How'd he die?"

"Just up and died, far as I could tell. Why?"

Charlie and Eddy continued to exchange uncomfortable looks. This time Eddy broke the silence. "Sorry 'bout this, Jesse. But Charlie and I got our orders. We have bring you in."

22

"Bring me in? What the hell is that supposed to mean?"

Charlie spat a plug of tobacco onto the ground. "Man showed up day before last. Name of Rosco Sr. Been in a huddle with the magistrate."

"What about?"

"Claims there's a warrant for your arrest for killing his son."

"Which one?" Jesse asked.

"How many you kill?" Eddy asked. His eyes were wide. He was enjoying this, Jesse thought.

Jesse held out his hands. "You want to cuff me?"

"I don't see as where that's necessary," Charlie said. "Y'all will come peaceable. Right?"

"Wouldn't have it any other way." As they made

their way past the recently deceased Rosco, Jesse
spoke up. "Tell Rosco Sr. I've delivered him
another son to bury."

It took a couple of days to verify that the warrant
was a forgery, but things got complicated from
there. Rosco Sr. started hollering how Jesse'd killed
his oldest boy, too. Denied him the right to a fair
trial. And the doc couldn't rightly determine just
how, exactly, the outlaw had died.

Jesse was too wrung out to much care what happened next. Anora hated him and some in the town
were set to brand him a murderer. He knew he ought
to start planning to defend himself against Rosco Sr.'s
accusations but right now he was just too weary to
bother. He collapsed on the bunk in one of the cells
and wondered if he'd ever feel like getting up.

Rumors abounded in the town. Jesse was under
arrest for killing Rosco Jr. No, he wasn't, someone
else said. He'd volunteered to stay in jail till things
were cleared up once and for all.

Anora's limbs felt leaden as she paused outside
the marshal's office, took a deep breath, and opened
the door. She told herself she wasn't afraid to face
Jesse. That he couldn't possibly hurt her any more
than he already had. Still, the sight of him on the
other side of the bars proved more wrenching than
she'd thought it would.

He lay on the bunk with his eyes closed. The
same bunk where they'd almost made love the night
of the dance. Her pulse leapt at the memory. At
first Jesse acted as if he didn't know she was there,

but after she cleared her throat for the third time he opened one eye. Even in the dim light she could tell he looked weary, as if he hadn't slept much. She told herself his lack of sleep was none of her concern.

"What brings you this way? I thought you weren't speaking to me ever again."

"I've come to tell you that I'm applying for an annulment."

Jesse's lips twisted humorlessly. "An annulment? On what grounds?"

She blushed. Glanced at her shoes. "You know."

Jesse rolled to his feet, crossed the cell, and brought his face to a level with hers. "I know we didn't have much of a marriage, you and I. One thing I sure as hell remember is that we consummated it. Or are you suffering a sudden convenient loss of memory of the times we made love?"

As if she'd ever forget.

"The night . . ." Her voice faltered. "When you left me that night, it was your intention to hunt Rosco down and kill him. Even though you knew it was wrong. Even though you knew it made you no better than him."

Jesse didn't move. Didn't speak. And his silence infuriated Anora. Why didn't he speak up in his own defense? He could say things such as how Rosco was no better than a rabid dog. He deserved to die. The man had killed their baby, along with countless other people. But Jesse just eyed her wordlessly, and Anora wished she hadn't come. If he wouldn't fight to save himself, then for sure he'd never fight for her. For them.

The magnitude of all they'd lost rippled through

her. Facing Jesse brought back everything she'd worked so hard to forget these past days. Including the fact that she still loved him.

"Sarah . . ." Her voice broke and she tried again. "Sarah was the one thing that brought us together. Gave us a chance. With her gone, there's . . . there's no more point in going on. No point in pretending to each other that we care."

She held her breath as she waited for Jesse to say something. Anything.

Admit that he cared.

Deny that he cared.

When the silence got to be more than she could bear, she turned and walked away, not sparing Jesse a backward glance.

Once clear of the jail, her feet carried her automatically to the burial park, where she made her way between the markers to the recently turned mound that covered the remains of baby Sarah. The fragile life she and Jesse had created together. Way back when she'd loved him with a senseless and consuming passion that defied reason. And gave herself willingly to him even though she didn't trust him. And didn't know that she ever could. What good was love without trust to give it strength?

Anora hunkered down on the frozen ground and hugged her knees. All her life, her men had let her down. Starting with her pa. After that it was Ben, when he got involved with Rosco's gang. Then Jesse. As she had lain there in the cabin, weak and bleeding from the birth, the lifeless body of her daughter for company, Jesse had denied her the one thing in the world she'd needed. His presence. His reassuring touch. His testimony of love. As long as Jesse believed love didn't exist, she'd always be alone.

It wasn't until she stood and brushed away her tears that Anora sensed she was no longer alone. A man stood a short distance from her. Once she spotted him he took a hesitant step forward, as if unsure of his welcome, and watching him move from the shadows Anora felt the blood drain from her face.

"Ben?"

He smiled and came toward her, walking with a sure, even stride the way she'd always dreamed. Was the whole encounter a dream? A ghostly Ben, risen from the grave?

His arms closed around her, real and solid, and Anora clung to her brother as if she'd been tossed a lifeline.

"Where . . . ? How . . . ?" She pulled back and stared into his newly matured features. "Who's in that grave over yonder with your name on the marker?"

Ben laughed and hugged her again. "What do you want to know first?"

"Mercy. I feel so light-headed, I scarcely know where to start."

"Then you better let me talk. I don't rightly know whose remains those are. I came across the body in the canyon last summer, and it started me thinking. I knew I couldn't just take off with Rosco's booty. The man would have hunted me down. But if I could somehow make him believe I was dead . . ."

"Where'd you go?"

"Boston, of course." He gave her a telling look. "You think I didn't know the real reason you were trying to save every penny you could put by? I heard about that famous surgeon too, you know, same as you."

"You never said a word."

"What? And ruin your surprise? Anyway, I figured if I was to up and disappear it'd also leave the way clear for you and the marshal. Hear you two got hitched."

"How'd you hear that?"

"I holed up a time in Indian Springs. Close enough to make sure you were okay." His touch gentled. "I'm real sorry about the baby. I came as soon as I heard. I also heard how the marshal's in jail."

"Rosco's dead. Now his pa's doing a fine job of causing grief in other folks' lives."

"I'm thinking maybe there's something I can do to help fix that."

"What can you do?"

"For starters, have a little talk with the magistrate. Explain to him how Rosco was dying long before Quantrill ever laid eyes on the man. Smelled so bad and coughing blood, the whole time I rode with him. Rosco was dying from the inside out. Bragged real good, he did, 'bout how if he didn't bring Quantrill down one way, he'd get him another."

"You think it'll work?" Her hopes fell as quickly as they rose. "Won't you get in trouble for riding with Rosco?"

Ben's face showed a thoughtful maturity she'd never seen before. "You leave me to worry about that."

She clutched his arm, still unable to believe he wouldn't disappear from her sight. "Those Boston doctors. They really did fix your leg?"

"Better than new." He touched a gloved finger to her cheek. "You've had a lot of sadness, Nory. Maybe, finally, life'll start to get happy for you."

Anora's heart filled with pride at the confident way Ben carried himself through town. He seemed taller than she recalled. "You grow some while you were away?"

"You could say I grew up."

They parted company in front of the magistrate's. Only then did Anora realize the full implication of Ben's return. If the fates were kind Jesse could well go free. Except he'd never speak to her again. He'd never forgive her for deceiving him about her and Ben.

Anora perched on the fluffy pink chair and sipped the brandy Ricki had insisted on serving her. The fiery liquor had warmed her insides, and before she knew it the whole story had come tumbling from her lips.

"And so you see, even if Jesse goes free, and I want him to, he'll be furious with me. Can't say as how I blame him. I could have easily told him the truth, back when he realized." She paused. Her face felt flushed, and she blamed the unaccustomed brandy.

"Realized?" Ricki waited for her to finish.

"That Ben and I . . . you know. Weren't really man and wife."

"Why didn't you come clean?" Ricki crossed her legs and the movement caused her robe to slip to one side, but she didn't seem to notice the way Anora stared in fascination at the sheerest stockings she'd ever laid eyes on.

"You'll probably think it sounds silly. But Jesse being so worldly and all, I would have felt downright foolish confessing to him how I only pretended to be married. Too proud to admit Ben was really my brother. Besides, I know how the truth is powerful important to a man like Jesse."

"Funny, hearing you you say that. 'Cause the Jesse I know lies all the time."

"Oh, I don't think so."

"Honey, I know so." Ricki tossed back her drink, then rose and crossed the room for a refill. "So Ben's come back. With information that can help clear Jesse. I don't see the problem."

"The problem's Jesse." Anora let out a frustrated sigh. She'd hoped that Ricki, having known Jesse for so long, might be able to suggest some magic way to make things right.

"True, Jesse might be pissed some. But trust me, that won't last. Man's crazy in love with you."

"In love? Oh, no. You're wrong about that. Jesse doesn't believe in love."

"I suppose he told you that himself?"

"All the time."

"See? Goes back to what I said earlier. About Jesse being a bigger liar than you are. And don't you hesitate to tell him so."

"I'm afraid I don't follow you."

"Jesse ever talk to you about his baby sister, Rose?"

"A little. I know she lives in Philly, with her son."

"Jesse was a teenager when baby Rose was born. That little moppet followed him everywhere, and he thought the sun rose and set on her. So when he learned she'd got herself in a family way, he was some kind of upset. Felt he'd failed in his duties to keep her chaste. You know. Menfolk. It's one thing for Jesse and the boys to be randy as hell. But his sister was expected to be a proper lady."

Ricki stared at the ceiling a second before continuing her story. "He went after the young man responsible, expecting him to marry Rose. Probably would have happened, too, except Jesse can be kind of hotheaded. The two men met and there was a scuffle. Jesse would never have hurt Cameron, you understand. I believe he was right fond of the boy. Unfortunately Cameron was accidentally killed."

"How?"

"Damn fool stabbed Jesse, then fell on his knife blade when he turned to run away."

"Cameron was Rosco's brother." Suddenly things became crystal clear.

"Half brother. Anyway, the reason I'm telling you this is because the Jesse I know is more than capable of love. I've seen how he loves Rose and Andrew. And, girl, any fool can see he loves you, too." She slanted Anora a look. "You love him?"

"Course I do."

Ricki sat back, lit a thin brown cigar and exhaled a stream of smoke. "So let me ask you this. What all are you prepared to do about it? Are you prepared to swallow your pride? To fight for Jesse's love?"

*   *   *

Jesse clattered down the steps and into the street, where he paused to look in both directions.

"King!" The other man wasn't the only one who heard him. Up and down both sides of the street, folks stopped in their tracks and turned to stare as their marshal faced off against Ben King.

The younger man slowly made his way back toward Jesse. "Something on your mind, Quantrill?"

"You know what's on my mind."

"Do I?"

Jesse hunched his shoulders against the cold blast of wind that blew down the back of his collar. A crowd started to gather. Once he would have preferred to keep this private, but he was past caring.

"Got some things need saying."

"Shoot," King said, then grinned. "Not literal-like, mind."

"It's about Anora."

"What about her?"

"I want to know what your intentions are."

King scratched his chin thoughtfully. "Strikes me as maybe I should be asking you the same thing."

"You don't love her the way she deserves."

"That's true enough," King said. "I do love the gal. Only different from you."

"You treated her poorly."

"There's no denying that."

"You don't deserve her."

"Do you?" King said, a challenge in his voice.

Jesse exhaled in a rush. "I make her a better husband."

King appeared to ponder his words. Suddenly he looked beyond Jesse and grinned. "Well, speak of the devil. Here she comes now. You best be taking this up with her."

Jesse stared, open-mouthed, as King made his way to Anora's side, where he gave her a hug and a chaste kiss on the forehead. Then he mounted his horse and rode away without a backward glance.

Jesse had eyes only for Anora. Till he realized they still had an audience.

"What are y'all looking at?" he bellowed in his best lawman's tone. "Go on. Get about your business." It seemed to take forever till the street cleared. Finally it was just the two of them. Him and Anora. And for once Jesse didn't have a clue what to say. He moved toward her, not too close.

Anora broke the silence. "What did Ben want?"

A scant two feet separated them physically. To Jesse, it seemed a chasm of a lifetime. "Told me he loved you. Only different from me. What did he mean by that?"

He watched Anora twist her hands together. "I have something to tell you. Only promise you won't get mad."

"Get mad? Why would I get mad?"

"Promise."

Jesse nodded.

"Your word?" Anora said. She seemed more anxious than usual.

"I said so, didn't I?"

Anora tilted her head back in order to look directly into his eyes. "You remember when you and

I . . . and you asked me why my marriage to Ben was different."

"I remember."

"Well, I kind of misled you."

"Misled me how?"

She watched his eyes grow wary and forced herself to go on. "I let you continue to think me and Ben were husband and wife when we weren't. I know I should have told you the truth. And I'm sorry. You'll never know just how sorry I am."

"You and King were never husband and wife? What the hell are you to each other?"

"Ben's my brother."

For a moment Jesse was too shocked to speak. "Why didn't you just tell me plain out?"

"Because I know how much you revere the truth. And I didn't want to lose you."

He let out a pent-up breath. "Damn you, Anora. This is one heck of a time to be telling me this."

"I know."

"Do you have any idea the hell I went through when he walked into the magistrate's and told his story about Rosco? I was cleared. And trapped in hell at the same time. 'Cause I believed King had a prior claim on you. And being set free didn't mean a plug nickel to me if it meant I couldn't have you."

"I knew you'd be mad," Anora said. "And I don't blame you." She remembered Ricki's words and forced herself to continue. "For that matter, I don't cotton to being lied to, myself."

"I ever lie to you?"

"Yeah, you did."

"When?"

"Every time you told me how you don't believe in love." She watched the play of emotions across his face. The doubts and uncertainties. And finally the surrender.

"I was some kind of fool. Tried to deny the way you made me feel, from the very first moment I laid eyes on you."

"You teased me about my freckles."

"I love your freckles."

"From the time you first came to town I was sorry I ever let anyone call me Mrs. King."

"You okay with folks calling you Mrs. Quantrill?"

"I'm very okay with that."

He swallowed thickly. "Do you still hate me for running out on you?"

"Hate you, Jesse?" Anora took a faltering step forward. Followed by a second. "I could never hate you." A mere arm's length separated them. One of them had to make the first move. Funny how she didn't mind that it would be her.

She cupped his face between her palms. His dear, dear face. As she gazed up at him, she resolved to put the light of laughter back in those tired, troubled eyes. To erase the lines of strain bracketing his kissable lips. To somehow ensure their future made good with all its promises.

"I love you, Jesse Quantrill."

"Not half so much as I love you." He dragged her against him. It felt so good. Where she belonged.

As she circled her arms around his neck and realized he was trembling, she was overcome with awe at the power she had over this strong, amazing lawman.

"I wouldn't expect you to leave Boulder Springs. I know how you feel about your home."

"My home is anyplace you are," Anora said softly, her eyes loving his. "As long as we're together."

"Kind of don't mind it here too much, myself."

She saw the answering light of love in his eyes and felt the ravenous hunger in his lips, as they caught and claimed hers. Returning his kiss, she felt an overwhelming outpouring of love and emotion. It flowed from him to her and back to him. A transfer and exchange so powerful she knew she'd never again have cause to doubt the strength of their love. Or the value that came from learning to trust, surrendering her pride.

23

Epilogue

A Few Years Later . . .

"Hold still," Anora said as she tugged on a corner of Penny's veil, straightening the sheer white mesh. "That's got it." She stepped back a pace and handed her friend the nosegay of roses. "You set?"

Penny's veil quivered. "Nory, I'm too nervous. I can't."

"Land sakes, girl. Of course you can. Nothing to it."

"Easy for you to say. You been married forever."

"Seems like it, anyway." At the patter of scampering feet she looked up in time to see the twins barrel through the room. "Hold up, there, you two. Where's your pa?"

Emily tugged at the ribbon on her special-made dress.

"He's wif Uncle Ben."

"Why aren't you both out front?"

Jesse junior piped up. "Sent us to see if y'all are ready."

"You tell those men to hold their horses. We'll be along presently."

"Okay, Ma." Hand in hand the twins ran from the room.

"Slow down and walk," Anora called after them, but her words fell on deaf ears.

"Those two don't walk anyplace," Penny said.

"Just like Ben." Anora hugged her friend. "I still can hardly believe you two are making a match."

"I can hardly believe it myself. But ever since he went away, it's like he came back a new person."

Anora beamed proudly. Ben had turned himself in, then struck a deal to lead the law to the gang's hideout. Since most of the outlaws' spoils had been recovered and returned, Ben was not only pardoned, he was hailed as a hero.

"I hope you both will be as happy as Jesse and I."

"I hope so, too. Never saw an old married couple behave like they're still on their honeymoon. The way you two carry on."

"That's the secret, Penny. Don't let the honeymoon ever end."

Jesse appeared in the doorway in time to hear her last sentence. "What's this talk about honeymoons? We haven't got to the marrying part yet. Poor old Ben's afraid you've gone and changed your mind."

Anora stepped into her husband's arms for a

quick kiss. "You run along and tell him we'll be right out."

"If you'd kept me waiting like this, I don't know whether or not I'd have hung around."

Anora cocked him a cheeky grin. "You'd have hung around, Jesse Quantrill. Long as I'd have set you to wait."

He grinned back. "I hate to admit it but, as usual, you're right. You know you got me well and truly hooked."

Behind them, Penny cleared her throat noisily. "Hey, you two. Just whose wedding is this?"

Anora turned to her friend. "You make the most beautiful bride. Doesn't she, Jess?"

"Second only to you, my love."

At that moment the first strains of organ music filled the room, underscoring the love Anora felt overflow her life. Surely no woman was more truly blessed, more truly loved than she.